# "Can you help my mom?"

"I will certainly try," Morgan answered. "A key to successful therapy is the patient's willingness to accept help."

"Well, she's not exactly jumping up and down at the idea," Wade admitted wryly. "Should we talk about the elephant in the room?" At Morgan's quizzical expression, he said, "Simone's death..."

"Ah, that. Yes, well, grief can cause all kinds of emotional as well as physical manifestations."

"Well, some people aren't as strong as others, I suppose."

"It's not a question of strength," she corrected him with a gentle smile. "Some people find a way to cope but that doesn't mean they've processed their feelings in a healthy manner."

Why did it feel as though she was talking about him? "Well, at any rate...she's ready for you. I just wanted to warn you before sending you into the lion's den."

"Thank you for trusting me with that information. Oh, and FYI, the coffee here will put hair on your chest. Very strong." And then she left, coffee cup in hand, inadvertently causing a flush of awareness to remind him that he was a man and she was a beautiful woman.

He rubbed at his eyes, embarrassed by his inappropriate thought about his mother's therapist.

Dear Reader,

I confess, when I first started writing Morgan O'Hare and Wade Sinclair's story, I wasn't quite sure who they were aside from the superficial. It wasn't until I dug deeper into their story that their hearts were revealed to me. That's what makes my job as a writer so rewarding. I love discovering deeper meaning in the words and honoring the characters' journey as they find love.

Wade and Morgan are two people who are strong, professional and capable, yet under the surface, they are seething with dark hurts which are preventing them from claiming their joy. The road to true happiness is never easy but it's the only road worth traveling, in my opinion, and I hope you agree as you turn the pages on Wade and Morgan's love affair.

I enjoy hearing from readers. I can be found on Facebook, Twitter and through my website at www.kimberlyvanmeter.com, or you can send me something in the mail at P.O. BOX 2210, Oakdale, CA 95361.

Kimberly Van Meter

# KIMBERLY
# VAN METER

—

## A Sinclair Homecoming

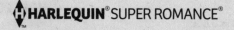
HARLEQUIN® SUPER ROMANCE®

Recycling programs
for this product may
not exist in your area.

ISBN-13: 978-0-373-60859-1

A SINCLAIR HOMECOMING

Copyright © 2014 by Kimberly Sheetz

**H** HARLEQUIN®

™ www.Harlequin.com

**Printed in U.S.A.**

## ABOUT THE AUTHOR

Kimberly Van Meter wrote her first book at sixteen and finally achieved publication in December 2006. She writes for the Harlequin Superromance and Harlequin Romantic Suspense lines. She and her husband of seventeen years have three children, three cats and always a houseful of friends, family and fun.

## Books by Kimberly Van Meter

### HARLEQUIN SUPERROMANCE

### HARLEQUIN ROMANTIC SUSPENSE

*Home in Emmett's Mill
**Mama Jo's Boys
***Family in Paradise
†The Sinclairs of Alaska
§Native Country

Other titles by this author available in ebook format.

# CHAPTER ONE

IF INSOMNIA WAS the devil's handmaiden then Wade Sinclair was her bitch most nights.

Like tonight.

He rolled to his side, refusing to look at the red numbers glowing from his digital alarm clock because he didn't want to know how much sleep he wasn't getting. Five a.m. came early when operating on very little sleep.

He squeezed his eyes shut and tried meditating but his mind was too unruly to cooperate.

Each time he came close to drifting to sleep, his baby sister's face popped into his mental theater, and sleep fled like a deer with a cougar on its tail.

Simone—pretty, charming, too smart for her britches—dead.

*It's been eight years,* he wanted to groan as if trying to negotiate with whatever demon prevented his eyes from closing and his mind from resting. How much longer was he supposed to carry this burden of unending grief and guilt?

He rolled to his feet and walked to the window to stare out across the forested land of the Yosemite National Park. But instead of California pines, he saw Alaskan hemlock and spruce, native to the Kenai mountains of his homeland. He saw the deep snow that had blanketed the ground and made the terrain hard to traverse. He saw his sister's body trundled into the body bag as they carried her away.

This was Trace's fault. If his brother hadn't kept bugging him about coming home, he wouldn't have been reminded daily of that awful day. No witnesses saw Simone climb into the car with her killer that night. No witnesses ever came forward to lend any clues.

And her killer continued to walk free.

Maybe that was what kept him awake at night.

No justice.

No closure.

And not even moving away to California had changed that.

His last conversation with Trace was too fresh in his mind to ignore, and he felt like a royal shit for being so curt with his younger

David's favorite brand of pinot grigio awaited her as it always did but she wanted a beer. In the early days of their marriage, David had lightly chastised her penchant for beer as low-class and had endeavored to educate her palate. She supposed he'd succeeded for she dutifully drank the finest wines and could appropriately pair wines with their courses. But she really still preferred a cold beer.

Her daddy had always said he couldn't trust a man who wouldn't share a beer with him.

Suffice to say, Daddy and David hadn't been the best of friends.

Maybe her daddy had seen something she'd completely missed because she'd had hearts in her eyes.

"I wish I'd listened, Daddy," Morgan murmured as she grabbed a beer by the neck and pulled it from the fridge. With two twists, she'd cracked the top and took a deep swig. "What do you think of that, David?" she asked to the empty kitchen. Nothing but silence answered. Great. She ought to get a cat if she was going to start having conversations with people who weren't there.

People thought she didn't date because she was afraid no one would be like David.

time to grieve any longer. Her client list was long and her practice well-established. Morgan O'Hare was a respectable authority on mental health. She'd even written a book on the subject! And she was a damn hypocrite.

Morgan managed to make it home in time for her favorite show, and after wiping off her makeup and twisting her hair in a ponytail she settled into her late husband's recliner and clicked on the television. *Let the good times roll,* she thought with a sigh, wondering if there would ever come a time when she didn't feel like a fraud living someone else's life.

Not likely if she couldn't get past this. David died three years ago.

She wasn't sure which stage of grief she was stuck in because she jumped between all the stages like a child playing hopscotch. Sometimes she was hurt; other times she was angry.

No, angry wasn't a strong enough word.

She was enraged.

But she couldn't show that side of her grief. People understood her tears; they wouldn't understand her rage.

Morgan rose abruptly and padded into the kitchen. She opened the refrigerator and reached for the wine but then stopped.

moment the fake name had slipped from her lips. She'd hoped that by making the commitment to drive all the way to Anchorage, she'd find the courage to cry in front of strangers, but when push came to shove, she couldn't. And as more time went on, how could she explain that she couldn't talk about the death of her husband without talking about that *other* thing that had happened, too?

"Melinda, are you coming?" Cora waved her over from the gathering circle of people as they took their seats, and Morgan nodded and waved but began backing toward the exit.

"I'll be right there after I visit the ladies' room," she answered with a bright, entirely false smile. As soon as Cora turned away, Morgan booked it out of there with her heart pounding and her palms sweating. She didn't feel halfway normal again until she'd put Anchorage miles behind her.

"Epic fail," she muttered, borrowing a phrase from her younger clients. And embarrassing. An instant replay bloomed in her mind and she cringed. Why couldn't she do this? Why couldn't she sit in that damn chair and tell her story? Share her grief? Because staying silent was easier, less painful and less messy than letting it all out. She didn't have

duced herself, saying, "I'm Cora. Is this your first time to our grief support circle? I haven't seen you before and I come every week."

"Yes, actually," Morgan answered, hesitating to strike up a conversation with the kind stranger. She knew support groups were useful—she often referred her own clients to such groups if the need arose—but she'd been unable to get herself to commit to one for herself. Even now, she'd traveled far from her own city of Homer to Anchorage to attend a meeting because she didn't want anyone to know that she still hadn't gotten over her husband's death from three years ago. Intellectually, she knew that there was no statute of limitations on grief, but people had a tendency to judge just the same. And she couldn't afford anyone in her own sphere to realize she was struggling when she counseled people every day on how to move on from their mental obstacles. Morgan focused a bright, engaging smile on Cora and said, "My name is Melinda."

"Melinda, such a pleasure to meet you. Grab a cookie and a seat. The circle will start in five minutes."

"Sounds good," Morgan said, but knew she wouldn't stay in spite of her best intentions the

He was the superintendent of a national park, not some paper-pushing, middle-management drone who could split at a moment's notice just because someone in the city housing authority deemed his mother a bad housekeeper.

Things would blow over and everything would revert to the way it was before— perhaps no better—but at least no worse.

Yeah, so why did he feel as if something really bad were just around the corner?

Wade finally glanced at the alarm clock and noted with weary relief that 4:00 a.m. wasn't the earliest he'd showered and started his day so he might as well get moving.

As he walked to the shower and turned the water on, he purposefully shoved all thought of his family to the bottom of his mental cache. He had his own life to live and he refused to feel guilty about it.

End of story.

Morgan O'Hare was an excellent example of the fact that fidgeting was not reserved for children.

"Nervous?" a soft voice inquired gently and caused Morgan to jump. A plump, older woman with graying hair smiled and intro-

brother, but he couldn't drop everything in his life just to play mediator between his siblings and his parents. Just because he was the oldest didn't mean he had the answers to every problem.

"It's bad, man," Trace had said emphatically. "I didn't want to believe it but Mom is going to die in that house if we don't do something. And Dad…he's in total denial and too stoned half the time to be of any help."

"I can appreciate that but I have responsibilities here that preclude me from hopping a plane anytime my family demands it," he replied, giving more attention to an environmental impact survey than to what his brother was saying. "I'm sure it'll blow over if you give it time."

"Stop giving me your practiced administrator rhetoric and start acting as if you actually give a damn," Trace said. "The house has been condemned. They wouldn't do that if it weren't necessary."

"What do you mean *condemned*? Surely, that's an overreaction to the situation," he said, frowning. How bad could it be? His mother had never been a terribly neat and tidy person but she'd never been an abject slob. Their home had been lived in, but never dirty. "On whose authority?"

Morgan always smiled and nodded, letting them go on thinking that.

The real truth? Morgan was afraid she'd find someone just like him.

# CHAPTER TWO

WADE WAS DEEP in a meeting with the local county's Native American leaders about passes for the indigenous people when his cell phone went off.

"Sorry about that," he murmured, chagrined at having forgotten to turn it to silent for the meeting. As he went to send the call to voice mail, he saw it was his sister, Miranda. Ordinarily, he would've ignored the call with the intent to call her back later but given everything that'd been going on lately with his family, he excused himself, saying, "I'm very sorry but I think I should take this call. I should only be about five minutes. Help yourself to a doughnut and some coffee." He ducked out of the conference room at the tribal center and into the hallway to answer. "Hello?"

"Wade, it's Miranda...something terrible has happened and you need to come home right away." Before he could launch a response, she said, "Mom's in the hospital."

"What happened?"

"She had a heart attack. The doctors were able to stabilize her but she's already had surgery to have two stents put in. But it gets worse…because the first responders couldn't get to her quickly, the heart muscle was damaged."

"Why couldn't the paramedics get to her?" he asked, rubbing at his forehead with his free hand. "Are the roads bad?"

"No, she was in that damn wreck of a house again and it was sheer dumb luck that she was able to call 911. But the paramedics could barely get inside the house and get to her."

Wade remained silent for a moment as Trace's conversation came back to him. He hadn't actually believed his brother when he'd said their mom was a hoarder. Could it really be that bad? Surely not as bad as those people on that TLC show. But if the paramedics couldn't get to her…the evidence seemed pretty damning. His gut ached as the realization hit that he couldn't put off a trip home. "I'll check the flights," he said, the words slow to fall from his mouth. "Can you meet me at the airport?"

"Yeah," she agreed, pausing to add, "we really needed you sooner. This is a worst-case scenario that I was hoping to avoid. I mean, there was no way of knowing that Mom was going to have a heart attack, but I had a feeling something bad was going to happen in that house with the way that it is."

"Okay, I'm coming home," Wade muttered, guilt causing irritation to leach into his tone. Did his sister have to pound it into his head that he should've taken her concerns more seriously? He got it. Move on. "I'll text you my flight information as I get it."

"Okay," she said, bristling a little. "Don't get pissy with me just because you're inconvenienced. You were raised better than that. You're the big brother. Time to act like it."

Now his little sister was schooling him? The day just kept getting better and better. "That's unnecessary. Are you finished?"

"Yes."

"Okay. Text me if Mom's condition worsens. I will text you with my flight information. Bye." He clicked off without waiting for Miranda's response. He wasn't about to trade words about his so-called lack of familial responsibility with either of his siblings. He had better things to do. He returned to the meeting with another brisk smile of apology and discussions continued around him but he had a hard time concentrating. He made appropriate responses but was glad when the meeting was over. After a few handshakes and exchanged pleasantries, Wade made a hasty exit straight to his office to book a flight.

MIRANDA TOSSED HER phone into her purse and tried to rein in her temper. Wade had balls the size of an elephant to be acting pissy with her after they'd tried and tried to get him to come home and help with their parents' situation. *Well, Mr. Big Shot, time to cancel that tee time because you're needed at home. Tough titty.* She didn't feel bad for him one iota.

Jeremiah entered the room just as she'd emitted a short growl of frustration and he frowned. "Everything okay?"

"No, everything is not okay. They are far from okay," she muttered, then skewed her gaze to her fiancé with apology. "I'm sorry. My brothers tend to bring out the worst in me. That was Wade. He's booking a flight… finally. It took a major catastrophe for him to board a damn plane, though, and that pisses me off. I've been dealing with Mom and Dad mostly on my own until Trace got involved, and now Wade is throwing a hissy fit—in his own controlled way—because we need him here. It drives me nuts that he manages to make me feel like the whiny nag because I need his help."

"So your brother hasn't been home since Simone died?" Jeremiah asked, making sure he had the facts straight about the family history. At Miranda's nod, he sighed. "Well, I know a thing or two about running away from pain. Chances are if someone had forced my hand into returning to Wyoming before I was ready, I'd be less than social, too."

Miranda cast Jeremiah a look of warning. "You're not allowed to be on his side, just so you know. He's wrong, and I'm right—drill that into your head and you won't find yourself sleeping alone."

"You're such a bossy broad," Jeremiah said, pulling her into his arms with a chuckle. "If I didn't know how much you enjoy my company at night, I'd take that threat with more seriousness. But before you get your panties twisted in a knot, know that I'm on your side—that goes without saying. However, your family has been through the ringer… and everyone deals with their pain differently. Cut him some slack. He might not be happy about it, but at least he's boarding that plane. Right?"

She grudgingly agreed, hearing the wisdom in Jeremiah's perspective. "Simone's been gone eight years. It's time everyone puts her to rest."

"Wise words from the woman who up until a few months ago was still drowning her pain in booze and men."

"Ouch. If being on my side means you don't pull your punches, don't be on my side," Miranda grumbled against his chest. She took a moment to enjoy the simple pleasure of being snuggled against the man she loved and then said, "Well, I guess you're right. Maybe we'll get lucky and whatever Wade needs to heal will come to him. Mamu says that the ancestors bring us what we need, when we need it."

"And do you believe that?" Jeremiah asked as Miranda pulled away.

"Maybe. It seems to have worked out that way for me and Trace. Maybe it'll be that way with Wade, too. Although, he's the most rigid out of all of us, so even if what he needed was standing right in front of him with a big neon sign, he'd probably refuse to see it."

"He has that Sinclair stubbornness in spades, huh?"

"Oh, yeah…my older brother could write a book on how to be a stubborn jackass."

"That's saying something because you and Trace… Well, I'd say you're both pretty stubborn."

"Only when people don't agree that our way is the best way," she quipped half joking. When Jeremiah's mouth lifted in a wry grin she conceded, "All right, I see your point but don't push your luck. No one likes to be reminded of their shortcomings. Shall I list a few of your less than desirable personality traits?"

"Point taken." He grinned. "Now, are we going to eat lunch or go straight to afternoon delight? Your tirade against your brother has eaten into our lunch breaks. I'm not sure we have time for both."

Miranda grabbed Jeremiah by the tie and began leading him to the bedroom. "I wasn't that hungry, anyway. C'mon, you big, sexy man o'mine. Let's see how well you perform under pressure."

"Baby, I eat pressure for lunch. I'm an administrator, remember?"

She laughed and they disappeared behind their bedroom door.

And for the next thirty minutes, Miranda's thoughts were blissfully free of any member of her damn family.

MORGAN WAS BUSY studying her case notes for her next client when her secretary, Remy, came into her office with a scandalized expression on his face. With Remy, she never knew if he was simply being theatrical or if there was something truly scandalous to share. At any rate, Remy was entertaining at the very least. And he was family so she'd long since given up trying to change him. Not that she would if she could. Remy kept her sane around a bunch of crazies, as he put it.

"Girlfriend, you are not going to believe what file just crossed my desk for processing." Without waiting for Morgan to guess, Remy said, "You remember those poor Sinclairs? You know the family whose girl was killed all those years ago by some psycho? Well, seems the mama has gone and had a heart attack and now Adult Protective Services is involved. They want a full evaluation of her mental status, if you know what I mean."

Morgan frowned and accepted the file from Remy. "Why would APS need an eval after a heart attack? What am I missing here?"

"Check out the pics in the file," Remy said.

Morgan opened the file and pulled aside the intake paperwork to see the enclosed pictures.

She stared in shock. "Oh, my…word…" Her gaze returned to Remy. "She's a hoarder?"

"Either that or she's auditioning for world's worst housekeeper," Remy quipped.

"Oh, dear…that poor family," Morgan said under her breath as she went through the pictures. Clutter of all sorts, from brand-new items to trash, littered every available space in the modest home and choked the halls. She returned to the intake paperwork. "It says here the paramedics couldn't get to her because of the mess. It's a wonder she was able to call 911. This is just awful. That family has been through so much already."

"Oh, and it gets worse," Remy said, delighted to have some relevant gossip. "On the day that APS booted her from the house and condemned it, police arrested the father for marijuana cultivation. He's been in jail for weeks. Wouldn't let anyone post bail. That's a weird thing. Why would anyone want to sit it out in jail?"

"Maybe he felt more in control there," Morgan answered, though her attention was on the Sinclair mom.

"How does being locked up make you feel more in control?" Remy asked. "I would say that's the opposite of being in control when someone else is telling you when to eat, when to sleep and when to go outside."

Morgan paused in her reading to answer her inquisitive cousin. "Well, if he has a substance-abuse problem and he doesn't think he has the willpower to stay clean, being in jail takes care of that problem, doesn't it?" Remy recognized the rhetorical nature of her question and shrugged.

"I suppose."

"Well, at any rate, the father's problems aren't my concern. Adult Protective Services wants me to evaluate the mom so that's what I'll do. I'll make time to do it tomorrow. In the meantime, I'm sure I don't have to remind you to keep your lip zipped about confidential cases, right?"

"Honey, now you're just being rude. Of course I don't talk about your crazies to anyone else."

"Please don't call them that. It's insulting."

"Oh, fine. You're in a mood today. Is it time for Aunt Flo to visit?" But Remy didn't stick around for an answer and sashayed from the room. That man drove her nuts at times but out of anyone in her family, Remy was the one who knew her secrets and never whispered them to a soul. For that, she was forever grateful.

Shaking off the odd vibe of her wandering thoughts, she shoved the file into her satchel to read at home tonight. In the meantime, her next client was scheduled in ten minutes and she still hadn't finished going over her notes. Time to get to work.

# CHAPTER THREE

THE TENSION BETWEEN Wade and his brother, Trace, was like a living, breathing thing, wedging itself in the open space as they traversed the sanitized halls of South Peninsula Hospital to their mother's recovery room.

"Whatever you do, don't go making promises that she can move back home," Trace said. "Until Adult Protective Services says the house is fit for human habitation, she can't move back, and trust me, it's going to take a whole lot of cleaning to put that house back together again."

"Fine. What's this about Dad refusing bail?"

"He doesn't want to come home, I guess," Trace answered with a shrug. "But he's not my concern. He can sit in that jail all he wants. Better for him, anyway. We have bigger problems and Dad's booming drug business isn't one of them."

Wade exhaled in irritation. Trace wasn't one to exaggerate but surely it couldn't be as bad as everyone was making it out to be. Seemed everyone was running around being Chicken Little. So the house was a mess. They'd clean it and set things to right. Shouldn't be a case for so much hand-wringing. He checked his watch. "After we see Mom, drop me off at the house and I'll pick up Mom's car to use while I'm here. No sense renting a car when there's one sitting in the driveway."

"Fine. But don't try to go into the house at night."

"And why is that?" he asked, irritated. "Is the boogeyman going to jump out from underneath the sofa?"

"No, smart-ass, you might trip and cause an avalanche and then we'll have two family members in the hospital. I know you don't believe me but you will when you see the house."

Trace was right; Wade didn't believe him. The house couldn't be that bad. He grew up in that house. There was no way his mother had turned into the kind of person who hoarded to a dangerous level. The idea—well, the idea was too much for him to imagine or accept.

"Just so I know…am I going to get the cold shoulder the entire time I'm here?" he asked Trace.

"Depends. Are you going to start being part of the solution or part of the problem?"

"What are you talking about? I'm here, aren't I?"

"Because our mother had a heart attack. Tell me if she hadn't, that you would be here like we asked you to be."

He couldn't rightly say that and Trace knew it. "Some of us have lives that we can't just drop because something is going on at home."

"Don't start acting like your job is superior to everyone else's. We all have personal lives that are being disrupted by the current situation. You haven't cornered the market on being inconvenienced."

"That's a pretty big glass house you're standing in, don't you think?" Wade said. "Seems to me you're being a bit of a hypocrite."

"I've already made amends and apologies for my actions. How about you? Besides, me and Miranda are square. I can't say the same for you. I was a dick for leaving her holding the bag with our parents and I own that. It's time for you to pony up, too."

"Don't lecture me, little brother. I'm in no mood."

"Well, step up and I won't have to. Did

it occur to you that I need my big brother? Yeah…well, I was counting on your support. Imagine my surprise when I was flatly denied. Didn't feel good."

"Are you finished crying? Jeez, Trace, when did you turn into such a girl?"

"Screw you, Wade. When did you turn into such a prick?"

A nurse shushed them with a warning look when their voices threatened to get louder. Trace buttoned up but looked filled with the need to say a whole lot more. Thank God for small favors. Wade's head was splitting from a long flight seated next to a crying kid and he was ready for a beer and bed. "Can we just get this over with? It's been a long day."

Trace nodded and they walked into their mother's room. Wade stared. Wires and tubes flowed in and out of his mother, while electronics monitored her every function. A bubble of fear rose in his throat at the realization that his mother could've truly died. Intellectually, he knew that as he grew older, so did his parents but in his mind, his parents were the same as they ever were. He was wrong.

"Mama." The word slipped from his mouth in a worried whisper, echoing the shock of seeing her so diminished and frail.

Her eyelids fluttered open and she focused on her sons. It took a moment for her to realize it was her oldest son before a wan but happy smile followed. "W-Wade?" She lifted her hand and motioned for him to come closer.

Wade forced a smile past his frozen lips and approached her bedside to hold her hand gingerly. "Hey there, Mama…what kind of trouble are you up to that I had to come all the way home?" he teased as he bent to kiss her cheek.

"My beautiful boy is home," Jennelle murmured, tears leaking from her eyes. "It's been too long, son."

The mild admonishment landed like a pair of cement boots and he had to force himself not to get defensive. "Not from choice, Mama," he lied. "But I'm here now so let's focus on that, okay?"

She smiled and weakly squeezed his hand. "Absolutely. My boy is home. That's all that matters."

In spite of being irritated as hell at Trace, he winced at their mother's exclusion of her other son. She must be pissed because she wouldn't even glance Trace's way. And if there was any confusion as to just how she felt, Jennelle clarified by saying to Trace,

"You can go, now. I'd like to speak with the one child who hasn't betrayed me."

"Ahhh, c'mon, Mom," Trace groaned, slapping his hand on his thigh. "Don't start that crap again."

She closed her eyes. "Make him go away, Wade."

Wade sighed, caught in a bad spot. He looked to Trace, beseeching him to give them a few minutes, and Trace muttered something unflattering under his breath but ducked out.

Once they were alone, Wade said, "Mama, aren't you being a bit harsh? You know Trace and Miranda are worried about you."

"Judases, the both of them," Jennelle said. "Kicked me out of my own home. Never thought I'd see the day when my own flesh and blood turned on me like that." A tear appeared at the corner of her eye, and Wade wiped it away gently. She smiled gratefully. "I know you'd never do something like that. You and Simone were always the ones who were on my side. No matter what."

He bit his tongue. He loved his mother dearly but she had a habit of being manipulative when it served her. Apparently, that hadn't changed. "Mama, tell me about what Adult Protective Services said. I don't understand how they could kick you from your home if there wasn't cause."

She withdrew her hand and shook her head, bewildered. "I don't know. It had to be Miranda's influence. She's so tight with those government types. She's been on a crusade to oust me from my home for months and she finally accomplished it!" Jennelle gasped, wincing with pain, and Wade knew he'd have to see for himself what was going on.

"It's okay, Mama…we'll get this figured out. I promise."

"Bless you, son," she said, her eyes watering. "I feel so much better knowing you're home. I've been so alone. Being attacked by your own children will do that to you."

Wade didn't believe that Trace and Miranda had deliberately ousted their mother, which meant there had to be more to the story than Jennelle was sharing. However, as weak as she was, now was not the time to drag it out of her.

He smiled and patted Jennelle's hand gently. "I want you to rest. Trace is going to take me to the house and I'm going to pick up your car to drive while I'm in town. Is that okay with you?"

"Of course, honey. No sense in spending

good money if you don't have to. That's my frugal boy." Her voice hardened. "But don't you let either of those turncoats into my house. Do you hear me?"

"Yes, Mama. I hear you. Now you rest. You hear me?"

Her eyelids closed on a relieved sigh, and Wade left the room to find Trace. He found Trace and Miranda talking with another woman in the lobby.

Miranda saw him first and motioned for him to join them. "Wade, perfect timing. This is Morgan O'Hare. She's been assigned Mom's case through Adult Protective Services."

He frowned, his gaze snagging on the attractive woman. She stopped talking to Miranda to smile at Wade, and he was struck by how blue her eyes were from behind elegant, dark-framed glasses. She came forward with her hand outstretched. "Hello. I'm Dr. O'Hare but you can call me Morgan if you like. I can appreciate the sensitive nature of the situation and I can assure you I will do my best to see that your mother gets the care she needs."

Wade accepted the perfunctory handshake but wasn't quite clear what was happening. "I don't understand…why is my mother being evaluated?" He looked to his siblings for answers but it was Dr. O'Hare who answered.

"Wade, because of the unique situation surrounding your mother's heart attack and the state of your mother's house, APS feels it's prudent to assess your mother's mental state to find if she's competent to assume responsibility for her care."

"Whoa, whoa…wait a minute…are you saying that my mother's mental health is being questioned simply because she's fallen down on her housekeeping?" he asked, horrified at this turn of events. It was one thing to deal with their family's problems internally and quite another to have complete strangers poking around. His family had suffered plenty of that when Simone had died. Seemed everyone had had a reason to poke, stare or flap their gums about business that was none of theirs. "I think we all just need to take a step back and stop overreacting."

Miranda glared. "You know it's not that. As if we'd be so petty as to go through all of this over a little clutter? Honestly, Wade, pull your head out of your butt for just a minute and hear what Dr. O'Hare is saying."

The pretty doctor smiled in spite of the tension and said, "A situation like this is rife with tension within the family. I can suggest a good family therapist if you'd like."

"I don't need a therapist. My mother doesn't need a therapist," he growled at the doctor and jerked his thumb at his siblings. "You two... may I have a moment, please?"

Miranda sent a quick look of apology to the doctor as they followed Wade a few feet away. "Don't make this harder than it already is," she said to Wade. "You haven't seen the house so you don't know what we've been dealing with. What *I've* been dealing with! I knew something like this was going to happen and I hate to say that it sucks to be right. That house is not the house you remember— because it's buried under a half ton of mess!"

"Settle down. I think we're jumping the gun a bit," Wade said, trying to rein his own temper. "Let's just stop a minute and assess before we run off half-cocked, making decisions that have long-reaching consequences."

"How much more of a consequence needs to happen before you realize what's going on? Our mother is a hoarder. She nearly died in her own house because the paramedics couldn't get to her," Trace added in a harsh whisper. "Remember how I asked if you were going to be part of the problem or the solution? Well, now's the time to decide."

"And I told you I'm here," Wade reminded him, trying hard not to clench his teeth. The Sinclairs had never been accused of suffering a shortage of stubbornness and that stubbornness was in full swing among all three. "But I'm not about to be reprimanded by the two of you for my supposed shortcomings. We have a situation that needs to be taken care of, so I suggest we do it without causing further embarrassment to our family."

Miranda flushed and nodded but she looked as if razors were stuck in her throat. "Fine. But you have to accept that Mom needs help and has needed that help for some time now."

"Perhaps. I am reserving judgment until I have seen for myself this supposed condemned situation at our parents' home."

Trace chuckled with a shake of his head. "Fine. You stubborn jackass. See for yourself. I'm done with this conversation and done with your holier-than-thou attitude. Miranda, he's all yours." And then Trace stalked off, leaving Wade and Miranda to deal with the doctor.

"That was real mature," he muttered, bracing his hands on his hips as Miranda shook her head as if ticked off with both her brothers. "Let's get this settled," he said and returned to the awaiting doctor.

"I apologize for the flared tempers. We don't always see eye to eye," Wade said. "Thank you for coming down but I don't think we'll be needing your services. My family prefers to handle the situation privately."

Dr. O'Hare blinked as if she didn't quite understand and then shook her head, puzzled. "Mr. Sinclair, I'm sorry if I didn't make myself clear but due to the circumstances, I am *required* to give your mother a full mental-health evaluation."

"She doesn't need a mental-health evaluation," he said, looking to Miranda for help, but she remained silent, and he knew he was on his own. "Listen, my mother has been under some strain but I think with the help of her family, we can mitigate whatever concerns Adult Protective Services has."

Morgan pushed her glasses farther on her nose with a small, precise movement and said, "I can appreciate the terrible strain your mother has been under as well as your entire family, given your circumstances, but the evaluation is mandatory."

Wade was losing ground quickly. He crossed his arms. "This is borderline ridiculous."

"I agree." She smiled but he got the distinct impression she was referring to him and not Adult Protective Services. Opening her file, she selected one of the glossy eight-by-ten photos taken by APS when the house was condemned. "Mr. Sinclair, I find a picture to be worth a thousand words in these types of situations." She handed him the photo with a brisk but apologetic smile. "It can be a shock to see a family member living like this, and denial is common. But as you can see…your mother was living in very dangerous conditions."

*What the…* Wade stared at the photo, unable to comprehend what he was staring at. Nothing looked remotely familiar from his childhood. He wasn't even sure what room he was staring at because everything was obliterated by floor-to-ceiling junk. "What the hell…?" he breathed, shooting a shocked look at his sister. "You've got to be kidding me."

Miranda was neither shocked nor surprised and proceeded to explain. "That's the living room. Or at least, it used to be. See that tiny, clogged walkway? That's the hallway toward what used to be our bedrooms. Simone's bedroom is off to the left. And the kitchen… well, you ought to be lucky that picture isn't a scratch-and-sniff. She's been sleeping in the bathtub for months."

Wade stared at his sister. His mother had been sleeping in a bathtub? "How do you know this?"

"Talen told me. She tried to deny it but it's true."

Wade returned the photo, sick to his stomach. The pounding behind his eyeball had turned into a battering ram against his skull. He'd wanted to believe that his siblings had exaggerated, that somehow this was all some big misunderstanding but there was no misinterpreting that picture. Mounds of unrecognizable garbage and clutter filled every nook and cranny that he could see. And if the entire house was like that? "How'd this happen?" he asked, talking out loud mostly to himself. He didn't expect an answer.

"It's too early to tell until I've done a full evaluation but I do know a little bit about your family's personal history, and I'd say this may stem from grief that never found an appropriate outlet."

Simone. Everything always spiraled back to Simone. Of course it did. "My sister."

"Yes."

Miranda piped in, saying, "Mom won't

let anyone into Simone's room anymore. It's weird, almost as if she's trying to forget that Simone is gone. She spends a lot of time in that room."

"Have you been in there?"

Miranda shook her head. "She guards it like a watchdog. I don't know what's going through that head of hers."

So much for a quick three-day trip to sort out details. "What do you need from us?" he asked, resigned.

"Just your cooperation. She'll need your support but she also needs to know that you're not going to enable her to hurt herself again. It's a delicate balance of support and tough love. I won't sugarcoat things…these types of situations are hard on everyone involved but I have seen positive outcomes with proper therapy."

"My mom will never agree to therapy," he said grimly. "I can tell you that right now."

"Well, you'd be surprised what motivates people. That's where the support comes in. I'll wait to introduce myself until tomorrow, seeing as I've already made contact with you. Likely, what I have to say is going to be upsetting."

*Upsetting?* That was too mild of a word. He nodded. "What time?"

"How's 10:00 a.m.?"

He looked to Miranda. "That works for me. How about you?"

She nodded. "I'll check with Trace."

"Thanks." He had no wish to talk to his brother at the moment. He returned to the doctor. "We'll be here."

Dr. O'Hare smiled. "Excellent. It was a pleasure to meet you. I wish it were under different circumstances."

It was probably a standard comment meant to relax people but Wade caught a flash of genuine emotion in her eyes. Or at least, he thought he did. Hell, maybe he was seeing things. Everything in his world had just been tipped on its ass. He ducked his head to the doctor in goodbye and he and Miranda left the hospital to go pick up his mom's car.

His last thought as Dr. O'Hare walked away—inappropriate and flustering—was how pretty she was and how he wished she'd been a wizened old man with a bald head and knobby knuckles.

If that were the case he surely wouldn't be spending undue time thinking of those deep blue eyes behind those designer frames.

And what the hell was he doing thinking of any woman in that capacity? He'd told himself he was going to take a breather in the romance department after suffering through a particularly uncomfortable breakup with Elizabeth, his mostly casual bed partner. Well, he'd thought what they were doing was casual. When he realized Elizabeth had different ideas, he'd decided to cut ties. Better that way than dragging out something that was never going to go where she'd hoped it would.

So that left the question: Why was he noticing how deep and blue Dr. O'Hare's eyes were? Had to be the strain of the moment because if he were thinking straight… Hell, no. It just wouldn't happen.

Besides, he had a feeling things were going to get worse before they got better—and that pretty doc was going to be in the center of it all.

And not in a good way.

## CHAPTER FOUR

Morgan left the hospital, thinking of the Sinclair family and everything they'd been through over the years. She remembered when the youngest Sinclair went missing and then was found the following day by Trace Sinclair, frozen to death on the mountain. The poor girl had been brutalized and left to die. So pretty, so young. It'd been a senseless tragedy that'd scared the entire town. For weeks everyone had been on hyperalert, terrified that the killer was among them. Her father had been paranoid, insisting on a strict curfew for his kids, particularly his daughters. Her younger sister, Mona, had actually known Simone. They hadn't been friends, per se, but Simone had been a tidal wave of charisma and it'd been difficult to prevent getting swept up in her energy. Mona had told her how pretty and sweet Simone had been.

Cheerleader, dance team, pep club, French club—the girl had been into everything.

And then, just like that, she was gone. Her

life snuffed out at the whim of a psychopath. Add in the fact that her killer had never been caught and well, it created a perfect cocktail for paranoia in a small town.

Morgan vaguely recalled Wade from school—he'd been older than she was in school—and of course everyone had had a crush on Trace, even though he'd been over the moon gaga for Delainey Clarke. But she remembered that Wade had been the quiet one. She also remembered that he drove a burgundy Chevy Blazer. Why she remembered that, she didn't know. Well, time had been kind to the Sinclairs in ways that fate had not. They were a good-looking bunch. No quirks of DNA in that chain.

She also remembered that David hadn't liked the Sinclairs, particularly Trace. More than likely because the Sinclair brothers were athletic, ruggedly handsome and smart and the girls were beautiful, both in different ways. Ahh, David and his opinions. He'd had so many of them. And of course, if she didn't share his opinions, he'd had ways of impressing upon her his wisdom. Morgan suppressed a shudder and couldn't help the glance over her shoulder, even though she knew her dead husband wasn't going to be behind her, watching.

He'd always been watching. Waiting for her to screw up so that he could correct her. Lovingly, of course.

*Stop thinking of him! He's gone. Gone. Gone. Gone.* Morgan climbed into her Lexus and closed the door a bit more forcefully than she intended, and the sharp sound caused her to jump. Her heart pounded, and she emitted a shaky laugh at her foolishness. All she needed was time. Time to heal. Time to forget.

But even as she rattled off to herself the same advice she gave others, she knew, in her case, it was a lie because there were some things that not even time could erase.

The punishments. The rigid adherence to certain rules. David's rules. That even now, three years later, she couldn't free herself from. A part of her lived in fear that David might pop from the shadows and discover that the towels in the downstairs bathroom were not lined up properly nor were they color coordinated. It was a small thing. But not in David's world. And subsequently not in hers. Usually, she could keep the memories from biting but tonight was proving more difficult as a particularly brutal one began nipping at her thoughts.

"Morgan…would you come here, please."

Morgan stilled the chopping of celery and swallowed, a familiar trickle of fear following the knowledge that he was in the bathroom. Hadn't she replaced the linens with fresh stock this morning? David preferred everything clean, particularly for the guest bathroom as that was the room others would see. Of course, it made sense to ensure the guest bathroom was spotless. Impressions were important.

"Coming," she answered, placing the knife on the cutting board and carefully wiping her hands on her apron and not on the dish towel as David had taught her.

She rounded the corner and saw David scowling in obvious displeasure at the spotless marble counter. "Can you tell me what is amiss here?"

Morgan tried not to tremble as her gaze quickly searched for what was out of place. Her stare settled on the tiny soap ooze from the dispenser. Hadn't she wiped it down after using it? A bead of sweat popped along her brow in spite of the subtle chill of the house. "I'm sorry. I'll fix it right away," she said, moving to clean the soap dispenser but he caught her hand in a tight grip, squeezing the bones until she winced. "I-I'm sorry...I didn't mean—"

"What would people think about our home if they saw this? Can we not keep a tidy home? Are we slobs?"

She shook her head, tears springing to her eyes.

"No, we are not," he agreed, tossing her hand away and grabbing a handful of hair in a move so fast she almost didn't see it coming. Almost. Pain exploded as he wrenched her to her knees, practically dragging her from the bathroom. "I do this because I love you," he yelled, his face livid with rage. "You must enjoy these punishments because you make me do these things." He shook her hard. "Do you hear me? I love you! Someday you will learn and I won't have to do these terrible things to you anymore. Don't you want that?"

"Y-yes! Please, David! Please!" She cried, her knees bruising from the hardwood floor. "I'll do better next time. I promise!"

"Lies...all you do is lie to me when I give you the best of everything. How did I get saddled with such an ungrateful bitch for a wife?" He tossed her away like garbage and she nearly shuddered with relief, believing his rage was spent but she was wrong. Suddenly, he buried his booted foot in her stomach and she blacked out from the pain.

The next day she'd bled out the remains of the child she hadn't known she was carrying.

Six weeks was barely pregnant, she'd told herself as she'd tried to get over her grief. If David hadn't been worried that he'd ruptured something internal when she wouldn't stop bleeding, she might never have known about the child.

And David had been so remorseful.

Almost sweet—for a time.

"Baby, you're my life. I am nothing without you," David had cried, clinging to her, demanding her comfort even though she was numb with shock. "I don't know what came over me. I am completely distraught over what happened. You know it was an accident, right?"

"Of course," she murmured, stroking his hair with mechanical motions. David liked his hair gently stroked in a certain way. Although the hospital had recommended that she stay overnight, David had been insistent that he would care for her. Lying in their bed as David wept, Morgan had wished for the solitude of a hospital room. "It's okay."

"Why do you push me to do those things?"

he asked plaintively. "And why didn't you tell me you were pregnant?"

"I didn't know."

He pressed a tender kiss to her belly and hugged her tightly. "To think…my child had been growing right here… I am beside myself over what happened." His words had seemed so sincere, so racked with grief that she'd actually begun to wonder if things were going to get better. Perhaps a child would heal what was broken between them. "Can you ever forgive me, my love?"

"Of course," she whispered, tears slipping down her cheeks. Six weeks pregnant was hardly pregnant at all. They could try again. They would try again. And everything would be wonderful again.

Morgan closed her eyes, hating that she was stuck remembering old history when she tried so hard to forget. Maybe it was the Sinclair case dredging up the past. Or maybe it was her failed attempt to go to grief counseling. But either way, she wanted to be done with it.

Startled, she realized tears were tracking down her face. *Damn it.* She wiped at her face with a tissue and forced a bright smile. *That's it. Smile. David is dead. No one knows your secret and everything is fine.*

Just fine.

Morgan squared her shoulders and put the car into Drive, making a mental note to order new tires before the snow season started.

WADE WAS SILENT most of the drive to their parents' house but his mind was anything but still. "I don't understand," he said finally, shifting in the passenger seat as he tried to make sense of everything. "How did this happen?"

"I don't know. It didn't happen overnight. You know me and Mom have always had a rocky relationship so I wasn't spending a lot of time at the house, plus with Dad doing his marijuana growing, I didn't want to know too much. And frankly, I had my own stuff I was going through. I didn't have time to try and figure out what was going wrong with Mom and Dad. I thought they'd work it out somehow. It wasn't until a few months ago that I realized that things had gotten way out of control. By that time, it was more than I could handle on my own."

"But this sort of hoarding takes years to accumulate, right?"

"Yes and no. I mean, Mom's always been a collector so I was used to seeing gobs of stuff piling up here and there but it didn't get to this point until the last year. I think it has a lot to do with Dad moving out to the shed to be closer to his marijuana. Maybe it was the final straw."

"And Dad is sitting things out in jail right now?"

"Yeah. Both Rhett Fowler and Trace tried to bail him out but Dad refused. So he's there to stay at least until we can get things figured out with Mom. Honestly, I'm glad I don't have to deal with him, too."

Wade agreed, rubbing at his eyes. "Do you have any aspirin? My head is splitting."

"Glove compartment."

Wade reached in and grabbed the bottle, shaking out two tablets and tossing them back without water. He'd crunch them like candy if he had to to make this pain stop. They rolled up to the house, and he hated how desolate and empty the place looked. Helluva homecoming. They exited the car, and he surveyed the land. Still beautiful. His parents' place was backed up to the national forest, which gave it an enviable backdrop but an unenviable position of fending off the wildlife at times. "Nothing changes about those mountains," he murmured mostly to himself. "Brings back memories."

"Yeah, tell me about it." Miranda smiled and then gestured grimly for him to follow. "Let's get this over with. The tour is a short one."

Wade followed his sister to the house and after unlocking the door, ducked under the caution tape stretched across it and walked into what used to be his childhood home.

*Used to be* was the appropriate phrase. "What the…" Ah, hell—the picture didn't do the actual situation justice. "She lived in this?" He covered his nose as the smell hit him. "Oh, God. What is that stench?"

"Your guess is as good as mine but as far as I can tell, it's coming from the kitchen." Miranda pushed past a pile of magazines and books and danced out of the way as they tumbled to the floor. "Careful. You never know what might come tumbling down." They pushed toward what had once been Simone's room and bracing himself, Wade opened the door.

"Are you kidding me?" he breathed against the reveal. In stark contrast to the rest of the house, Simone's room looked as it did the day she died. He looked to Miranda and she appeared just as stricken. "What the hell is going on? It feels like a shrine."

"That's because it is." Miranda was just as horrified. "I can't believe that dotty woman would do this. Simone didn't even live here anymore when she died! She lived with me that summer."

As Wade surveyed the room, creeped out by the feeling that Simone might pop from a shadow, he realized any hope he might have harbored of a quick resolution died as the knowledge that their mother might very well need professional help, after all, sank in.

"I've seen enough," he said curtly, motioning for Miranda to leave. He closed the door behind them, and they made their way free from the claustrophobic clutter of their parents' home. Once clear, Miranda locked the front door and handed Wade the keys, which also had the car keys. He accepted the keys and drew a deep breath, even though his chest felt as if an elephant had stomped on it. He opened his mouth but didn't have the words. Miranda seemed to understand. She hugged him tightly and simply nodded. He appreciated her silence. He didn't want to talk about it. He didn't want to stay. In the end, he knew he'd have to do both.

"Where are you staying?" she asked as they broke apart. "You can stay with me if you want. I live in town. Trace and Delainey live outside of town. Both of us have a spare bedroom. Take your pick."

"Thanks but I booked a hotel. I managed to find something in town that was reasonable."

"Talen is going to be bummed. He was looking forward to meeting Uncle Wade in person."

Wade always made sure to send his only nephew a birthday card with money but he'd actually never met the kid. He forced a smile. "I'd love to but I think I need a little time to process. But let Talen know that I will definitely see him before I leave, okay?"

"He'll be so excited. He said you always send the best presents. How about dinner tomorrow night?"

Well, his secretary, Nancy, deserved most of the credit for his gift choices as she had a son around the same age and always pitched in with suggestions when Wade was unsure. He ought to come clean but he was tired and ready to put an end to this day. "Dinner sounds good," he agreed, and they hugged again before climbing into separate cars and driving off in separate directions.

He needed to put some distance between himself and everything he'd just discovered.

Hell, he needed a beer and sleep.

Tomorrow would come all too soon—and with it, one helluva fight.

# CHAPTER FIVE

"I DON'T UNDERSTAND," Jennelle started, her lip trembling as her gaze darted from Wade to Morgan O'Hare. "This is ridiculous. I don't need an evaluation. I'm not crazy!"

"No one is saying you're crazy," Morgan assured Jennelle with a pleasant smile that was completely lost on Jennelle because she was getting mad. "Due to the state of your home and your refusal to stay out of the home until it's been cleared, APS felt it prudent to do a mental-health evaluation. I assure you, nobody thinks you're crazy. You've been through an ordeal and everyone, including your children, has your best interests at heart. Isn't that right, Wade?"

Pulled into the conversation, Wade had no choice but to pick a side. And if he wasn't telling that woman to go stick her mental eval up her backside, he wasn't on his mother's side. But he'd prefer to do this without the audience of a stranger. He looked to Morgan and asked, "Can I have a moment with my mother, please?"

"Of course," she said. "How about I grab a coffee in the lounge? Would that give you enough time?"

He nodded, and Morgan exited the room, the sharp click of her heels receding down the hall. Wade sighed as he came around to his mother's side, saying, "Here's the deal, Mama…I've seen the house. No more games. No more lies."

"What are you saying? Are you calling me a liar? Wade Neal Sinclair, shame on you. I've never lied to you in my life."

"Mama, that house ought to be burned to the ground," he said, shocking her. "I don't even have words to describe the mess you've got going on in that place. And the smell? I nearly threw up. I couldn't handle being in there for longer than five minutes. And then Miranda tells me that you've been sleeping in the bathtub? What the hell is that about? C'mon, Mama…you've gotta know that's not okay."

Her chin lifted. "That Miranda is the problem. She's got you all riled up."

"No. Miranda isn't the problem. I hate to say this but it seems, right now, you're the problem." At her pale and wounded expression, Wade tried to soften the blow. "Mama... I know you've had a rough time of things with Simone dying but she wasn't your only child. We all loved her but we have to let her go."

"Don't tell me about letting go. I'm sick and tired of everyone talking about things they know nothing about. You don't have children and I pray that when you do, you never know the pain of losing one." Tears welled in Jennelle's eyes and her heart monitor began to beep in warning.

*Ah, hell, that can't be good.* He'd gone and upset her. He started to apologize but Jennelle's watery cry strangled the life out of him. "Simone was my special g-girl and you can't tell me to s-stop missing her."

Helplessness overwhelmed him at the evidence of his mother's unhealthy grief, and he didn't know what to do or say that wouldn't make it worse—*was that possible?*—but he knew things had to change. "Of course not, Mama," he said in a conciliatory manner meant to be soothing. "We all miss her. But...there was something creepy about that room." He knew instinctively that he probably shouldn't mention he'd seen the room but damn it, something had to be said and done about it. "You can't keep a shrine to her. It's not right. Simone wouldn't have wanted that."

"You obviously think I'm crazy just like your brother and sister. Go ahead and join the Judas team. I'm used to the feeling of this knife in my back."

He bit back a hot retort. "Listen, Dr. O'Hare seems like a really nice lady. Why not just give her what she needs so we can start fixing this mess you're caught up in."

"What if she says I'm crazy? What then? Will you believe her?"

*Ahhh, that was a good question.* He didn't want to believe any of this but after seeing what he saw last night, he couldn't ignore that his mother may very well need some professional help. "Just because you need a little help doesn't mean people are going to cart you off to a mental institution," he said, dodging her question a bit. "I don't pretend to know anything about what creates a hoarder—"

"Don't call me that word."

"Mama, face facts. You are a hoarder."

"I am not. I'm a collector and have been since you were a boy. Was I a hoarder then, too?"

"Of course not, but you can't try and tell me that your house was this bad when we were growing up. I couldn't walk through the living room without tripping on something, and there is definitely something dead in that kitchen," he said, trying for patience but Lord, his mother could push a saint. He'd forgotten how difficult she could be when she dug her heels in. Now he knew why Miranda wanted to push her into oncoming traffic at times.

"Don't be ridiculous," she said with a sniff as if he'd just uttered complete nonsense. "Something dead. There's no need to exaggerate to the extreme. Yes, the house is a bit disorganized but I am not a hoarder and I will not sit here and allow people to put a label on me that doesn't belong."

"Mama," he said sharply when he realized they were going nowhere fast. "I'm not going to debate semantics with you. APS has determined you are a hoarder. Whether you agree with the term or not is immaterial. I'm dealing in facts, not feelings at the moment. You want to get back into your house?" She nodded petulantly. "Okay, then. The plan to accomplish that is to do whatever needs to be done and that includes talking to Dr. O'Hare, cleaning up that house and getting rid of that damn shrine to your dead daughter."

"I don't see what Simone's room has to do

with anything," Jennelle muttered. "Her room was spotless."

"Which only makes it doubly creepy because the rest of the house is a trash dump." She gasped and looked away, hurt. He stopped, biting his tongue at his harsh words. He was no better than Trace if he couldn't rein in his temper. His mother needed understanding, not shaming. He drew a deep breath and tried again. "I'm sorry, Mama…I don't mean to hurt your feelings. I'm just frustrated is all and worried, too," he said.

Her dull answer, "Don't worry, I'm used to it," cut him deep but he supposed he had it coming. She sighed, heavy and wounded, as she added with a small shrug, "I don't know what I did to deserve this but there's not much I can do about it except suffer through it, I suppose."

"I didn't mean to sound so harsh. I'm just trying to get you back into your house." At that she nodded, and he felt the first tiny concession on her part. "So you'll talk to Dr. O'Hare?"

A long pause stretched between them until Jennelle offered a grudging "Yes," but there remained that mulish expression on her face that never boded well, and Wade knew better than to hope for smooth sailing but he'd take it.

"Excellent." He breathed a sigh of relief. "I'll go get her."

Although Morgan had said she'd return after coffee, he needed out of that room with his mother. The knowledge that he'd been happy to leave the situation resting on his siblings' shoulders didn't feel good. He didn't know how Miranda handled this day in and day out. He was already looking to bail and he'd only been dealing with his mother for a day. He figured a trip to the jail to see his dad was also on the schedule. Truthfully, he'd rather eat raw monkey brains than see his dad in those orange jail smocks. Simone's death had tipped everyone's world upside down and he hadn't realized that not everyone had found their equilibrium again.

He spotted Dr. O'Hare pouring creamer into her coffee and reluctantly drew her attention. "She's ready for you," he said, but stopped her with a gentle touch on her arm. "Dr. O'Hare, may I have a private word with you before you go in?"

She smiled. "Of course. I can imagine this ordeal is very trying for your entire family."

"Yeah, something like that. Listen, I'm just

going to come out and say it—my mom is difficult. Hell, my whole family is difficult. If you looked the word up in the dictionary, our family picture would probably be staring right back at you. But I can't even imagine what my mom has been going through because frankly, I haven't been here. I feel bad about that now that I see what's been going on. All I'm saying is, please try not to take anything she may say personally. Sometimes my mom's filter is nonexistent."

"First, please call me Morgan. I like my patients and their families to feel comfortable with me. Unless you're more comfortable with Dr. O'Hare, of course. Either way is fine with me."

He ought to keep things professional and with a certain amount of distance but he liked her name. It rolled off his tongue nicely. And he did feel less stiff when he used her given name. "All right, Morgan it is," he agreed with a small smile in return, but he really needed to ask what was truly worrying him. "Can you help my mom? Please tell me you've seen worse cases."

"I will certainly try to help," Morgan answered, but sidestepped his other question, probably because it wasn't professional to answer and he respected that, even if he'd hoped for a reassurance. "A major key to successful therapy is the patient's willingness to accept help."

"Well, she's not exactly jumping up and down at the idea," he admitted wryly. "But she really wants to move back home so maybe that will motivate her into accepting the help she needs."

"Perhaps. You'd be surprised how some people are tied to their past in an integral way. Letting go will feel like losing a part of herself."

"Wow. That's deep." He chuckled out of discomfort. Well, seeing as it was going to come up at some point, anyway, he decided to beat her to the punch. "Should we talk about the elephant in the room?" At Morgan's quizzical expression, he said, "Simone's death…it seems my parents can't let her go."

Understanding dawned and she said, "Ah, that. Yes, well, grief is a powerful emotion and can cause all kinds of emotional as well as physical manifestations. Hoarding, phobias, even insomnia—their roots can often be traced to an extreme emotional upset in the patient's past."

Insomnia. That was something he knew

about. But it wasn't because of his grief. He'd long since put to rest his feelings about losing his baby sister. "Well, some people aren't as strong as others, I suppose."

"It's not a question of strength," she corrected him with a gentle smile. "Some people are so strong that they find a way to cope with the side effects but that doesn't mean they processed their feelings in a productive and healthy manner."

Why did it feel as though she was talking about him? That was ridiculous. He was being defensive. "Well, at any rate…she's ready for you. I just wanted to warn you before sending you into the lion's den."

"Additional insight from family members is always appreciated. Thank you for trusting me with that information. Oh, and FYI, the coffee here will put hair on your chest. Very strong." And then she left, coffee cup in hand, out the door and down the hall, inadvertently causing a flush of awareness to remind him that he was a man and she was a beautiful woman.

Where'd that come from? Catching an eyeful of that pert behind twitching beneath her pencil skirt? He rubbed at his eyes, embarrassed by his inappropriate thought about his mother's therapist. Maybe he'd jumped the gun in breaking up with Elizabeth. Having Elizabeth here might've been a distraction he seemed to need, he thought wryly, even if he knew he couldn't possibly have brought Elizabeth to his hometown without creating mixed signals. Elizabeth…it would've been so much simpler if he'd felt the same way about her that she had about him. But when he realized the deeper emotions she'd craved weren't going to happen, he couldn't, in good conscience, keep seeing her.

He exhaled and shook his head as his gaze wandered to the coffeepot. Well, maybe a cup of strong, bracing coffee would put his thoughts back on the straight and narrow. It was worth a shot.

MORGAN ENTERED JENNELLE Sinclair's room with a ready smile, hoping to start off on the right foot with the matriarch but judging by the tight press of the older woman's lips, an easy time of things wasn't in the cards. No worries, she thought. She'd definitely weathered more difficult challenges than one stubborn, older woman.

"Good morning, Mrs. Sinclair. How are you feeling today?" she asked, setting down her coffee cup and taking a seat beside Jennelle's bed. "May I call you Jennelle?"

"No, you may not. I prefer Mrs. Sinclair."

Morgan smiled. Jennelle Sinclair was going to be one tough nut to crack but then she'd known that from the start. At least Jennelle didn't give her false hope of an easy case. "Of course. No problem. My name is Dr. Morgan O'Hare and I've been assigned your case by Adult Protective Services."

"And what case would that be?"

"Well, you've recently had a health scare and the state of your home was a contributing factor—"

"I don't believe that for a second. That's a bunch of rubbish."

"Well, no, actually, it isn't. Your home has been condemned due to unsafe conditions and yet, you went back to the house, which then put your health at risk when the paramedics couldn't quite get to you in time."

Jennelle looked away, angry brackets forming around her mouth when she couldn't refute the evidence. "I guess you have all the answers. What do you need me for?"

"Well, I am going to evaluate your mental health status to determine if you are competent to make decisions for your health and well-being."

"I never heard of such poppycock," Jennelle exclaimed, two high points of color flushing her pale cheeks. "Of all the rude, intrusive and ridiculous statements. My mental health is just fine. So I'm a terrible housekeeper. Is that a crime nowadays?"

"No, of course not. But it's our job to make sure you're not putting yourself in harm's way."

For a long, tense moment Jennelle seemed to struggle with all the pent-up fire in her chest but her health simply wasn't up to the challenge and she sagged against her pillow, wincing as she lost the strength to rage. "Do whatever you need to do," she said with weary bitterness. "I'm tired of fighting a losing battle. You people are going to do what you want, anyway. My consent is hardly necessary."

Morgan frowned. "I'm sorry you feel that way, Mrs. Sinclair. Perhaps within a few days you'll feel better about the process. Change is always difficult but once you embrace the therapy, good things can happen."

Jennelle sent Morgan a withering glance, and Morgan withheld a private sigh. She was definitely going to earn every penny with this case. But there was something about the older woman that struck her as terribly sad, in spite of her bark. She settled more comfortably in her chair then said, "Tell me about Simone…" At the mention of her youngest daughter's name, Jennelle softened and her shoulders relaxed but the overwhelming sadness remained in her eyes. When Jennelle didn't volunteer any information, Morgan tried to help her along. "My younger sister, Mona, knew Simone in school. She said Simone was the prettiest and nicest girl in their grade."

At the kind words, a tiny, almost imperceptible smile curved Jennelle's lips. "Yes, that was my Simone. Everyone loved her. She had a light that shone from her soul," Jennelle said, choking a little. "Sh-she was the light of my life. I miss her so much. I don't understand who would've done such a horrible thing to her."

Ah, there it was—the pain, the sadness, lurking ever so close to the surface, a demon of grief and impotent fury, twisting everything good and sweet into a pulpy, bleeding mess. What would it take to draw out that poison? Would Jennelle be willing to let it go? Some people clung to their misery, too afraid of the unknown to set it free. Only time would tell which camp Jennelle called home. Morgan commiserated with the older woman. "And as I understand it, her killer was never brought to justice?"

"No, the trail went cold and then interest dropped. Simone's case was shoved into a file and never touched again. I tried to resurrect the case, even posted a reward for information, but nothing came of it. Nobody cared anymore. They didn't want to hear about Simone's murder any longer, unless it was to gossip about it."

Morgan knew that much was true but hearing it from a family member plucked at her heartstrings. "Cold cases are hard to solve without a major break in the case. Technology simply hasn't caught up."

"They took DNA samples from her body but nothing came up in their databases. How could someone who would do something so heinous not show up in the police database? Surely, this wasn't their first time. What if there are other girls out there who've been victimized by the same psychopath?"

The anguish in Jennelle's voice was real. The questions in her head and heart gave her no peace. Morgan suspected this was the root of Jennelle's hoarding—trying to hold on to things as a surrogate for her dead daughter, who was ripped from her without warning.

"Sometimes answers don't come to us in a timely manner but we can't let those questions rule our lives," Morgan said carefully. "There are many questions surrounding Simone's death and there might be an answer someday but then again, there might not. It's a cruel twist of fate, for sure, but tearing your own life apart and pushing away your remaining children will not bring her back. Was Simone close to her siblings?"

"Yes. All the kids were close. We all used to be so close."

"And then she died."

"Yes."

"Your other children didn't give you comfort?"

"There is no replacing one child with the other. Besides, no one was like my Simone. She was my baby."

"How does Miranda feel about that?"

"She's jealous."

"Jealous? Or perhaps hurt?" Morgan suggested, and Jennelle closed her eyes, refusing to comment. Morgan jotted down some notes. "You are very angry with your daughter Miranda. Why?"

"Because she's a wretched human being."

"Okay. Why? I've spoken with Miranda and she seems very worried about you. Does that seem like the actions of a bad person? I can tell you that I've met and worked with bad people and she doesn't seem to fit the criteria."

The door that had opened briefly once again slammed shut and Morgan knew sharing time was finished when Jennelle said, "I'm tired. I did just have surgery. Surely, APS will take that into consideration."

Morgan snapped shut her notebook and deposited it into her satchel. "Of course. I've enjoyed talking with you. I'll come back tomorrow to finish my evaluation."

Jennelle's mouth tightened, but she shrugged as if she was helpless to stop Morgan.

Morgan gathered her things and let herself out of the room quietly.

The poor woman was eaten by bitterness and grief. She needed lots of intensive therapy to breach the walls she'd erected around herself to guard against the pain.

A walk in the park, it wouldn't be.

But she wanted to help this family. For some reason this case mattered to her on a personal level.

Perhaps that wasn't wise, but she needed to help this family heal. One thing was for sure; when she was busy with tough cases, it quieted the ghosts of her own past.

At least for a little while.

# CHAPTER SIX

MORGAN SIPPED HER WINE, enjoying the warmth from the crackling fire as her younger sister, Mona, returned from the kitchen, carrying a variety of cheeses on a small plate. "I noticed you still keep that nasty Limburger around. I thought you hated that cheese?"

"I do," Morgan agreed, reaching for a slice of regular cheddar with a cracker.

"Then why do you keep buying it? All it does is stink up your fridge."

Morgan shrugged. "Habit, I guess."

"Well, that's a dumb habit. It stinks and you don't even eat it."

Morgan smiled but remained silent. She couldn't help herself. She tried not to buy that stupid cheese but David's voice was in her head and before she knew it, the cheese was in her basket.

"Only a sophisticated palate can appreciate the robust flavor of a European cheese. If you want to elevate yourself, you have to stop gravitating toward the white-trash fare." The subtle sneer in David's voice rang in Morgan's memory and she forced a smile. Mona didn't know about David's peculiar opinions nor did she know about who he really was. What made it worse was that Mona had adored David.

"So what's new?"

"Not much. Just the same old stuff."

Mona wrinkled her nose. "Sounds riveting."

Morgan laughed. "Not everyone lives the exciting life of an artist, sweet sister. Speaking of art, how did your latest gallery showing go? I'm sorry I missed it. I had a client run overly long and I couldn't seem to get out of the office on time after that."

Another lie. That was the night she'd driven to Anchorage in the hopes of attending a grief support group but she'd chickened out—as she always did—and lost out on supporting her sister for nothing. Morgan busied herself with sipping her wine as she listened to her sister chatter on about this and that, as well as a bit of gossip.

"I made a few sales, which will keep me in ramen noodles for the next couple of months if I don't live too extravagantly," Mona ended with a twist of her mouth. "I definitely have that starving-artist thing down. It's not what it's cracked up to be, for sure."

"You could supplement your income with a second job," Morgan suggested cautiously, and hoped her sister didn't fly off the handle as she sometimes did whenever anyone in the family gave her grief about her career choice. "I mean, just a temporary thing to bolster your budget, of course."

"An artist can't split her creativity between the mundane and the sublime. C'mon, Morgan, you know there's really nothing out there that I would enjoy. Can you see me working for a fishing outfit or behind a cash register? I would die inside."

"Yeah, but paying your rent on time and being able to buy groceries is a nice thing," she reminded her sister then raised her hand to stop Mona before she got on a roll. "You know I support your artistic endeavors so don't lose your cool…all I'm saying is, you're not a kid anymore and I know you'd catch less flack from Dad if you finally picked a career that paid in actual money and not just exposure and goodwill."

"What would Dad know about being an artist? He's a third-generation fisherman like every other guy in this town. I think you managed to snag the one and only man who had any sophistication and class. It's probably because he wasn't from here originally."

Morgan refrained from comment and chose to sip her wine instead, not that Mona noticed.

"I mean, David was the kind of guy who knew what wine to pair with food and recognized that there was a difference between red and burgundy on the color wheel. The guys around here have one color palette—and it's the eight basic colors of a crayon box." Mona sighed and took a sip of her wine, ending with a grumpy, "I miss David."

Morgan nodded and downed her wine, forcing a brief smile, and Mona's eyes widened with sympathy. "Oh, my God, I've been such a selfish jerk going on about David when I know you're still not over his death. That's why you keep that stinky cheese, isn't it? It was David's favorite. How could I forget that? I'm sorry, sis."

"You're fine. I'm fine. I'm getting over David's death. I really am." Something caught in her throat and Mona became alarmed when Morgan choked a little. "I'm okay. It's been a long day is all. I have a new case that's a little sad and I've been thinking a lot about it."

"New case? What's it about?"

Morgan hesitated, then relented, saying, "Do you remember Simone Sinclair?"

"Of course. Why?"

Morgan shared only what had likely already made the rounds within town gossip. "Her family is having some real troubles and I've been called in by Adult Protective Services to evaluate the mom."

"Why?"

"She's a hoarder."

"Eww. As in living-in-a-garbage-dump type of hoarder?"

Morgan made a face. "Well, not exactly but she put herself in harm's way and I need to determine if she's competent to make decisions for herself. It's all very sad. The mom is still grieving for her lost daughter, so much so that she's pushing away her remaining children."

"That sucks."

"Yes, it does. What do you remember about the Sinclairs? I only knew them peripherally."

Mona leaned back and tucked her feet under her as she settled into a more comfortable position on the sofa. "Well, Simone was drop-dead gorgeous. I don't know of any guy who didn't have a major crush on her. She was super involved in school and really nice. I mean, some girls who seem to have it all have rotten personalities but Simone was sweet. At least, she was to me. I liked her. We didn't run in the same circles but, I don't know, she was never rude to me."

"Yeah, I think her sister, Miranda, was in my class and Trace was a class above me but we didn't know each other. Wade was three years above me. I remember he drove a burgundy Blazer, which I thought was cool."

"Hmm…have you met with the family yet?"

"Yes, I met with the siblings yesterday and the mom today. I feel bad for the family. So broken up with pain from the past. It's a tragedy." Sometimes when Morgan talked she felt as if someone else were moving her mouth and she was watching herself from the outside. Here she was talking about the Sinclairs being unable to move on and that was exactly her problem, too. She glanced at her empty glass. Another? Sure, why not? David wasn't going to pop from the bedroom and stare her down for indulging. She reached for the bottle and poured herself another glass.

"Are you okay?" Mona asked. "You seem off today."

Morgan chuckled. "You worry too much. I'm fine. Just tired."

"Should I go?"

"No, of course not. I love your visits. Helps take my mind off my troubles for the time being."

"Well, having a screw-up sister will do that for you." Mona raised her own glass. "Happy to help." A companionable silence passed between them until Mona said, "You know I loved David and he was probably the most amazing husband ever but you're still really young and I hate the idea of you being all alone. I almost wasn't going to tell you but if you're interested, I have somebody who might be your type."

"I don't have a type."

"Well, he's kind of like David. He's too old for me but he might be perfect for you."

"Are you saying that I like to date old men?"

"Of course not. I'm just saying as much as I love a sophisticated man, I'm thinking me and this guy just wouldn't be a good match."

Morgan sighed. She wasn't ready to date, not yet. Maybe not ever. David had broken something inside her and there was no putting it back together again because she didn't even know which pieces were missing. The fact that she couldn't tell anyone—couldn't bring herself to tell anyone—made it all that much worse.

To outsiders, she appeared the grieving widow. But her private self was a raging inferno of guilt, shame and yes, even grief. Why did she mourn him? Did she miss him? A little. Before things got really bad, David had been a good husband. It's just that the bad times had eventually eclipsed the good. By the time she realized she was living in an abusive marriage, she was locked into it. Only Remy knew. To everyone else, David had been a doting husband and pillar of the community. His funeral had been standing-room only, which had shocked her numb. "I appreciate the offer but I'm just not ready to date right now," she murmured, ready to drop the subject.

Mona nodded vigorously but there was a desperation to the action that made Morgan wary. "Of course you're not. I totally understand. David is a hard act to follow. But what would going to dinner hurt? Let me at least tell you about this guy and then I'll leave you alone, I promise."

Morgan sighed, humoring her sister. "All right, tell me about this guy," she relented.

Maybe if she let Mona get it out of her system they could put it to rest.

"Well, he actually owns the gallery that I just had my showing in. His name is George Founder and he sort of looks like Sean Connery but without the Scottish accent. He's very distinguished. I think you guys would hit it off."

Morgan frowned. George Founder? He had to be at least sixty years old. "I know of George and I think he's a little old for me." What was her sister thinking? Did Mona actually think she'd consider a man so much older than she as a romantic possibility? Morgan would've been mildly offended if it hadn't been coming from Mona. "I do like a man who is a fair bit younger than sixty."

"But he's a spry sixty," Mona insisted. "It's not as if he's wheeling around in a wheelchair. Besides, he happened to mention that he'd seen you around and wondered if you would like to go to dinner."

She was on the radar of George Founder? She didn't know whether to be flattered or embarrassed. "He's not my type," she said, hoping to put an end to this conversation. "When I'm ready to date I'll let you know, I promise. But I just can't right now. Besides, I don't have time to date. I have so much going on in my life with my job and my clients and putting this house up for sale that I just can't even think about dating."

"You're selling the house?" Mona asked, surprised.

Morgan cursed her slip of the tongue. She hadn't told her family yet that she was listing the house. She couldn't live in it a single moment longer. It was like a prison, more so than it ever had been when David was alive. His ghost was everywhere and she refused to live in it anymore.

"This house is gorgeous. It's probably the nicest house in Homer. Why would you want to sell? Are you having financial problems?" Mona's faint note of alarm was likely self-centered but Morgan didn't fault her for it. She ought to let the woman worry a little, though, she thought with a small hint of sisterly pique but instead, she forced a little light laughter to ease Mona's fear that Morgan's checkbook might slam shut.

"Why does there have to be a problem for me to want a change? No, to answer your question. I don't have financial problems. David made sure that I was taken care of.

But if you must know, it's very hard to live here and not see David around every corner."

That was the absolute truth. Except unlike what her sister envisioned, Morgan saw the opposite.

Sorrow followed as Mona nodded. "You poor thing. I can't even imagine. Here I was thinking that being in the house would be a comfort but I could see how it could be the opposite. Why didn't you put the house on the market right after he died?"

"Good question. I'm not sure. I think I was in shock for a long while and then I thought that having the house would be a comfort but it's been three years and I realize now that it's time to make a change. So I've listed the house with one of the Realtors here in town but it hasn't gone live yet, so it's not on any actual listings."

"I'm sure the house will sell. It's very well taken care of and it's just beautiful."

"Yes, but my Realtor has said that we're still in a down economy and people aren't buying high-end homes right now so there's a possibility that it might sit."

"Well, it's not like you have to be out. You can afford to wait for the right offer, right?"

Morgan nodded. She didn't want to wait.

She'd be willing to take a loss if she had to. Some nights she was so desperate to be free of this giant monstrosity that she was half tempted to give it away. But if she did that people would start questioning why she was so eager to be free of it. No one knew about that night, not the true events. All anyone knew about were the fictitious events that she'd made up, and she was done with that secret following her around, lurking in the shadows of this cursed house.

"If I had the money I'd buy it," Mona said wistfully. "But I can hardly afford ramen. Speaking of, I hate to ask this, especially in light of our earlier conversation but can you spot me a couple hundred bucks?"

Morgan wasn't surprised. Mona always needed money. "How much?" she asked, reaching for her purse.

"Four hundred would be nice but I could make do with three."

"Sure. Is this a loan or a gift?" Morgan looked at her sister with a raised brow. "Let's just call it a gift," Morgan decided. "I don't want to be chasing you around town for my money. But in light of this, now I have to gently insist that you start looking for something to supplement your income."

Mona accepted the check and tucked it into her pocket. "Given the fact that I just accepted money from you, I guess I have to listen to your advice. Yes, I realize I probably need a second job. But I'm not excited about it, and please don't tell Mom and Dad that I got money from you. I catch enough grief from them as it is."

"They're just worried about you."

"Well, they can stop worrying. It's not like I'm a drug addict or anything. I'm an artist, that's all. I like to create things. I like beauty and metaphor and seeking a deeper meaning in things. I want my life to mean something. Why is that so hard to grasp?"

"You can still do all of those things and hold a job that pays your bills. I hate being the bad guy here but I'm not looking forward to the prospect of supporting you for the rest of your life. I'm not having money troubles but there may come a day when I'm not flush. Clients don't always pay on time, this house is very expensive to maintain and David's life insurance will run out one of these days so I would like to know that my baby sister isn't living on the street if I can't give her a little bit of money now and then."

"I'll never be on the street," she said. "Besides, if worse came to worst you and I can at least get an apartment together."

Morgan shuddered at the thought. "Oh, hell, no. I remember sharing a bedroom with you and you're a terrible roommate."

Mona scowled. "Okay, fine."

"Just think about the job, please?" Morgan smiled, wishing she had her sister's verve for life and her thirst for meaning in her life, even though she could be a bit of an irresponsible mooch at times. "Listen, I won't tell Mom about the money you borrowed if you won't tell our parents about my putting the house on the market. I know I'm going to get a bunch of protests from them. Particularly from Dad because he might call it foolish to let go of the house that I own for emotional reasons."

"Sure. Your secret is safe with me. I got your back." Mona paused, then surprised her by going back to her original topic. "Can I please set you up with George?"

"Mona," she groaned, irritated. "I already told you—"

"Yes, yes, I know and I'm sorry but here's the thing, I kinda already promised him that you would *probably* go to dinner with him."

"And why would you do that?"

"Because George wasn't going to let me

into the gallery without the promise that I would ask you out for him."

Morgan stared at her little sister. "Are you kidding me? I definitely wouldn't go out with someone who would use that type of extortion to get a date. That really doesn't say much for his character."

"No, no, no, no, he's a really good guy. I'm sorry it came out that way. He really is a good guy but he's intimidated by you, I think."

"Intimidated? I'm the last person who would intimidate anyone."

"That's not true. You're highly successful, beautiful and you're very independent. Men can be very intimidated by those qualities in a woman."

That's how her sister saw her? Talk about living a lie. "I don't know, Mona—"

"Please just give him a chance. One date. That's all. And then you can walk away and I won't feel like I reneged on a deal and everyone is happy."

Morgan made a sound of exasperation. "You know who's not happy? Me. I don't want to go on a date with this man. I feel like I'm being forced into it through emotional blackmail. Which I don't appreciate, by the way."

"Duly noted. And I really appreciate this.

You're the best sister ever. And who knows, you might really like him. And you know they say the first act toward making a change is taking a leap of faith."

"Please don't. I will go out with this man on one date. A dinner. And then I never want you to put me in this position again. Are we clear?"

Mona nodded, solemn. "I understand. I'm sorry. I know I shouldn't have but I am in a pickle."

"Yeah, yeah. You're always in a pickle, Mona. That's nothing new." Morgan couldn't help the frustration in her voice. "Why was it so important that you get into this gallery? I'm sure you could've gotten into a dozen other galleries on your own steam."

"You have no idea how cutthroat it is out there in the art world. It's all about who you know, not just about your art. You have to network and Facebook and Twitter and mingle and do all these things that I don't want to bother with. I just want to get my work on the walls of somebody's gallery without constantly kissing ass to make it happen. It's exhausting. Who has time to actually make art if you're so busy mingling?"

"Yes, the world has been taken over by

social media," she mused in agreement. Remy lived on Facebook, often when he should be working. His excuse was that without his involvement in social media, Morgan would never know what was going on in the world. She sighed and asked, "Why was this gallery so important?"

"Well, I was hoping this one particular art critic would take a liking to my work and possibly feature me in this magazine for artists. But as it turned out, my style wasn't her cup of tea so she didn't write something very flattering about my work."

"So basically you traded me for no gain?"

"Yeah, but I didn't know that at the time. Besides, you need to get out more. Life is about more than just work and sleep."

"What am I going to do with you?" Morgan buried her head in her hands. "You make it so hard to be on your side sometimes."

"Yeah, yeah, I know."

Well, at least Mona didn't dispute that fact. "I hate to cut this visit short but I'm pretty tired. I have an early client tomorrow morning and I still have notes to go over."

Mona nodded and then gestured at the cheese plate. "You mind if I take this with me? Kind of 'ramened out' right now. I could use some protein."

Morgan nodded. "Yes, take the cheese and crackers. Would you like to look in my pantry to see if there's anything else you'd like to take home?"

Mona allowed a tiny smile. "If you wouldn't mind…"

"I don't mind." She stood and hugged her sister. "Just leave me the chocolate chip cookies. Anything else is fair game."

"You're the best. I really mean that." Mona kissed Morgan on the cheek. "I really hope that you meet someone as great as David again. You deserve it."

Morgan's smile froze but she managed to nod. "Well, we'll see."

Good God, would fate be that cruel? It was the one thing Morgan feared more than anything.

*Please, don't let anyone like David in my life ever again.*

Perhaps it was her sister's talk about dating or maybe she was just tired after a long day but Wade popped into her thoughts, momentarily blotting out David.

If she were looking to date—and he wasn't her patient's son—Wade might be the kind of man she'd like to enjoy an evening out with. Strong, smart and ruggedly handsome, Wade was a man who would make any woman take a second look. She withheld a wistful sigh when she reluctantly allowed reality to intrude. Who was she kidding? She couldn't trust the knowledge of her past with anyone, much less a potential date. She had to protect her public persona at all costs. There was no way she was going to allow David—or the threat of his influence—to derail another moment in her life. Was it lonely? At times. But then she remembered the pain, the humiliation, and the fear of living with David, and suddenly, being lonely wasn't that bad.

So dating? Not even a blip on her radar.

Which meant Wade—that hunky mountain of sexy potential—would remain forever out of reach for her.

But a girl could dream, right?

As long as dreams never became a reality.

# CHAPTER SEVEN

"SO TELL ME about California," he heard his sister say before she stuffed a bite of her steak into her mouth. He realized he'd only been listening with half an ear to his sister's conversation and he grimaced when she realized the same. She graced him with a scowl that he deserved and he started to apologize but she cut him off. "Come on, you have to at least make an effort, Wade. I'm trying to do eight years of catching up within one dinner, all the while trying to steer clear of topics that are triggers for us both, and you're making me do all the work. At least make the effort, okay?"

"I'm sorry, sis. I'm being a jerk. There's a lot of stuff running around in my head."

She nodded in understanding. "Yeah, I get it. Being home is hard after a long time away, I would imagine."

"Nothing's changed," he said, allowing his stare to wander the small steakhouse. "I remember our parents used to take us here on special occasions."

"Which wasn't very often because feeding four carnivore kids steak dinners was hard on the pocketbook," Miranda quipped around her next bite.

He smiled. "I always loved this place, though. Made me feel important whenever we came to eat here."

"Important? Why?"

He chuckled at his nostalgia. "Because when it first opened it seemed all the bigwigs ate here. I remember Mayor Gibbons used to eat here all the time and the Masons used to gather here for their monthly meetings." He shrugged when he realized his own childish reasoning didn't actually make much sense. He returned to her original question. "California is good. I'm very happy. My job is very fulfilling and I can't wait to get back."

"Wow, impersonal much? I'm not interviewing you for a job position. Relax. I want to know about the *real* California. I mean, Delainey's told me a few things about Los Angeles but you're on opposite ends of the state, way up in the mountains. I'm sure that's gotta be different."

"It's vastly different. I personally don't care for Los Angeles. I've had to go there a few times for meetings with other federal park officials but I much prefer my neck of the woods. You ought to come visit sometime, and bring Talen and Jeremiah. Speaking of Jeremiah…when do I get to meet this guy?"

"Oh, now you want to be the big brother?" she teased. "You'll meet him. Don't worry. You do plan to come to the wedding, right?"

He didn't want to make promises but he'd sound like a real jerk if he didn't agree to come to his sister's wedding. "Of course, if I can get the time off. I'm using up a lot of my banked personal time right now for this impromptu trip."

"Right. Well, you have some time to pencil that date in so I'm not too worried. What do you think of Morgan O'Hare?" she asked, somehow zeroing in on the topic that he'd just been thinking about when he'd zoned out. "You probably don't remember her from school but she actually knew Simone. Well, not her, exactly, but her sister."

"That's not saying much. I think everyone knew Simone."

"That's true. She did have a way about her, huh?" Miranda paused and then said, "This whole situation with Mom has hammered home the fact that none of us has really dealt with Simone's death. It doesn't seem right that it's been eight years and yet none of us has accepted the fact that it wasn't our fault."

He shifted in discomfort. He hated talking about Simone. "Not to be rude but I've moved on just fine. I miss her every day. She was a great kid but like you said, it's been eight years. It's time to move on."

"I don't think it's a coincidence that you have not been home since she died," Miranda pointed out gently. "I think we all know why you've stayed away."

"I thought we were going to avoid touchy subjects?" he reminded her with a slight smile. He didn't want to pick a fight with his sister over dinner. And he also didn't want to talk about the things that kept him up at night. "Do you think Morgan O'Hare can be objective in Mom's case? I know she was assigned the case by APS but I wonder if we can make an appeal to get someone else, maybe someone from another town to do the evaluation."

Miranda frowned. "What's wrong with Morgan? I like her. She seems nice. Although maybe we'd be doing Morgan a solid by requesting someone else," she said wryly. "Mom's not exactly a peach to be around. Especially now."

Yeah, he hated to admit it but Miranda was

right. He'd never seen their mother so eaten up with bitterness and pain and she didn't hesitate to take it out on whoever was closest.

"Simone's case was such a polarizing event in this town. I just wonder if we would be better served if we brought in someone who had no connection whatsoever to Simone."

"I don't think it's right to hold that against Morgan. I believe she can be objective. Besides, if APS had concerns, they wouldn't have assigned Morgan the case."

"We have one shot to make this work with Mom. If we make one wrong move, she's going to withdraw and shut us all out."

"Um, hello? Have you not seen how she's treating us? She's already shut us out. So I don't think it could get any worse."

"It can always get worse."

"Ugh. I'd forgotten what a stick in the mud you can be." She tossed a tiny crumb of bread at Wade's head. "I think you're being foolish. Sorry, but that's just dumb. Morgan is highly qualified to handle Mom's case and not to mention, she specializes in this sort of thing. Mom is not the first hoarder she's ever had to evaluate."

Wade winced. He hated that term *hoarder*. When he heard that word, he envisioned someone far worse than his mother but then, he couldn't deny that his mother's house had been pretty disgusting. "Fine. If you think she's qualified then I'll let it go. It was just a thought."

"Speak of the devil," Miranda said in surprise, peering past him. "Looks like someone's on a dinner date."

Wade tried concentrating on his own dinner, but in the end curiosity won out and he nonchalantly turned around. It was hard not to notice how pretty Morgan was outside of a clinical, professional setting. Her hair was down, curled in lazy waves that she had tucked off to one side. She wasn't wearing her glasses, which softened her face and the pink-champagne blouse she wore brought up the roses in her cheeks. He returned to his dinner plate and shoveled a bite of food into his mouth. "I guess all work and no play makes Dr. O'Hare a dull girl."

"Something tells me the date isn't going very well. She has a look on her face like she wants to escape."

"Maybe it's because her date looks old enough to be her father. I can't imagine they have much in common."

Miranda narrowed her gaze then her eyes

widened with recognition. "I thought that's who that was. That's George Founder. He owns one of the nicest galleries in town. He mostly specializes in art that I don't really care for but he has big-name clients. I'm talking big money."

Wade shrugged. "Good for her. I guess money is the great equalizer."

"That wasn't nice. How do you know she wasn't coerced into a dinner date with him? Or maybe she's just being polite because basically the expression on her face right now is that she'd rather poke her own eye out with her salad fork than remain another minute with George."

"Sounds like her problem, not mine."

"Okay, okay. I get the hint. So tell me, are you dating anyone in California? You never talk about a girl so we never know. I have to ask, are you gay?"

He nearly choked on his mashed potatoes. "What do you mean, 'am I gay?' What the hell kind of question is that?"

"Not that there's a problem with it if you are. You're still my brother no matter what. It's just a little weird that you never talk about your romantic relationships, which makes me wonder if you were afraid to admit something."

"And neither do you. Up until a few months ago you were pretty single, as well. It's not my fault that suddenly you're all fired up to get settled down. Don't drag me into that."

She looked guilty and nodded. "Okay, you got me there. Up until Jeremiah I probably never would've imagined tying the knot with anyone. Or being tied down in any way. But now that I have Jeremiah, he's made me realize that I was living a really lonely life. And now that Trace has Delainey, of course I think about what you're doing and how your emotional life is going. And now that I'm in love I realized that it's kinda weird that you have not had a steady girlfriend in a really long time. So the next logical question popped up."

"Could it be that I'm just too busy to settle down? You have to jump to 'are you gay'?" He wiped his mouth and took a drink of water. "To answer your question, no, I am not gay. I don't have a problem with gay people but I'm not one of them. I'm not attracted to men in any way. Does that clear things up?"

"Well, it clears that question up. But you're really not dating anyone? I mean, I'm sure you have *needs,* right?"

Did his sister just ask him about his sex life? *Please tell me this is not happening.* "Not that I wouldn't love to have a conversation with my little sister about my sex life, I don't have a juicy story to tell. If you must know I was dating someone on and off but I broke it off before I left. Her name is Elizabeth and she's an attorney. We're both busy, our schedules are hectic and neither one of us is interested or even available for anything more than casual."

That wasn't entirely true. Elizabeth had been lobbying pretty hard to push their relationship to the next level but frankly, the idea just gave Wade hives. It was easier to keep people at a distance than bring them in close. He didn't have time for romantic entanglements. Not to mention, the last serious girlfriend had wanted him to see a counselor because of his insomnia. She'd had a crazy idea that his sleeping problems were because of Simone. He found her idea to be ludicrous and when she wouldn't let it go, he let her go.

"I'll settle down eventually. I'll need something to do when I retire," he joked. "Besides, with you and Trace both looking to get married this year I don't think there is any thunder left for a third wedding."

"Well, shows how much you know. Trace and Delainey already got married."

"They're married? Hell, I didn't even rate a phone call?"

"Oh, stop, like you were going to drop everything and show up for a quickie ceremony at the courthouse?"

"Well, no," he admitted. "But it would've been nice to know."

"Take it up with Trace but honestly, you and I both know that Delainey and Trace should've married years ago. It was just a formality and they weren't interested in wasting more time."

He supposed he could understand that, and Miranda had a point. Likely, even if Trace had called, he probably would've sent his brother to voice mail. Guess there was no reason to ruffle feathers over something already done and gone. "A quickie wedding, huh?"

"Yep. Lucky dogs. Nothing but a justice of the peace to make it official. I envy them. Jeremiah wants to have a big wedding so no quickie wedding for us," she added with a grumble. "Frankly, this wedding stuff is exhausting. And then add in all of our parents' crap…it's murder on my sanity. Do you have any idea how many types of wedding cake there are? I think I've gained ten pounds just taste testing. And why does it have to be cake? I say let's have pumpkin pie."

He laughed. "I dare you to have pumpkin pie at your wedding. That would be awesome."

"Right? Who likes wedding cake, anyway? The buttercream is always too sweet and half of the cake goes to waste. Oh, and those cakes are expensive. Our small wedding is quickly approaching the $10,000 mark. That's ridiculous. I'd rather go to Tahiti."

"Why does Jeremiah want to have a large wedding?"

Miranda sighed. "Well, he said it's probably the one and only time he'll ever see me in a dress so he wants to do it up big."

Wade belly laughed at that. "You know, he's probably right. The guy's pretty smart."

"Yeah, he's a keeper." At the warm smile on his sister's face, Wade suffered a pang of envy and damn if his gaze didn't stray briefly to Morgan before darting back to his sister. For some reason, the knowledge that Morgan was on a date kept sticking in his thoughts like a bee frantically struggling against a spider web. Did Morgan prefer older guys? He straightened and squared his shoulders until he realized he had no business thinking—or caring—what turned Morgan O'Hare's crank. If she liked older guys, more power to her. Wade forced his attention back to Miranda, barely catching the tail end of her conversation but he must have covered well as Miranda didn't miss a beat. "Of course, all this wedding planning could be a waste of time. How am I supposed to pull off a wedding when my family is imploding? What if Dad isn't out of jail? Or what if Mom continues to go off the rails? It's times like these that I want to beg Jeremiah to elope. Honestly, I just want to have a normal family again."

At the quiet pain in his sister's voice, Wade cringed and tried not to hear recrimination, but he'd left soon after Simone had died, and he hadn't been around to help pick up the pieces. He hadn't expected to be gone this long but circumstances had put him in California and he hadn't made an effort to return. He liked California. And he loved his job. But his family needed him and he had to stick around. He purposefully brought the focus back to safe topics. "Tell me about my nephew. What does he like? It's hard to get to know someone over the telephone. Do you think it would be okay if I picked him up from school and we went to the park?"

"Oh, he'd like that," she said, lighting up with the kind of love that only a mother possessed, and he realized he didn't know his little sister as a mother. He'd left before Talen was born and had only seen him in pictures. "He's such a great kid. He and Jeremiah have really hit it off. It was hard for Jeremiah at first because he lost his only son in an ATV accident but Talen wiggled his way into Jeremiah's heart and has been there ever since. I wasn't looking for a father for Talen but I lucked out and got one, anyway."

"Planning on having any more?"

"I don't know…maybe down the road but for now we're just focusing on being happy and healthy—both emotionally and physically."

"Look at you, all spiritual now." He grinned, teasing. "I'm kidding. I'm glad to see you so happy. Makes me think I'm actually missing out by remaining a lone wolf."

She rolled her eyes. "Lone wolf. In your dreams. More like strange squirrel."

"Hey!" Wade lobbed a pea at her, and she dodged with a gasp.

"We're in a restaurant," she said with mock outrage. "What would our parents say?"

"Well, if our mother was in her right mind

and our father wasn't in jail, I'd probably get an earful or a thump on the head—then again, I'm not twelve so…"

"Yeah, yeah…" Miranda laughed and sighed as they both realized the evening was drawing to a close. "What if Mom doesn't respond to therapy?" she asked.

"I don't know. Guess we'll cross that bridge when we come to it."

"Are you going to visit Dad in jail?"

He sighed; seeing his father behind bars wasn't something he was looking forward to. "I suppose. Doesn't seem right to come all the way home and not see him, right?"

"It's up to you. But I can't help but think that it will make a difference if he sees you. I think he's taken it personal that you haven't come home in so long."

"Why is that?"

She shrugged. "I don't know. Just a feeling."

"Have you gone to see him?"

"Of course. I can't *not* visit him. Even though Trace is pretty mad at him, he still offered to bail him out, which Dad refused, and now Trace won't talk to him at all."

"I never in a million years imagined that I'd someday visit my dad in jail. What happened to our family?" It was a rhetorical question; they both knew what happened. He pulled some cash from his wallet but Miranda stopped him and put her credit card down instead. "You have a wedding to pay for. Let me get this one," he protested.

"Nope. I asked you to dinner and so I'll pay. You can catch the next one."

He grudgingly agreed but he was happy to see his sister doing so well. There'd been a time when he'd been worried about her. Her old boyfriend Johnny had been a real treat from what he'd heard. Maybe it'd been a blessing that he hadn't been here to see the crap he put Miranda through. He couldn't say he wouldn't have punched the loser in the face.

They said their goodbyes, and Wade forcefully refrained from glancing in Morgan's direction as they exited the restaurant. He didn't want to try and gauge how her date was going by her body language or facial expression and he just knew that he might if he dared to send a single look her way. He walked Miranda to her car and hugged her again, thanking her for talking him into dinner. The air had a serious bite and he sensed snow on the way. Funny how he could leave and come back, and the old instincts returned.

# CHAPTER EIGHT

THAT WAS THE longest dinner date of her life. Morgan yawned and placed her purse on the entry table, rubbing her eyes, intent on a single objective—a glass of wine and bed.

But as she went toward the kitchen, she heard the distinct sound of laughter coming from her living room. Mona, she realized as she recognized the laugh, must have been using her house as a place to entertain. It was something her sister often did when she wanted to impress someone. Ordinarily, Morgan didn't mind as long as she received a courtesy call to let her know but tonight she was tired, grouchy and irritated that Mona hadn't even given her a heads-up. But as she rounded the corner, ready to give her sister a piece of her mind, she startled when she saw who Mona was entertaining.

"Wade Sinclair?" The name escaped her mouth in a shocked gasp, immediately followed by intense discomfort over what she deduced was happening. "What is going on here? Please tell me this isn't what it looks like."

Mona glanced up at Morgan's sharp query, and Wade's gaze widened in recognition as he immediately put distance between himself and Mona. "Um…this is awkward," he said, looking as embarrassed as a teenaged boy who'd been caught by his parents making out with a girl.

Ugh. Had he been about to make a move on her sister? She shouldn't care—but she did.

"I didn't realize…"

She waved away his attempts to explain, definitely not interested in suffering through the uncomfortable stumblings of this awkward social encounter. Instead, she directed her comment to Mona, lasering her with a stern glare. "The next time you bring someone to my house to *entertain,* you have to let me know. Those are the rules and they haven't changed."

"Geesh, party pooper. You're in a fine mood," Mona groused then gestured to Morgan. "Wade, I believe you've already met my sister, Morgan."

"Sister…" The word slipped from Wade's mouth as understanding hit him between the eyes, and Morgan graced him with a brief but ultimately aggrieved smile. "This is… I'm so sorry. I didn't realize…"

"I know. It's fine." No, it wasn't. "But if you wouldn't mind calling it an evening…I would appreciate it."

"Of course," he said, bobbing a nod and grabbing his coat, but Mona wasn't too happy to lose her companion and abruptly stood, her hands going to her hips in an annoyed fashion.

"Hey, hold on now," Mona said, glaring at Morgan. "Just because you're in a pissy mood doesn't mean you have to come in and rain on my parade. Wade and I were having a wonderful conversation before you busted in and went all mean face on us. Weren't we?" She looked at Wade for confirmation, then added, "Don't mind my sister. She can be a giant wet blanket at times."

*A wet blanket?* Oh, that girl had balls. "Excuse me, I'm not in the mood for your shenanigans, Mona. I'm tired and I just want to go to bed."

"I think Morgan is right. We should call it a night," Wade said, going to the door in spite of Mona's protests.

Morgan spared him the awkward goodbyes. "I'm sorry, this must be very uncomfortable for you," she allowed. "But my sister has a bad habit of bringing home people she shouldn't."

Mona gasped, offended. "Okay, now you're just being a jerk. What are you talking about? How was I supposed to know that Wade was *your* Wade?"

"Whoa," Wade exclaimed, shifting his gaze from one woman to the other. "I'm no one's Wade. I think there's some confusion here."

"Settle down. It's just a saying. I didn't know that you were the one my sister was talking about the other night."

"You've been talking about my mother's case?" He scowled, immediately on guard. "Isn't that a breach of patient confidentiality?"

"Please, nothing was said that was a breach of anyone's confidentiality." Morgan tried to assure Wade but she could see a storm gathering behind his eyes. Not that she blamed him; if she thought someone was talking about her personal business, she'd be pretty upset, too. *Damn you, Mona, for making a mess of things.* Maybe she'd erred in judgment in the small details she'd shared with Mona the other day. She worried her bottom lip, concerned but ultimately, just eager to put a pin in this day. "Let's just put an end to this evening and start fresh in the morning. Everything will look better with the rise of a new day."

Mona rolled her eyes. "There you go, my sister's solution to everything." She turned to Wade and said, "Come on, we can go back to my place, my *real* place. I guess you figured out that this is my sister's house."

But Wade wasn't about to do that. "Sorry, I think this has gotten a little too uncomfortable for my tastes." Wade put his hand on the doorknob but stopped as if he wanted to apologize or comment but in the end he just left with a chagrined expression. As soon as the door closed behind him Mona whirled on her sister.

"What the hell? Why did you do that? I really liked him. You're the world's most effective chastity belt."

"Don't start with me. For one, there's a conflict of interest. Two, there is no way in hell you need to be messing around with Wade Sinclair. I think the poor man has enough problems without you entering into the mix."

Mona gasped, outraged. "Unbelievable. My own sister—stabbing me in the back. Nice. And for your information there is no conflict of interest—not for me. He's the first guy that I've felt a real connection with and then you come along and stomp on it. Who cares if he's the son of one of your clients? Big deal. In a small town that's bound to happen at some point. Besides, did you see the way that man was looking at me like I was a cheesecake and he was coming off a sugar withdrawal? Do you know how long it's been since I've had a man look at me like that?"

It was Morgan's turn to groan. "I'm not going to waste time debating your love life. Bottom line is, back off. Did *you* see how uncomfortable he was? Now I'll have to work twice as hard to gain his confidence because of this situation. You just made my job harder, as if it wasn't hard enough as it is. I really don't appreciate this, Mona. Sometimes you're so incredibly selfish."

"Ugh. You sound just like Mom. And here I thought you would always have my back."

"Don't you pull that with me. I do have your back. But it seems to be a one-way street with you. What happened to calling me when you plan to use my house? What happened to that courtesy?"

Mona shrugged as if it couldn't have been helped. "It happened on the fly. He walked into my gallery and it was like kismet. We connected on this level that defies explanation and of course, I can't take him back to my place because it's smaller than a closet. And besides, why are you home so early? You were supposed to be on a date with George."

Morgan threw her hands up. "I *was* on a date with George! And by the end of it I wanted to run screaming from the restaurant. We don't have anything in common, something that I knew already, and the dinner was excruciating for both of us. So I came home early. I was looking forward to a glass of wine and a quiet evening at home. And instead I got this."

"Well, sorry! How was I supposed to know that you were going to have such a crappy time? And speaking of selfish, you haven't even asked me how my second night went."

Morgan pinched the bridge of her nose, just wanting to be done with this conversation and this night. But one look at her sister's disappointed expression and she caved. "All right, I'll bite. How did the second showing go?"

Mona sniffed as if only mildly mollified. "Marginally better. Tonight had a different crowd and there were actually a few people who seemed interested in purchasing a few of my more expensive prints."

*Hallelujah.* Morgan was beginning to think

that Mona would never make a living from any of her art. "Well, that's good, I suppose."

"Yeah, it is. Felt good, actually. It kind of made up for some of the other opinions that were voiced."

"Let me guess. You overheard some people saying they didn't like it."

"Worse. One guy actually called my art confusing and mildly disturbing."

Morgan shrugged, yawning again. "Well, I don't know if that's bad. Picasso's art makes me feel that way and he's a classic so maybe you're in good company."

"Aww, you're sweet. But you're still not off the hook for ruining my date with Wade."

"It wasn't a date," Morgan corrected her as she walked into the kitchen to grab the wine. "That was a booty call that I interrupted and I'm glad."

"Booty call? Now that's just rude. Maybe he was my soul mate."

Morgan poured herself a glass of wine and took a deep swallow before answering. "He was not your soul mate," she said, finding the very idea absurd. "Any man you would bring home on the spur of the moment is not your soul mate. That's a booty call." To be honest, she hated that notion, too. Morgan contemplated her internal knee-jerk reaction at the thought and found it troubling. Did she feel this way because of the professional ramifications or something far more personal?

Mona poured herself another glass of wine, as always, making herself completely at home, completely oblivious to Morgan's troubled silence. "Okay, Miss Smarty-Pants, how exactly do you recognize a soul mate? It's not like they walk around wearing name badges."

Morgan was really the last person to counsel anyone on appropriate relationships but she had to keep up the pretense with her sister. She couldn't bear to devastate Mona's opinion of David, even if it was pure fiction. "Well, your soul mate is someone who is loyal, kind, generous with his time and heart and he doesn't sleep with you on the first date."

"Your version of a soul mate is boring. I think your soul mate is someone who sets your soul on fire. Someone who ignites your blood and makes you hunger for something that only they can provide." Mona's eyes lit up with her own description, falling in love with an ideal and certainly not reality.

Morgan wished things happened like that. In real life, it was hardly that explosive or earth shattering. "I think you missed your calling. Maybe you shouldn't be painting but writing because this stuff is golden. Talk about fairy tales. I hate to break it to you but love is not all hearts and rainbows every second of the day. Sometimes love sucks."

"How can you say that? You and David had a love affair. I've never seen anyone more in love with you than David. When you were in a room, his eyes never left you. It was as if he was consumed by you. I want that kind of love."

"No, you don't," Morgan said before she could stop herself. She closed her eyes, realizing she'd made a mistake. Trying to recover, she smiled and said, "You're right. Everyone's experience with love is different. And David was very attentive," Morgan added, choosing her words carefully. "I hope you meet someone who does all those things for you, but I just don't want you to be pining for something that might be unrealistic. That's all I'm saying."

Mona sighed, sipping her wine. "I guess." A moment of silence passed between them, and then Mona said, "So tell me your real opinion of Wade Sinclair…he's handsome, right?"

"I suppose," she answered carefully. Morgan had shut off that part of herself a long time ago and she was afraid what would happen if the switch were flipped. But there was something about Wade Sinclair that she found intriguing. There was a stoic strength about him that drew her with a glance and she sensed a great passion behind his eyes, and someday the right woman would benefit from it. But that woman wasn't her. "I really don't look at my clients that way, or the sons of my clients. It's unethical." That much was true, except the rules she set for herself seemed to bend when Wade was concerned. She shouldn't notice or care how handsome he was—but she did. However, she'd chew off her own hand before she admitted that fact to Mona.

"You and the rules. Haven't you ever just wanted to break the rules? I mean, come on, life isn't about coloring inside the lines every single day. Besides, that guy is hot. He has this buttoned-down look but when he loosens up he's really sexy with an utterly charming smile. Did you know he has a dimple?"

She was a sucker for dimples. Not that it mattered that Wade had a dimple. "Really? Well, I hate to be the bearer of bad news, but

Wade isn't going to be sticking around for long. Unless you want to split Alaska and go back to California where he lives, it's an ill-fated venture."

Mona wrinkled her nose. "California? Yuck. Can't stand that place."

"To be fair, you had one bad experience. Actually, California would probably suit you very well. I've heard Berkeley is very friendly to artists."

"Yeah, but then I wouldn't really stand out then, would I? I would just be one more quirky artist running around Berkeley. Here, everyone knows who I am—I'm Mona, the artist. And I like being a big fish in a small pond. I get more dinner dates that way."

"Mona, you're incorrigible."

"No, I think the word you're searching for is *adorable*."

Morgan couldn't help but laugh. She couldn't stay mad at Mona, no matter what she did. "Are you staying here tonight or are you borrowing one of my cars to go home, seeing as your ride left without you?"

"I think I'll just stay in the guest bedroom tonight. I'm out of wood for the woodstove."

"Ahh, and the truth comes out."

"Well, that definitely played a part. It's hard to get busy when your teeth are chattering."

"Fine, you can stay. But I have to leave early in the morning. If you make breakfast in the kitchen please clean up your mess. The last time you left splattered eggs everywhere and it took me all night to scrape it off."

"Are you really mad at me for bringing Wade here?" Mona asked.

"No. But I don't want you to date him, okay?"

"Are you attracted to him?" Mona asked, shocking her with the sudden question. "I mean, I would be willing to step aside if you had your eye on him. You deserve a little fun. I mean, Wade looks like he could boogie down, if you know what I mean."

Morgan actually blushed and uttered a tiny laugh at Mona's assessment. "I have no doubt Wade can handle himself in the bedroom… but no, he's not my type."

"Really? Then what is your type?" Mona asked, mildly confused. "You haven't dated anyone since David died. Have you really been celibate for the past three years? I would die. Maybe I ought to buy you a vibrator for Christmas so you don't grow cobwebs down there."

"Mona! That's enough already. Jeez, good night." She rinsed her wineglass and put it in the dishwasher, gesturing for Mona to do the same when she was finished, and headed off to bed.

But as she washed her face and applied her facial cream, her thoughts stubbornly refused to settle and it was all Mona's fault. Wade was a very attractive man. The idea of him in her bedroom, pressed up against her in a not-so-professional manner made her breath hitch. An unfamiliar tension curled inside her and she spent a minute organizing her vanity until everything was exactly in its place but the tension remained. Then she pulled a faint memory from her mental cache and startled when she realized what she was feeling.

Attraction.

*Sexual attraction.*

She closed her eyes and allowed a tiny bit of fantasy to play out in her head: Wade pushing her up against the wall, his tall, firm body aligning with hers perfectly, his tongue tangling with hers until she was left writhing with need. Her eyes popped open and she pressed a hand to her forehead, wiping away the sudden beads of moisture. She squeezed her thighs together to ease the aching emptiness and when that didn't help, she abruptly rose with a tiny cry of frustration and turned off the light, determined to go to sleep and put this whole silliness behind her.

She was wrong to think of Wade in a sexual manner. It was unethical. And it wouldn't happen again.

But as her eyelids finally drifted shut, Wade was there, naked, smiling, showing off that one adorable dimple and reaching for her.

It was going to be hard to leave this particular dream behind.

And even harder to face Wade in the morning.

# CHAPTER NINE

WADE RETURNED TO his hotel room, still rattled by what had just happened. He should've listened to his intuition and declined Mona's offer but what could he say? He was a man and she was a sexy woman—sometimes the libido got in the way of rational thought.

He shoved a hand through his hair, groaning as he fell to the bed. That was no excuse for what almost happened. Seconds before Morgan had walked through the door, he and Mona had been in a pretty hot and heavy liplock. He'd been fairly certain they were going to end up in the bedroom. Good God, he was so glad that hadn't happened. How embarrassing.

He stared up at the ceiling and wondered what Morgan was thinking at this very moment. Was she disgusted with him for going home with her sister? By the looks of things, Morgan hadn't been surprised to find Mona entertaining a stranger in her home. Did Mona do this sort of thing often? When he'd thought that Mona reminded him of someone, he hadn't expected that Mona and Morgan were related. But the minute Morgan entered the room, he saw the resemblance and wanted to die.

Mona had been amenable to taking the party elsewhere but the idea made him recoil now that he knew Mona was Morgan's sister. Why did it matter, exactly? He wasn't sure but it did.

Those excruciating five minutes were carved into his memory and would likely remain there until he died. Damn, he hadn't felt this kind of adrenaline rush in years. He searched his memory. Hell, the last time his heart had raced like this was when he was seventeen and he and Angelica Ramon had nearly been caught naked in her shower together. Her parents were supposed to be gone for the day. Well, they'd come home early. Oh, that'd been a race to safety, for sure. Angelica had pushed him out of the bathroom window—thank the Lord for a single-story home—and he'd run to his Blazer clutching his clothes. All her parents had ended up seeing was the cloud of dust from his squealing tires as he beat a trail out of there.

Too bad everyone knew that he drove a

burgundy Blazer. His dad had been waiting for him.

"A minute, son," his dad had called out when he'd tried to sneak to his bedroom. Wet hair plastered to his head, Wade cursed under his breath and did an about-face.

"Yes, sir."

Wade entered the den with slow feet, reluctant to meet his dad's stare. He probably looked guilty as hell but he couldn't help it. He knew Angelica's parents had given his dad an earful and now it was time to pay the piper. "You're never going to guess who just called…"

"Dad…"

"No, actually, on second thought, you probably know exactly who called, don't you?"

For a split second he considered playing dumb but he was caught. "Yeah," he answered. "Probably Mr. Ramon."

"A very angry Mr. Ramon. He seems to think that you and his little girl were up to no good. Is this true?"

He shrugged. "Depends on your perspective, I guess."

"How about from the perspective of Mr. Ramon?"

Wade shrugged again, hating that his dad

was drawing this out. *Just punish me already and be done with it.*

"All I can say is, you're lucky Ben Ramon doesn't own a gun, 'cause otherwise, I might be looking at a son with buckshot buried in his ass."

Wade cracked an inappropriate smile and quickly smothered it.

"So here's the deal…I remember what it was like to be a randy teenager but you gotta be more careful and more respectful of who you're playing around with. First thing tomorrow, you're going to go to Ben and mend fences. You're gonna apologize and be the respectful young man I raised you to be."

Wade looked to his dad, appalled. "You want me to go back there? He'll beat me to a pulp."

"Naww…he won't do that but he's going to give you an earful, and you're going to listen. That's his baby girl. Always remember that, son. For every girl you think you can mess with without consequence, she's someone's daughter. That ought to put things in perspective."

And it had. Angelica had had a reputation around school and he'd gone to her house without further thought beyond the exciting possibility of getting laid.

His dad had always been filled with quiet wisdom like that.

Wade sighed as the wave of nostalgia brought an unexpected crack of pain.

And now Zed was in jail.

What the hell happened?

How had their family disintegrated so completely?

"Simone…" he said softly, her name drifting from his lips like a prayer, and that was all that needed to be said. Life wasn't fair and he'd never suffered under the assumption that it was, but damn, if that message hadn't been drilled into his family with brute force.

He supposed there was no point in putting off the inevitable. Tomorrow, after he took Talen to the park, he would visit his father in jail. A small groan escaped as he squeezed his eyes shut, not looking forward to the visit. He'd rather eat nails.

Or relive that excruciatingly embarrassing dressing down from Ben Ramon.

Anything but talking to his father with bars between them.

He rolled to his side and tugged his clothes off. Without bothering to find his pajamas, he climbed into bed nude and clicked off the light. Sleep, as always, was a long time in coming.

But then, he was used to that.

THE NEXT DAY, Wade picked Talen up after school, smiling as memories of his own childhood spent within those walls came back to him. Talen, an adorable tyke with impossibly dark eyes native to his Yupik heritage, squealed with excitement when he saw Wade, even though they'd never actually met face-to-face.

"Uncle Wade!" Talen ran and jumped into his arms without reservation. Wade swung him up and placed him on his shoulders as they walked to the car. "Mom said you were picking me up today and that's all I thought about all day."

"All day? What about your schoolwork?"

"Yeah, I wasn't paying a lot of attention. My teacher said I was *woolgathering*. Whatever that means."

He laughed. "It means you were daydreaming."

"Oh, yeah, I guess I was."

"Who is your teacher?"

"Mrs. Eagan," he answered as Wade helped

him from his shoulders and into the car. "She's nice."

"Yeah? That's a good trait in a teacher. I remember my third-grade teacher. Her name was Mrs. Winchell. She was real nice, too. I remember she always had a graham cracker for the kids who'd forgotten to bring a snack."

"My mom always packs fruit. I wish I had a graham cracker."

"Graham crackers are good, I'm not going to lie, but fruit is so much better," he said, pulling away from the school and heading for the park. The boy didn't look anything like Miranda but he was a good-looking kid nonetheless, which made him think that Talen took after Johnny. Thankfully, the kid would never have to know what a pathetic asshole his biological father had been. Wade had to give Miranda credit; even when her head wasn't on straight, she always managed to put Talen first and it showed. "So what do you think of Jeremiah and your mom getting married?" he asked, maneuvering the streets toward the park.

"It's good. Mamu says that Great Spirit puts people in our lives for a reason and I think Jeremiah helped my mom not be so sad," Talen said.

"Your mom was sad?" Wade prompted, curious. "What was she sad about?"

"I don't know but she didn't get a lot of sleep. Sometimes when I would wake up for a glass of water, she'd be awake still. That happened a lot."

Insomnia. *God, did they all suffer from that wretched curse?* "I'm sorry to hear that, buddy. Does she sleep okay now?"

"Oh, yeah, she sleeps good. Jeremiah puts her right to bed."

Wade swallowed a guffaw. *Ah, the perception of kids. Gotta love it.* "I'm glad your mom is sleeping again. Sleep is important." *Wish I could get some. Just a wink would be great.* "Your Mamu seems pretty smart. What else does she say?"

"All kinds of stuff. She's full of smart stuff because she's real old."

He chuckled. "Yep. Wisdom often comes with age."

Talen turned to Wade, his dark eyes curious. "Are you here because of what happened to Grandma Jennelle?"

Mamu wasn't the only smart one. He smiled at Talen. "Yeah, buddy. Grandma Jennelle needs a lot of help right now."

"Yeah, it makes me sad because she's so sad inside."

"You think she's sad?"

"Don't you?"

He nodded. "Yeah, I do. I'm just surprised you can see that."

"It's easy to see. Grandma Jennelle seems mad but it's really sadness. Her heart is hurting. That's why it decided to stop working."

Wade regarded his nephew, amazed at how intuitive the kid was for such a young age. "I think you're right. We need to help Grandma Jennelle get past the hurt and sadness. Has your mom talked to you about what's happening at Grandma's house?"

"Sort of. Grandma Jennelle's house is a mess and it smells terrible but she showed me how to take care of the plants outside. She's fun sometimes."

"Yeah, she used to be a different person," Wade said wistfully, remembering when his mother used to smile, laugh and bake like there was no tomorrow. He swallowed the sudden lump that had risen in his throat and blinked back a wash of tears that came from an unexpected place. "Man, how about we put a pin in all this serious talk and hit the swings?" he told Talen as he put the car in

Park and shut off the engine. "We have a mission to have as much fun as possible for the hour that we're together. Sound good?" Talen gave Wade a thumbs-up with a gap-toothed grin, and Wade nodded in approval. "All right, then, let's get this party started, my little man. Time's wasting."

"Race you to the swings!" Talen dashed from the car and was sprinting to the swings before Wade could even get his car door open. He laughed at the boy's boundless energy and followed, realizing with a pang Skype wasn't nearly enough when it came to spending time with his nephew. He'd missed out on too much. But he supposed that was how it had to be. At least he had Skype. It was better than nothing.

WADE WALKED INTO the small jail building and after the requisite security checks he was led into a small visiting room where he awaited his father. His stomach churned, but he tried to keep his mind focused on what he wanted to accomplish today. He needed Zed to agree to let Rhett or Trace or him bail him out. That was the objective.

But even as he gave himself a mental pep talk, an immediate frown formed on his face the minute the guards escorted his shuffling father into the room and directed him to the metal chair opposite the table where Wade was sitting. The jail-issued clothing hung on his father's formerly robust frame and he looked a shell of the man Wade remembered.

Zed, upon seeing who was visiting him, let out a long exhale as if he'd known this moment was coming but hadn't been looking forward to it any more than Wade. A guard remained close by, hands folded but watchful as if Wade was going to slip Zed something to pick his handcuffs with, which Wade tried to ignore. "Hey, son." Zed stretched back in the chair, his manacles rattling on the metal table. "Wish you'd picked a better time to come visit."

"Yeah, me, too. What do you want me to say, Dad?" Wade asked, unable to play the polite card as he'd rehearsed in his mind. He knew he'd catch more bees with honey but all he had was vinegar in his blood at the moment. He was too bound up at seeing his father—correction, the man who used to be his father—in this situation. Where was the man with the quiet wisdom? Where was the man who'd taught him everything he knew about being a man? Gone. And in his place was a stranger. "Miranda tells me that you won't let anyone bail you out, even though Rhett and Trace both offered. Why?"

"It's like this, son. I'm better off in here."

"That's a matter of opinion. Did it occur to you that we could use your help with Mom? Things are falling apart. We need your help to get her to see reason."

Zed shook his head. "You don't need me. You guys got this in hand. Besides, I need to be in here."

Wade didn't hide his impatience. "No, what you're doing is hiding in here. I see what you're doing. You don't want to face the mess that our family has become so you're hiding out in this jail cell. Well, that's bullshit. You need to let one of us bail you out so you can lend a hand."

"I know it looks that way and maybe it is that way but I can't leave yet."

"Why?"

"I guess you could say I lost my way. And I finally found some clarity right here. I'm not ready to let that go yet."

Damn, that meant Miranda was right. Zed was fighting addiction and this was the best way for him to do it. What could Wade say to that? If his dad was truly trying to get clean and right in the head then who was he to force him out into the cold? But that meant it was just more work for them, and Wade wasn't okay with that. "Mom has a problem. Why didn't you help her? Why did you leave her in that place? She had a heart attack, Dad. Do you understand she almost died? Your wife nearly died in that train wreck of a house. And what's with that room of Simone's? She's made a shrine of that bedroom and it's creepy. Surely you had to have known about what was going on?"

But Zed remained silent. Whether he didn't have the strength to protest or he was silenced by shame Wade didn't know, but it didn't matter because his father's silence spoke volumes to Wade.

"Dad, I can't believe how bad things have gotten. I can't believe you let this happen. The dad who raised me would've never let his wife disintegrate like this. He would've taken the situation in hand and helped his wife find the closure she needed. But instead, you buried yourself in that shed and spent all of your time tending to an illegal garden." Wade shook his head. "Dad, you used to have talent. You were an artist, for crying out loud. But now you're just a criminal. How am I supposed to make peace with that?"

"That's your own struggle. I can't take that on."

"Yeah, that's rich. Seems to me you can't take anything on. Somewhere along the way you turned into a selfish bastard."

"Is that all you have to say? I haven't seen you in eight years and all you want to do is bust my balls? If so, you can take yourself right back out the door. I've got enough on my plate than listening to a pup like you give me *what for*. I screwed up. Sure, I know that. What about you? I raised you to stand up and all you did was run away, so don't sit there and lecture me about doing what's right. Because you sure as hell didn't. You split the minute things got hard. And don't you try to deny it. Maybe we all needed to stick together. Who knows? Too late now."

"I had a job opportunity," Wade shot back, refusing to take that on. "What was I supposed to do? Give up on my dreams because we had a tragedy in the family? I was trying to hold my life together, too."

Zed shrugged. "Well, I guess we've all got reasons for acting the way we did."

Yeah, that was probably true, but Wade

didn't like the way Zed made his statement. Somehow it made Wade feel guilty. And he had nothing to feel guilty over. "If we don't get the house cleaned up, she's never going to be able to move home. Trace is spending some of his money that he got from that reality show to hire a team of professionals to go in and clean. And they're likely to throw everything away because it's all ruined. You okay with that?"

"I guess I have to be. You do whatever you need to do to help your mom. She needs you."

"She *needs* her husband. She needs the man she married to stop hiding behind excuses and take control of the situation."

"You're delusional if you thought I was in control of anything when it concerns your mom. Your mom was always the boss so what makes you think I can stop her from doing anything that she wants? She fixed up that room to remember Simone. I didn't see the harm in it. By the time I realized she was spending too much time in there and everything else was going to hell, it was too late. It was like trying to stop a train that'd already jumped the track. When that happens, the wreck is imminent."

"Yeah, but at least you can check for survivors. You don't just leave the scene and wipe your hands. I don't care what you say, Dad. You screwed up. You abandoned us. Worse, you abandoned Mom. And I'm not letting you off the hook on that."

"If that's the way you feel, then so be it. I got my reasons and they're my own."

They could go on all day arguing like this. Neither would back down nor concede to the other. Both were stubborn and assured of their own position. Wade supposed there was only one thing left to say and he didn't mince words. "I'm disappointed in you, Dad. I never thought in a million years I'd say that to you. I never thought that this kind of situation would ever touch my family but here we are. So while you're in here licking your wounds and coddling yourself, I'll be out here taking care of your family. If you're all right with that, then you're definitely not the man who raised me."

The only indication that Wade's statement had touched Zed at all was the subtle tremble of his bottom lip, but he said nothing. Zed ducked his head as if accepting Wade's opinion and signaled to the guard. "I think my son and I have said all that needs to be said. I'm ready to go back to my cell."

The metal chair scraped against the tile floor as Zed rose and allowed the guard to lead him from the room. Wade watched him go, a burn in his chest spreading throughout his body as he realized his hero was dead. The visit hadn't gone as he'd hoped but it'd gone as he'd expected. Childish tears welled in his eyes but he wouldn't let them fall. He wouldn't cry for that man. He wouldn't waste a single tear.

As he left the building, he fought the urge to run. He could be on a plane and flying home within a few hours. Miranda and Trace could handle this. But even as he leaned dangerously close to making that decision, he knew he couldn't do it. He wouldn't abandon his family like that again. He wouldn't give that man the opportunity to say that he had run away. Not this time. He'd been wrong to leave the first time—he saw that now. There was nothing he could do about the past but he could do something about the present. *So buck up,* he told himself. *You're going to see this through. Your family needs you and you will be the man that your father couldn't be.*

It wasn't until he was halfway to his hotel room that he realized his cheeks were wet after all. Some pain just wouldn't stay down, no matter how hard you tried to stuff it in a private place.

# CHAPTER TEN

MORGAN SETTLED IN the uncomfortable chair across from Jennelle Sinclair and turned on her recorder. Later, she would transcribe her notes and she didn't want to miss anything important. "Jennelle, let's talk about how you feel today."

Jennelle sighed, as if irritated by the entire process and shrugged. "How *should* I feel today? Well, let's see, I've been tossed from my home, my children have betrayed me and my husband is a criminal. I'd say I'm feeling pretty low. And how are you today?"

Morgan ignored the bite in Jennelle's voice. "Well, I think we can address some of those issues if we work together. As for how I'm feeling, I'm feeling fairly well. Thank you." That was a complete lie. She was actually rattled today but she'd made a successful career out of pushing her own feelings aside and focusing on the feelings of others and today would be no different. The fact was, she was still upset at her sister, Mona, for bringing home Wade Sinclair. And the fact that she was bothered, bothered her. She shouldn't care. Wade was the son of her client. She never crossed those kinds of boundaries—ever. And yet here she was, suffering the pangs of jealousy. She forced a smile. "How are you feeling healthwise?"

"As good as can be expected for a woman who's just gone through open-heart surgery, I suppose. But what does it matter? My heart is broken and I'm not sure the surgeons could do much more damage, anyway."

The surgeon saved her life but Jennelle wasn't about to recognize that fact in her current frame of mind so Morgan let it go. "Let's talk about your home, shall we?"

Jennelle's expression shuttered so quickly Morgan thought she heard the slam echoing in the room. "What is there to say? Apparently, my home doesn't belong to me any longer."

"That's not true. It's still your home, and we want to do our best to return you to it. But you have to understand that your children are very concerned—rightfully so—and you cannot return to the home the way that it is now. But let's not focus on that right this second. Let's talk about what your home meant to you when all four of your children were alive. Talk to me about Jennelle as the mother and the homemaker. What was it like then?"

Jennelle startled at the question, caught off guard by her request. And that was the point. Morgan needed Jennelle to start talking so they could reach those painful places through back doors if needed, and the best way to do that was to go before the trauma, back when things were good.

"Why do you want to know? Everyone keeps telling me we can't live in the past. They've accused me of living in the past and now you want me to go there?"

"This is just you and me, talking. Woman to woman. I want to know you as a person, not a patient. Can we do that?"

"I suppose." Jennelle looked away, focusing her gaze on that scene outside her window, but it was several moments before she started talking and when she did, Morgan could hear the wistfulness in her tone. "It was an active house," she began, halting as if afraid of touching on those memories. Morgan maintained a respectful silence, waiting for Jennelle to continue. A slow breath rattled out of Jennelle as she slowly continued, dragging the memories from her locked box. "There was always something going on. Between sports, school activities, clubs and organizations, Zed's carving business, there was never a moment in our house that wasn't filled with life." Jennelle stopped as if buffeted by the echo of the past, and when she started talking again there was a subtle tremble to her voice. "So much love. Do you have children?" Morgan shook her head, and Jennelle sighed. "There's nothing like the energy of children to fill a house with love. I have always wanted kids. Back in my day it was perfectly acceptable to be a homemaker. Nowadays, it's almost a bad word. But I liked keeping a home. We grew our own fresh vegetables and fruits, Zed and the kids hunted in the mountains for fresh meat and we had plenty to keep everyone busy. Life was good."

"Tell me about your children, such as their individual personalities and what made them stand out."

"Oh, that was so long ago, I don't remember." Morgan knew the opposite was true. Jennelle remembered quite clearly who her children were. She was having a hard time reconciling who her children were back then and who they were now. Jennelle shifted in discomfort. "I don't understand the point of this. How is this going to put me back in my house?"

Morgan straightened, ignoring the pinch in her back and said, "Generally, people who hoard have emotional trauma in common. We're trying to get at the root of that pain and if we're able to do that, I think we can heal the wound causing you to hold on to things that you should let go."

"I don't understand why everyone else has to determine what I should and shouldn't hold on to. It's my life and my business."

"Yes, it is. However, when your safety became an issue then that's when outside forces had to come in and evaluate. Your children love you very much and they're worried about you. You are their mother and at one time I suspect you were all very close. I want to see that happen again. In spite of the hurt on all sides, healing is possible."

"You've never known the pain of a betrayal by your own flesh and blood," Jennelle said, dismissing Morgan's assurances. "It's a pain so deep, it can never heal."

Morgan knew better than to openly disagree, particularly when a patient was hell-bent on seeing things their way, but Morgan felt bad for Wade and his siblings. Jennelle was being intractable in her thinking. It was still early in the therapy but Morgan worried that Jennelle was so far deep in her grief that she was blind to the damage she was doing. Frankly, they all probably needed therapy at this point.

"Share with me a treasured memory," Morgan suggested. "Something when the kids were young perhaps."

"This is nonsense and a waste of time."

"Humor me. I enjoy hearing family stories."

Jennelle shrugged and said, "Well, it's not my dime you're wasting so, here goes nothing. The one memory that stands out more than the rest is blueberry season. We used to go picking blueberries in late July. Zed loves blueberry jam so we'd take a picnic and go fill our buckets with all the blueberries we could carry. I'd make pies and jam and cobbler and whatever we couldn't eat we would freeze for later. I could always tell when the kids were sneaking blueberries out of the bucket because their teeth were stained purple. But I didn't mind. I acted like I did but I really didn't. They were rascals, all of them. Zed was no different. In fact, I think he encouraged them to get into mischief because he thought it was funny. And sometimes it was."

"Sounds like one big, happy, loving family. Did you pass on your recipes to your girls?"

"I tried. But Miranda was such a tomboy she never wanted to be in the kitchen with me and Simone was such a social butterfly that she wanted to spend more time with her friends than learn how to cook. In fact, the only one who really wanted to learn my recipes was Trace's high school girlfriend, Delainey. I taught her how to make my strawberry jam."

"That was very sweet of you."

"I suppose. At least it wasn't wasted effort. Trace and Delainey just recently got married."

"Oh? I hadn't heard."

"Of course not. They ran off and did a quickie wedding at the courthouse. I guess they didn't want any family or friends around when they tied the knot. Pretty selfish, if you ask me."

"Or perhaps they felt they'd waited long enough? As I recall, they broke up and only recently got back together?"

Jennelle only sniffed in response. Boy, Jennelle was a tough nut to crack. She could only imagine how frustrated her children were.

Morgan drew a deep breath and followed with a smile. "At any rate, it must be nice to keep the recipe in the family. Now Delainey can teach any children they might have and keep the tradition alive."

At the mention of potential grandchildren, Jennelle softened ever so slightly. "That would be nice." *Ah, a subtle crack in her armor.* Jennelle examined a cuticle and then admitted, "It'd be nice to have more grandkids. I always envisioned my house filled with them. Things just didn't work out that way."

"No, but they could still," Morgan said. "Your children are still young enough to give you plenty of grandchildren."

"Perhaps."

"Do you have a good relationship with Miranda's son?"

"As good as can be expected. She prefers that he spend all his spare time with his other grandmother. That Yupik woman."

*Ouch. Another painful topic, apparently.* Morgan made a note and steered the conversation back to safer ground. "So Miranda was a tomboy and Simone was very social. What were the boys like?"

"Boys are boys. They liked dirt and bugs and hanging out with their father. They were always tracking and killing something. I always said boys were like a big cloud of dirt with legs."

Morgan caught the subtle smile before Jennelle could smother it, and Morgan capitalized on it. "Your boys turned out really well. I'm sure you're very proud of them."

"I was. Until they betrayed me."

"Here's something to consider—what if they didn't actually betray you but in the ultimate act of love made a difficult choice to protect their mother?"

"I suppose everyone can choose to look at a situation however they want. Doesn't change the facts."

"Correct. Facts are facts. And if we look at the facts in your case, you nearly died in your house. Yes?"

Jennelle looked away, stubborn as hell. "I'm tired. Are we done for the day?"

And just like that, Morgan lost her. "Of course," she said with a sigh. "I'll be back tomorrow, same time."

"I guess I can't stop you while I'm stuck in this bed."

Morgan gathered her things and rose. "I just want to say that although you may disagree, I feel you and your husband did a very good job in raising your children. And I feel confident we can fix what is broken between you all."

"We'll see."

Morgan left it at that. Jennelle wasn't in the mood to hear anything else and Morgan had enough experience to know when a patient had reached their limit.

Morgan exited the room and nearly ran into Wade. Mentally in her own world, she was completely startled and dropped everything in her hands, scattering notes and her recorder, grimacing when it shattered. "Crap!" she muttered, bending to pick up the pieces.

"Here, let me help you," Wade offered, bending, as well.

She was so embarrassed that she didn't protest, and when he handed her the pieces of her recorder she smiled briefly, too thrown off her game to react appropriately. Images from her imagination assaulted her brain and she was momentarily too flustered to speak.

"Are you okay?" Wade asked, concerned.

She flashed him a quick smile and tried to keep moving. "Yes, thank you," she answered brightly. "I'm fine. Nice to see you!" And then she hustled away from him as if the devil were on her heels.

By the time she reached her car, she was breathing heavily and feeling like an idiot.

Even worse? Her gaze strayed to the broken bits of her recorder and realized she'd have to try and remember everything Jennelle had said but her mind had gone blank.

"Son of a bitch," she muttered.

She needed to get her head on straight. And that meant no more allowing any inappropriate mental images of Wade Sinclair.

# CHAPTER ELEVEN

WADE WATCHED, PUZZLEDÁ as Morgan hurried down the hall and wondered if his unfortunate experience with her sister had upset her more than she'd let on. He had half a mind to chase after her just to make sure everything was okay but he had to talk to his mom. Wade was still out of sorts but he wanted to see what his mom's perspective was on his dad's voluntary jail stay. He could probably guess what her opinion was but he needed to be sure. He walked in and found his mom staring out the window, her expression wounded and lost and he gentled his voice to ask, "Is everything okay, Mom?"

She glanced at him briefly before returning her gaze to the view. "I'm sure you saw that woman leaving. I don't understand why she has to keep poking at me. Haven't I gone through enough?"

"Mama, do we have to go through this again? She's here because she's *required* to be. If you hadn't ruined your house none of this would be happening. But I'm not here to talk about your house. I need to talk about your husband."

At the mention of Zed, Wade snagged her attention. "What's wrong? Is he okay?"

"He's fine. I just saw him at the jail. But I have to say I'm incredibly disappointed. He's choosing to stay in that place instead of letting anyone bail him out. We could really use his help in this situation but he's digging his heels in and refusing to budge. Sort of like you," he added with a mild frown. "I don't understand what's wrong with the two of you."

Jennelle took immediate issue with his statement. "What do you mean, what's wrong with us? What kind of question is that? Your father is his own man. I'm not his boss. If he doesn't want to help it's his choice. Besides, has it ever occurred to you, all of you are making a big deal about nothing? Maybe your father realizes that and just wants to let the dust settle so things can get back to normal."

*"Normal?* Which normal would that be? The one where you live like a hermit crab, piling on more and more crap until it topples over onto you and Dad remains oblivious to what's going on under his nose because he's stoned half the time? That normal?" At

Jennelle's disapproving stare, Wade threw his hands up in frustration. "Because I've lost sight of what normal is in this family and I think you have, too."

"You're in a fine mood. Nobody asked you to get involved."

"Stop it. This is serious. I put my life on hold to come out here to help you and him. The least that he can do is accept the help to bail him out."

She shrugged. "Zed's never been one to accept a handout. I would've thought you would remember that."

"It's not a handout. In one instance it's a friend being there for another friend, and in the other it's his son."

"Well, either way it doesn't matter, does it? Because he's perfectly content to sit there and if that's the case then that is where he will remain until he's ready to leave."

"Mama, did you know that Dad had a drug problem?" he asked, going straight for the hard question.

She scowled. "A drug problem? Really? I think that's a little extreme, don't you? Your father doesn't have a drug problem. He has a gardening problem."

"Well, the *garden* he was tending is illegal.

So I would say it's a problem no matter what. And that doesn't bother you?"

"I don't like it," she admitted stiffly. "But he's a grown man. I can't chase after him and make him do what's right, any more than I could make you children do what's right."

"Yeah, that's the thing. We *are* doing what's right. And the fact that both my parents are acting like children is really disheartening."

Jennelle glared. "I did not raise my son to talk to his mother that way."

Wade took a moment to collect himself. "You're right. I apologize but I'm frustrated. I feel we are all killing ourselves to help you both and neither of you will lift a finger."

Jennelle's eyes flashed. "Oh, that's rich. Nobody said that you needed to come out here and police what we were doing. If your sister hadn't poked her nose where it didn't belong none of this would've happened. If you feel the need to blame someone, blame your sister."

It killed him that his mother was being so hard on Miranda because he knew it was unwarranted and coming out sidewise from a different place. Thank God Miranda had found Jeremiah and straightened herself out. Otherwise, Jennelle's wrath might've ruined her. "Please stop being so harsh to Miranda. She's the one who's been doing the heavy lifting around here and you've done nothing but run her down. It's gotta stop, Mama. For Miranda's sake, please. It's almost as if you hate her and that hurts my heart to even think because she loves you very much. We all love you and I wish you could see that."

"Parenting advice from a man who has never had any children? That's hilarious. I don't hate your sister. I'm very disappointed in her—there's a difference."

"Well, it's sort of hard to tell. Because what comes out of your mouth sounds like hatred. And the situation with Simone's room has definitely gotten out of hand. Everything in it needs to be boxed up and put in the attic."

"Don't you dare touch a single item in that room. Do you hear me? Not a single item."

"Why? So you can stay in there and pretend that Simone is alive? She's not," he said, adding in a lowered tone, "she died eight years ago. It's time to let the past go."

Jennelle gasped as if Wade had just sliced her with a knife, and her eyes watered. "How dare you. How dare you speak to me like this. A mother can never forget her child. And you are cruel to ask for me to do so. Now get out of my room. I no longer want to look at your face."

"Mama…"

"Get out."

Wade was flabbergasted by how stubbornly difficult his mother was being. She flat-out refused to give him an inch. He'd never seen her so closed off to her children. Just as the man rotting in jail was not the man who'd raised him, this bitter and mean woman was not the woman of his childhood. He didn't know this woman. And frankly, at the moment, he didn't want to.

Wade left, needing to put some distance between him and that room. He didn't know who to talk to or how to handle the situation. All he knew was that he was one big ball of stress. He could really use a beer. By the time he reached his car he already knew he was headed to The Rusty Anchor. He wasn't much of a drinker but right about now he could use a little bump in the chillout factor.

He walked into the old bar, assaulted by the smell of frozen boots, spilled beer and the subtle odor of fish but the pungent aroma somehow soothed his ragged nerves. The Rusty Anchor never changed. This place was an integral part of Homer and his childhood. Back in the day, the rules were a bit more lax than they were now. His mom used to send him into The Rusty Anchor to go bring Zed home on the occasion that he'd spent a little too much time with his buddies. One time he and Trace had seen Delainey's dad, Harlan, passed out at the bar and they'd helped him home for Delainey's sake. Not all the memories were good. He sidled up to the bar and gestured. The old bartender was a face he recognized and he smiled. "Hey, Russ, it's been a while. Do you remember me?"

Russ squinted at Wade and then nodded in recognition. "There's no mistaking a Sinclair but it's been a while since I saw your mug around. How you been, Wade? I heard about your dad. Tough break. But we all knew he was gonna get caught sooner or later. Part of me wondered if that's what he wanted all along."

"Was it pretty much common knowledge that my dad was growing and dealing pot?"

"Pretty much." He paused then asked, "What'll you have?"

"Whatever's on tap."

"You got it." Russ turned and filled a stein with amber liquid and pushed it toward him. "So I take it you're here to help out your parents?"

Wade took a drink of his beer. "I guess you

could say that. Things have fallen to crap. Not sure what to do about it, either."

"Probably not much you can do about it until they want to change. Your dad, he just sort of fell apart after Simone, you know? And I do know about your mom but there certainly has been a lot of change in her life that hasn't been for the better."

"Yeah, you can say that again. It's like I don't even recognize them anymore."

"Death will do that to you. Tragedy sucks the life out of you and leaves an empty shell behind."

"Do you remember Simone?"

Russ nodded. "Cute kid. Didn't know her very well, though. We didn't exactly run in the same circles."

Wade smiled. "Yeah, I guess not. You want to know something? I can't remember the sound of her voice. It's just gone from my memory and I'll never get it back. Sometimes I wonder if that's what my mom is going through. She's got her room all fixed up as if Simone hadn't died. Maybe she's just trying to hold on to everything because she's afraid she'll wake up one morning and everything she thought she remembered about Simone will be gone."

"It's possible. But life goes on. That's a fact that she's going to have to get used to. No matter how many trinkets she holds on to, it ain't gonna bring the girl back."

"Yeah, that's the part she's having trouble with."

Russ smiled. "Take it easy, kid. Don't OD on home stuff. Take it one step at a time. Good to see you."

Wade rubbed his forehead in an attempt to relieve the pain that had begun to throb. He needed more sleep. This insomnia was killing him. He'd hoped that a different bed, perhaps the change in scenery, would help with his sleep issues but it hadn't. He'd spent just as much time staring up at the ceiling as he did when he was at home. And he was exhausted.

Unbidden, Morgan's image popped into his head, and he was too tired to push it away. Maybe he really needed to smooth things out with her. He probably should've handled himself better the other night but in truth, he'd been embarrassed to his toes. It wasn't often that he caught himself in that kind of compromising position.

Yeah, that was probably what he needed to do. Clear the air and start fresh. Maybe even apologize. If he was embarrassed, likely she was even more so. He wished he'd noticed the similarities between the two women before he'd allowed Mona to take him to Morgan's home. Too late now. The only thing he could do was try to make amends.

He finished his beer, left a nice tip for Russ and, pulling Morgan's business card from his pocket, he checked her address and headed for her office. No time like the present to get things done.

# CHAPTER TWELVE

MORGAN WAS SURPRISED to see Wade walk into her office. And for a split second her heart beat just a little bit faster, and that made Morgan highly aware that she had an awkward situation brewing. Remy ushered Wade in with an openly impressed expression that only Morgan could see, as well as a quick appraising glance at his backside that made Morgan want to wring his neck. "Thank you, Remy. That will be all."

"Look at you, keeping all that sugar to yourself. I don't blame you," Remy said with a wink as he closed the door behind him.

Morgan shook her head, embarrassed. It was times like this that she questioned her decision to hire Remy at all. "I'm sorry. He's a little flamboyant. And he's also family. But believe it or not he's a good secretary." She was rambling. She took a moment to collect herself. "What can I do for you, Mr. Sinclair?"

"Please call me Wade. I feel I need to clear the air over what happened the other night."

"No need. It's none of my business. And my sister can be very persuasive." Now, if only she could slow her fluttering heart to a normal level. She hadn't felt this flustered around a man in God only knew how long, and the fact that it was Wade made it worse. She swallowed and tried a brief smile. "Truly. No worries," she assured him. "My sister can be a force of nature."

"Yes, that I would agree with." He had the grace to appear chagrined, which she found a point in his favor. There was something about Wade that spoke of integrity; perhaps it was the fact that he was voluntarily suffering through a terribly awkward moment in order to clear the air. She didn't know many men who would do that.

Her gaze snagged on the minute slivers of premature gray threading through his hair, and she was caught by the urge to run her fingers through it. The man must have a very stressful job to have a bit of gray already.

Wade continued and she realized she'd drifted. "However," he said with a frown, "I don't want you to get the wrong impression of me. I rarely go home with women I just met. She caught me at a weak point in the night and I want to apologize for possibly putting you in an awkward position."

"Oh, it's fine." Why was she lying? It wasn't fine. She was *very* bothered by the fact that Wade had left with her sister but how was she supposed to defend her opinion? She really had no right to be bothered. It wasn't as if she had any claim to Wade and it would be inappropriate if she did. But when she thought about her sister kissing those lips it drove her mad. She forced a tight smile. "Really, Wade, I assure you, I've already forgotten about the incident. You aren't the first man my sister has entertained in my home. I was just thrown off guard because we have an arrangement where she is supposed to call me if she is going to be entertaining, and she neglected to do that. I'd just come off a really wretched blind date and I just wanted some peace and quiet. So it really wasn't you…it was just a situation that was a little unfortunate."

"Why do you let your sister bring home strange men to your house? I mean, I know it's none of my business but it does seem a little unorthodox."

She sighed, shrugging. "I don't know. She's my sister and she usually gets her way. It's easier to agree than to fight with her but I'm selling the house as soon as I can and then the issue will resolve itself because I'm downsizing."

A memory flashed across his handsome features as he murmured, "My sister Simone was like that. She had the tenacity of a bulldog. She could never understand why anyone would tell her no." Wade caught himself when he must've realized he didn't want to open a conversation up about his dead sister and cleared his throat to focus on something else. "Why would you want to sell your home? It's a real show-stopper and unique for this area."

She really wanted to know more about Wade and his relationship with Simone but she didn't want to pry too hard into business that wasn't her own. "It has too many memories," she answered, which was the truth. But was *memory* the right word? More like nightmares. She couldn't wait to unload that house and everything associated with it. "Anyway, it's too big for one person. I want to simplify my life. I'd love a cottage or small cabin, something that's easy to maintain. A five-bedroom house with 4,000 square feet is ridiculous for one person."

"What does your husband say?"

"My husband is dead." She flushed, realizing she'd answered brusquely. Ordinarily, she was cool and calm when people asked about David because it was an act that she put on. But for some reason she had a hard time slipping into the role she was so familiar with when it was Wade asking the questions. That certainly didn't bode well. "I'm sorry. I didn't sleep well last night and I'm a little out of sorts."

"No need to apologize. I was asking questions that were none of my business. I don't know why I asked. I mainly wanted to clear the air about the situation with your sister. I should've just left it at that."

"No, I'm really sorry. I appreciate your concern. But I want you to know that I would never hold that situation against you because if Mona is involved, chances are, you didn't have a chance. She's a bit of a man-eater."

"Is that so?"

"Oh, yes. Mona knows how to get what she needs and what she wants from pretty much everyone who crosses her path—particularly the men." She laughed. "Actually, I might've saved you from being another notch in a long line of notches on her bedpost."

"Oh, that's a sobering thought."

"Isn't it, though?" She chuckled at his open look of distaste. "Anyway, no hard feelings."

"Great. Happy to hear that." He started to go for the door and then stopped. "You know, I have a hard time sleeping, too. Insomnia runs in my family and it's riding me pretty hard lately. Do you have anything that could help me sleep? I'm not talking about drugs, just some alternate suggestions. I'm a little desperate at this point."

"Have you tried meditation? Yoga? I find when I really can't sleep, yoga helps."

"I did yoga once. I think I pulled a groin muscle. I'm not sure I'm flexible enough for that kind of therapy."

"You don't have to be super flexible. You just have to learn how to breathe and listen to your body. It gets better with time and practice. If you want, you can come with me to my yoga class. It's a very gentle class, and I can almost guarantee you no one is going to twist you into a pretzel."

Was she insane? Inviting him to yoga? But the words had popped out of her mouth before she could stop them. And now she couldn't take them back. And even worse? She really wanted him to accept her invitation. This was insanity. And yet she was waiting for his answer.

"Really? Yoga? I can't believe I'm going to say this but I think I'm ready to try anything. I'm starting to hallucinate from lack of sleep and I need my wits about me to deal with my family. One inadvertent slip of the tongue and it's Armageddon."

She smiled. "Being on your guard takes a certain level of energy, for sure," she said, realizing she liked the sound of his voice. Unlike David, whose voice had been hard and unyielding, brooking no argument, Wade's voice was soothing. "Well, perhaps a good stretch is all you need. Try it out. What could it hurt?"

"I'll try anything once—or twice. What should I wear?"

"Something comfortable and something that breathes. Oh, and I should mention it gets a little warm in this class so be prepared to sweat."

"When is the class and where?"

She tried to hide her excitement. "The class is tonight at six o'clock. I hope to see you there."

"Address?"

She blushed at how fluttery he made her. "1456 Ginger Street."

"I'll be there."

She held her breath and her smile until Wade left the room. And then she sank into her chair wondering what the hell she'd just done. She shouldn't be socializing with him. She shouldn't be spending extracurricular time with him.

But she was excited and she couldn't wait.

HAD HE REALLY just agreed to go to yoga? He hadn't been lying about the fact that he'd tried it once and really had pulled something. The memory still had the power to make him wince. But there was something about Morgan that he wanted to know better. He sensed something about her that felt familiar. Maybe it was a terrible idea—one he would pay for later—but this trip home had been filled with instances that he was likely to regret later.

He rubbed the grit from his eyes. He hadn't been lying about the insomnia. He was about ready to lose his mind. There was a reason why sleep deprivation was a form of torture.

Had Morgan always been so pretty? How had he not noticed? Her hair hung in long, tumbling, feminine waves that made him itch to explore the texture between his fingertips. And while he'd been momentarily intrigued by Mona he realized now what he found most alluring about Mona was that she reminded him of Morgan.

His phone rang, and he picked it up, hesitating when he saw who it was on the caller ID: Elizabeth. He didn't really want to talk to her right now. When he'd left for Alaska she'd been insisting upon a conversation but he'd seen little point as he felt they'd made a clean break. He exhaled in irritation.

While Elizabeth was a sweet, sexy lady and he'd thoroughly enjoyed spending time with her, they lacked that special spark between them to push their relationship to the next level. At least, the spark was missing on *his* end. Elizabeth hadn't agreed.

He sent the call to voice mail and went to shower and get ready for his yoga class. But just as he went to get in the shower his phone rang again and against his better judgment he checked the caller ID. This time it was his brother, Trace, and he felt compelled to take the call. He and Trace hadn't spoken since the day he arrived, and Wade felt they needed to hash things out before a rift started that never ended.

"I haven't heard from Miranda about the evaluation on Mom. How's it going?"

"As good as can be expected. Mom is being difficult."

"So has Dr. O'Hare decided whether or not she's competent?"

"I don't think she's made that determination yet. Like I said, Mom isn't exactly being cooperative. I suspect she'll have her evaluation done by the end of the week, though."

"Good. This whole thing is dragging on and I just want it to be done. I need to be able to give a date to the professional organizers and cleaning crew. Right now the situation is in limbo and it's putting me on edge."

"It's going to be hell going in and cleaning the house. Frankly, it might be easier to mow it down and build a new one."

"Yeah, probably. But you know Mom would freak out even more if we did that."

"Is it possible for her to freak out more than she already is? I don't know. Scary prospect."

"Hey, I know we got off to a rocky start when I picked you up from the airport, and I'm sorry if I said a few things that were brutal."

"It's okay. I understand it was said out of frustration."

"Yeah, but that doesn't make it right. You're

here now and you're helping and I just need to let the past go. At least that's what Delainey says."

"Well, you might not want to let me off the hook just yet because I don't how long I can stay. It's different for you guys because you live here. My life and career are in California, and I can't put both of those things on indefinite hold while our parents continue to act like irresponsible children. I know it might sound like I'm placing it all on you and Miranda but honestly, I just don't know how long I can stay here and I want to be honest."

"I understand that you can't move home indefinitely but we're going to need you to help us at least until Mom comes home and the house is cleaned up. Surely you have some kind of leave or vacation time built up that you can use."

He did. But that's not exactly how he envisioned using his banked-up personal time. "That's not the point. I can't put my life on hold for this situation. I just can't do it. I'll do what I can but I don't want to make false promises."

Silence filled the space between them, and Wade knew Trace wasn't happy with what he'd said but Wade didn't want to lie about how he felt.

In the end, Trace sighed and said, "Whatever, Wade. I guess we just need to be thankful for whatever time you can give us."

Was that sarcasm? It had sounded a lot like sarcasm. "I didn't say I was leaving tomorrow. I just wanted to be up-front with you."

"I know." Trace released a pent-up breath. "I understand. The whole situation is screwed. It's not exactly how I envisioned starting my life with my wife."

"I'm sorry, little brother. I don't know what else to say. I wish it were different."

"Yeah, me, too."

"At least Delainey is familiar with the family. It might be overwhelming for someone new."

Trace agreed. "Delainey's been great. I don't know what I'd do without her. She keeps me grounded when I want to run off and disappear."

For a moment, Wade suffered a pang of envy for what Trace and Miranda had in their significant others. To have someone in your life who had your back and kept you centered…that had to be something special. Elizabeth had tried to insert herself in that role but he hadn't wanted her there. To be fair, he hadn't been interested in *anyone* fulfilling that role but maybe he'd been blind to the benefits of having someone there for more than just a bed warmer. "You're a lucky man," he told his brother. "Don't let her go."

"No chance of that," Trace said. "Well, I gotta go. Let me know what the doctor says about Mom."

"I will."

Trace clicked off, and Wade tossed the phone onto the bed as he strode to the shower. Why hadn't he told his brother that the reason he couldn't stay was because each moment that he stayed in Homer was another moment that he absolutely could not escape the crushing guilt he felt at failing? Even though it had been Trace who'd been the unfortunate one to find Simone's body, all three of the Sinclair siblings had been out there looking for her. And each of them had failed. Logic told him it wasn't his fault any more than it was Miranda's or Trace's fault. But that's not what his heart said. He was the big brother; he was the one who had always looked out for Simone and he hadn't been able to save her. Everywhere he went, he saw Simone and the memories of when she was alive. And he just couldn't take it. It's why he'd left in the first place.

And if he thought his insomnia was bad back in California…here in Homer, it was bound to kill him.

*Please God, let yoga be the answer to finding some blessed sleep.*

# CHAPTER THIRTEEN

WADE STEPPED INTO the softly lit room and nearly choked when he realized it had to be 100 degrees in that room. "Someone forgot to turn off the heater?" he joked to Morgan when she joined him, looking even cuter in her yoga pants and sports top. "It's hot enough to get a sunburn in here."

"Oh, it's supposed to be," Morgan answered with a smile as she spread her mat on the floor. "This is *hot* yoga. The heat will help your muscles to stretch and oxygenate."

"And it might help my body to clock out," he retorted, wiping the sweat already beading on his brow. "Is it normal to feel a little claustrophobic?" he asked, drawing a deep breath of the heated air and feeling light-headed as Morgan grabbed a guest mat and spread it out for him. "I'm not sure if this is my thing. I know I need sleep but I didn't plan on getting it by passing out."

"Give it a try at least once. If it's not your thing, then you don't have to do it again. But what if after this class, you experience the best sleep of your life?"

Ah, hell. That was a compelling argument. He desperately wanted a little vacation in Nodsville. "What if I my eyes roll into the back of my head and I fall over in a heap?"

"No one will judge."

He did a double take. That wasn't the answer he was looking for.

"Come on, scaredy-cat." Morgan grasped his hand and drew him toward their mats. "Stay by me. I'll help you through it."

"Is there a paramedic in the room in case, you know, someone dies?"

"No one has died yet."

He took a seat cross-legged, following Morgan's lead, and when the instructor started talking in soft, modulated tones, he realized if his friends back in California could see him now he'd never hear the end of it.

"I am Rainbow Aurora. I will be your guide through this journey to wellness this evening," the instructor said, and Wade had the presence of mind not to roll his eyes. Rainbow Aurora? He wanted to ask if her parents had graced her with that name or was that the name she'd taken on when she started her journey to Stretchy Pants Land. *Okay, stop being a jerk and try to make a go of this,* he told himself when the voice in his head became incredibly snarky. "If at any time you feel panicked and can't breathe, go into child's pose and give yourself over to the sensations your body is creating."

He shot a look at Morgan. *Are you kidding me?* She simply smiled and squared her shoulders with a blissful, anticipatory expression that made his insides tremble a little. Or maybe it was impending heatstroke.

Within the first five minutes of the class Wade wanted to escape except his legs had turned to jelly and he was pretty sure his lungs were sticking together. Why did he stay? Simple. Because watching Morgan perform her yoga poses managed to make the heat in the room seem like a cool breeze. While he struggled, Morgan floated from pose to pose in utter peace, demonstrating how flexible she was and how deplorably stiff he was. He was fairly certain he'd spent almost the entire class stuck in child pose, and even then he felt as if he'd been folded into the shape of a pretzel because it had to be unnatural for a man to remain in that pose for too long.

By the time the hour was up he had to admit his muscles felt looser than they'd been in years and exhilaration followed at having survived the class. He followed Morgan gratefully out of that hotbox and drank from his water bottle in big, greedy gulps. "I think I just sweated out a whole person," he said when he could speak. "That was insane and I think you tricked me into going. That was no peaceful, gentle class."

She smiled but didn't deny it. "If I'd told you that you were about to go to a class where the room was heated to ninety-five degrees and do stretches what would you have said?"

"I would've told you no way." He grinned. "You're a crafty woman. I better watch out for you."

"How do you feel?"

"Actually, I feel pretty good. I think this is my body's reaction to still being alive after a brush with death."

She laughed, the sound tickling his insides. He liked the way her face lit up with a smile and how she seemed far different from the buttoned-up therapist she presented at first. "Well, you said you wanted help sleeping. This always works for me. Every time I go to yoga class, by bedtime I'm ready to hit the sheets."

"That'd be a miracle. I'll let you know how

it goes." Sweat tricked from every pore, and he probably looked like a human faucet but he really wanted to invite her out for a nightcap. However, he knew that wasn't going to happen. He mopped his face with the small towel she'd instructed him to bring and said, "This has been…fun. *I think.* But now I have to go take a shower before I turn into a pillar of salt."

She smiled and wiped her own face. "Drink lots of water. You could dehydrate easily after a class like this. The water will also help with the soreness that you'll feel tomorrow."

"Soreness? You mean the torture continues?"

"Well, my guess is that you stretched muscles that haven't been stretched in a very long time. Chances are you will be very sore tomorrow and possibly worse the following day."

"That's something to look forward to. Sore tomorrow and worse the day after that. Tell me again why I did this?" He was joking and he loved the way her eyes sparkled with mirth as they bantered back and forth. She intrigued him. There was something about her that lit a spark deep inside him that should have been a warning but he wasn't in the frame of mind to listen. No, in fact, he wanted to know even more about her. "Hey, I know this is probably an inappropriate suggestion and if you shoot me down I won't hold it against you but would you like to go get coffee tomorrow morning? I promise to be showered and not dripping with sweat. I'm told I clean up pretty well."

"I'm sure you clean up very well, Wade Sinclair. You know you're a very handsome man," she said with a mild tease to her voice but soon enough she sobered, as if compelled to throw out a disclaimer, and added, "It probably goes without saying that we shouldn't, given my connection to your mom's case."

"What if I promise not to talk about my mom at all?" he suggested, determined to get that coffee date. "It's a small town. I'm sure you run into this situation a lot. If you never had anything to do with any of your clients' relations, I suspect you'd end up very lonely because there wouldn't be anyone left to talk to. Besides, it's just coffee. It's been a long time since I've been home and I didn't really keep ties so it'd be nice to talk with somebody who knows what's going on around town."

"And your sister and brother can't do that for you?" A tiny smile played with the corners of her mouth. Was she flirting with him? God, he hoped so because he was fairly certain he was flirting with her a tiny bit.

"Let's just say my siblings and I have some unfinished business from the past that makes it hard to just chat."

She seemed to consider his offer and he could tell she was wavering. *Please say yes.* He'd never been so keen on getting a woman to go to coffee with him before. In fact, he'd never actually chased a woman before. She played with her bottom lip with her front teeth and just when he was fairly certain she was going to turn him down, she relented with a small exhale as if going against her better judgment and said, "I'm sure this is *not* a good idea. I just want to go on record as to say we probably should keep the lines drawn between us but coffee seems harmless enough. What time would you like to meet?"

A wild thought occurred to him as he said, "How about this…I'll meet you at your place and we can enjoy coffee without the threat of people staring or whispering or making things seem less than professional."

"Are you asking to come to my house in the morning and have coffee with me? Or are you asking to come home with me tonight and share coffee with me over breakfast?"

A jolt of awareness went straight to his groin and even though he hadn't been thinking along those lines, that one simple question was like an adrenaline shot to the heart. Pulse thundering, and his mind gleefully throwing all sorts of images that weren't appropriate into his mental theater, he stammered an apology, worried that he'd offended her. "I…I'm sorry if I've overstepped myself. I was just trying to think of a way that might work for us both, given our situation. I didn't mean to imply—" Heat crawled into his cheeks as he struggled to redeem himself but Morgan's light laughter put him at ease.

"Relax, Wade. I was kidding."

"Oh, thank goodness. For a second I really thought I'd offended you."

"No, not at all. It's been a long time since I've bantered with anyone of the opposite sex, and sometimes I forget how to do it successfully." She blushed. "Wow, this conversation just deteriorated, didn't it?"

"No, it's fine. It's my fault. I should've never suggested going to your house for coffee. Now that I think about it, I realize how that must've sounded. We can meet at the coffee shop. If anyone has anything to say they can just keep it to themselves."

She released a shaky breath and nodded, but if Wade wasn't mistaken, he detected a tiny bit of disappointment in her expression. Was it possible that she'd briefly entertained the inappropriate version of his suggestion? Chances were, he'd never know. "Yes, the coffee shop would be best," she said, switching things up with an almost too-bright smile. "I will meet you at 8:30 for a little friendly chat."

In a parallel universe, he would've pulled her into his arms, sweat and all, and planted an exploratory kiss right on that sweetly curving mouth. In that universe, he didn't care about how it looked or why he shouldn't. In that world, his hotel bed that night would've remained made and untouched. But he didn't live in that world. He lived in this world and he'd just have to settle for something far less satisfactory with the alluring Morgan O'Hare.

He returned her smile and, feeling as if he'd just penciled in a business meeting, said, "I look forward to it. Again, I'm sorry if I made you uncomfortable. I wish we could just erase that last couple of moments. I hope you don't hold it against me. My dad used to say the reason God created women was because men needed someone to smooth out the rough edges that men had created with their mouths. I never understood that saying until just now."

To his surprise, she laughed. "That's a good one. No worries. I will see you at eight-thirty. And stop beating yourself up. It was an innocent comment that just came out wrong."

He nodded and slipped on his jacket while she did the same. "I'll walk you to your car," he offered, and she started to decline but he shook his head, knowing his offer was non-negotiable. "It's dark and God knows who's out there watching. Please allow me to walk you to your car so that I know you're safe."

At that she nodded, and he knew he didn't need to spell out his reasons for his apparent chivalry. It was impossible for him to allow a woman to walk alone in a darkened parking lot if he was within a reasonable distance to escort her. Maybe if someone had been with Simone that night, she'd still be here and this entire mess his family was in wouldn't have happened. Another instance of the parallel universe.

"Thank you," she said, pausing at her car door. Her breath plumed before her and he had to root his feet so he didn't close the distance to sweep a kiss across her lips. "I'm glad to see gentlemen still exist in this modern world," she said.

He smiled and gave a mock bow as if he were her knight in shining armor, and once she was safely inside her car, he got into his own.

His plans had included watching some television after showering but his conversation with Morgan stayed with him far longer than he expected it to. In fact, as he slipped into the shower his thoughts were firmly on Morgan's flexible body and they were decidedly Rated R.

Wade enjoyed sex but he'd never been ruled by the pursuit of it. He'd often gone long stretches between relationships and he wasn't one to seek out a one-night stand, so when he had the urge for a little carnal activity, if he wasn't in a relationship, he simply buried himself in work until the urge went away.

But he didn't want to bury this urge. He closed his eyes and allowed his hand to stray to his erection, remembering every line and curve in Morgan's body, and the way her eyes closed in peaceful bliss as she held her poses. The downward dog had been particularly engaging as he pictured himself behind her, framing that perfect backside with his hands on her hips, guiding his aching length into her ready and willing heat.

Was it wrong, fantasizing about his mother's therapist? Surely, there was something wrong with that—but something about Morgan worked for him in a way that he'd never experienced. She was a brainy beauty without an ounce of guile—in fact, he wasn't even sure if she was aware of how sexy she really was. She hid behind those glasses and conservative clothing but beneath was a woman bursting at the seams with raw sexuality, and the men in Homer were fools if they didn't see it.

Hell, if the situation were different, he might've enjoyed the early-morning coffee suggestion—the one that wasn't based in friendship.

He shuddered and nearly fell against the shower wall as his knees threatened to buckle. Several minutes passed before he could stand without trembling and when he could, he quickly washed and exited the shower, not sure what had come over him. He climbed into bed and snapped off the light, prepared to fight the insomnia as usual, but within five minutes, his eyelids began to droop and he drifted into dreamland. His last thought before dropping off being, *tomorrow I'm buying that girl's coffee! Hallulejah! Sleep!*

# CHAPTER FOURTEEN

MORGAN ADJUSTED HER purse on her shoulder for at least the tenth time as she waited for Wade and wondered briefly if she looked half as nervous as she felt on the inside. She'd paid particular attention to her wardrobe this morning and had actually spent a little extra time with some mascara and blush before heading out the door.

David had always insisted that she look perfect whenever she stepped outside their house, and after he'd died, she'd eschewed makeup in favor of a clean face, blemishes and all. It fit the part of the grieving widow to pay so little attention to her makeup but that wasn't the reason she'd thrown away nearly every bit of high-priced toiletries David had purchased for her. She'd wanted to reclaim some part of herself and that included her dislike for heavily made-up faces. She rather liked seeing people's flaws. Maybe if she'd caught a glimpse of David's secret flaws she would've looked past the flattery and the seemingly polished exterior and run far, far away.

*Stop thinking about David,* she told herself sharply, swallowing a lump in her throat. He was gone and he wasn't coming back. He couldn't control what she wore, how she did her hair or how she chose to wear her makeup. Maybe this was a mistake, a different voice piped into her thoughts. What was she thinking going to coffee with Wade? It wasn't ethical. Or was it? Was she breaking any rules? Was she not allowed to have friends?

Just as she was about to walk out the door and call Wade with an excuse, she nearly collided with him, forcing a laugh at her own private neuroses that he had no clue she was mired in. "I'm sorry! I was just…"

"Leaving?" he supplied, and she blushed at being caught, but his warm smile dissolved the apprehension spilling over in her brain. Why shouldn't she enjoy coffee with Wade? They were consenting adults and as far as she knew there was no law against it, nor was there an ethical quandary caused by enjoying polite conversation over a dark brew.

But one good look at Wade and she couldn't ignore the little flutters of awareness that tickled her insides. Damn, he was handsome.

Classic Sinclair good looks. Wade's expression faltered and she realized she'd taken too long of a pause and flat out lied to cover up her actions.

"No, not at all. I was just going to step outside to check my voice mail because the service in the building is spotty."

"Oh, do you still need to check your voice mail?" he asked courteously, and she purposefully dropped her phone into her purse.

"Nope. I was just killing time. I can check my messages later."

"Great," he said with a smile as they got into line. "Because I am determined to buy you coffee this morning as a thank-you for tricking me into that horrendous class."

"Oh? And why is that?"

He leaned down to murmur in her ear. "Because I slept like a baby last night for the first time in years. I feel like a new man and it's all because of you."

Morgan suppressed a shudder of pure hunger that lanced straight through her and fought the urge to lean into him and angle her lips for a kiss. She imagined he was a great kisser. There was something sensual about his mouth that tugged at the part of her imagination that she'd long ago shut down, reawakening urges and needs.

Her breath caught and for a long moment she forgot they were standing in a coffee shop in front of everyone who had eyes to see. She licked her lips and managed to say, "I'm so happy for you," but her mind was suggesting a different way to expend energy. "You could come with me next week if you're still in town."

His eyes briefly sparked with something aside from polite friendship, and Morgan knew with a certainty that she wasn't alone in her less-than-neighborly feelings. What would it be like to throw caution to the wind and do something so reckless, so wild and out of character, that it left a mark on her psyche? Would that one single action have the power to break the walls she'd erected to protect herself? *Danger.* She had enough marks on her soul. *Back away, don't go there,* a voice warned, but she felt drugged with the potential she saw in his eyes. "I have better coffee at home," she murmured, almost unable to believe that the words had made it past her lips. *Who was she? And who was in control of her mouth?* She held her breath, wondering if he would read between the lines and hear what she hadn't said.

"Are you sure?" he asked, and she knew neither were talking about coffee. She jerked a small nod, and he said in a low tone that only she could hear. "I would love to sample your coffee but I feel compelled to ask... should we?"

"It would complicate things," Morgan agreed, slowly crashing back to reality. What was she thinking? She was losing her mind. "I don't know why I said that. Now I'm the one making things weird. I'm so sorry." Heat flooded her cheeks, and she wanted to sink through the floor. When had she become so inept at talking like a normal person with someone of the opposite sex? She abruptly turned back around to face the coffee line, relieved to see she was next up. "The coffee here is excellent," she said, putting an end to the strange walkabout they'd taken together. "Best in town."

WADE DIDN'T WANT COFFEE. He wanted Morgan. Yeah, that was a sure-fire way to muck things up, and he wasn't the wild one in the family, so why was he itching to break the rules? He'd always considered himself the stable one. And stable people don't go off trying to bed their mother's therapist—no matter how badly his hands shook with the desire to roam her beautiful body.

They managed to order their coffee and find a nice, private area to enjoy their early-morning kickstart and as expected, their conversation was decidedly benign and boring. It was as if each of them was so intent on preserving propriety that they knowingly engaged in completely ridiculous fluff just to avoid talking about what they both wanted.

Finally, after a third go-around about the weather—yeah, snow's coming, it's Alaska. Snow is always coming at some point—Wade cut to the chase and simply threw it out there. "I'm attracted to you, Morgan. What do you think about that?"

Morgan flushed and took a moment to return her cup to the table before answering, and he knew she'd taken that time to formulate a perfectly safe answer to a very unsafe question so he didn't give her the chance. "I don't want to hear the acceptable answer to my question. We both know it's a bad idea. But I feel something and I think you do, too. We're both adults and we both know the risks. I'm not going to be in town for long. I'm not looking for commitment and I suspect you're not looking for a boyfriend, right? Let's enjoy each other and leave it at that because here's the situation…when I say that I'm attracted to you, I don't mean it in a passing, polite way. I mean it in a ravenous way. I've never felt this kind of hunger before and frankly, I'm not entirely comfortable with it but if you feel the same, let's indulge and it'll just be between us."

Had he actually said all that? Just put it out on the table like he was serving up breakfast? Judging by the two bright spots appearing in her cheeks, yes, he had said all that and either she liked his blunt assessment or she was mortified. It could go either way, and for a second he suffered the terrible feeling that he was about to get slapped. But instead, she rose and shouldered her purse and said, "My first client isn't until ten and I just remembered that I left some paperwork at home. You recall where I live?" His pulse went bananas, but he managed to nod. She graced him with a tremulous smile and said, "Good." Then she walked out the front door.

He waited five minutes then followed. Within fifteen minutes, he was at her house and she was waiting for him, framed by the dancing light of the gas fireplace—wearing very little aside from a welcoming smile.

MORGAN PURPOSEFULLY IGNORED every voice of reason trying to force her to change her mind and rescind her offer but the minute Wade entered her house, she discarded everything but the desire to touch and feel.

She'd made the bold decision to wait for Wade in the living room, nude, because she didn't want to allow herself any opportunity to back out. She needed this. And not just because she needed the physical release but because she desperately needed David out of her head and out of her life forever.

Wade's Adam's apple bobbed as he stared, his hands going to his buttons to undress. "You look amazing. More beautiful than I imagined." He practically ripped his shirt off and tossed it, going immediately to his pants as he kicked off his shoes. "I just want you to know that I don't do this sort of thing. I'm not the kind of guy who has random one-night stands."

She smiled at his nervousness, finding it endearing. Knowing that Wade was fighting his own internal demons strengthened her desire to feel him inside her.

"Did you bring protection?" she asked, liking what she saw. His body type appealed to her, loving that it was distinctly different from David's. Whereas Wade had a thin smattering of chest hair spread across his pectorals that narrowed to a trail to his groin, David had been covered in hair that he often shaved, which had made his skin prickly to the touch. Her question cleared some of the lustful haze from his eyes as he retrieved his discarded pants to dig around in the pocket.

"You mean these?" He pulled three condoms free with a playful twist of his mouth. "I like to come prepared."

"Excellent," she murmured, going up on her toes as he wrapped his arms around her and pulled her tightly against him. They fit together well and it felt natural to be in his arms. Wade brushed her lips with his in an exploratory kiss that sent tingles of sweet sensation tripping down her vertebrae, and when she responded by flicking her tongue lightly against his, he deepened the kiss with the right amount of pressure.

Morgan allowed herself to free fall into the pleasure Wade was offering and for the first time in a very long time, she remembered that sex with the right partner could change a person. Somehow they found the sofa, and she ended up on her back with Wade pressing soft, urgent kisses down her front, taking time to lave each breast with the attendant care of a man intent on wringing every last bit of pleasure from the action.

She covered her eyes with her hand as she gasped, delirious with the sweetness of the moment. As if that wasn't enough, Wade made his way down her belly, and she gasped in shock when his mouth touched her feminine folds. Heat raced to her cheeks as she fought the urge to cover herself. David had always believed that a woman's genital area was dirty and anyone who put his mouth there was nuts. Plus, David had been fairly certain that no man enjoyed going down on a woman and only pretended to enjoy it. And after being under his thumb for so long, Morgan heard his sneer even though he was long gone.

Wade sensed something was wrong and stopped, glancing up at her with a quizzical expression. "Do you not want me to…?" he asked, a subtle frown creasing his brow, as if he were disappointed at the prospect of being denied.

"You don't have to," she started, shaking her head but then she'd really liked what he'd been doing. She more than liked it. The touch of his tongue against her flesh had been like the zap of a live wire—electrifying. She swallowed and ventured to admit, "But I liked it..."

A slow grin spread across Wade's face as if relieved, and he wasted little time in talk as he returned to business.

Within moments, Morgan forgot all about David and his peculiar ideas about sex and how it should or should not be performed and lost herself to the pleasure Wade was creating with his clever tongue and fingers.

Her last rational thought? From now on, this was going on her sexual menu because it was awesome.

# CHAPTER FIFTEEN

WADE HAD NEVER been one to lounge in the nude but doing it with Morgan seemed perfectly natural. If someone were to catch a glimpse of them, they'd assume Wade and Morgan were a long-term couple who were nudists on the side because they both seemed comfortable in their skin with one another.

"You have a beautiful body," he said, openly admiring Morgan as she returned to the sofa with a plate of sliced fruits. He accepted a pear and bit into it, grinning when she gave him a cheeky smile. "And no, I don't say that to every naked girl I'm with."

"No?" She bit into a green apple slice. "Then thank you. The yoga is paying off, I see."

"From my vantage point, I would say a definite yes. You are very flexible," he said, wiggling his brows in a comically lascivious manner that made her giggle like a young girl. "And I can see now that I should've sprung for the bigger condom package."

Morgan laughed and nodded as she finished her apple. "I should probably get back to work. In fact, Remy is probably fretting as we speak. I don't take off like this," she said, reaching over to grab her cell phone. Seeing how many missed calls she had, she lifted her phone as proof. "See? Remy is probably calling the National Guard. He's a little dramatic."

"Remy…is that short for anything?"

"Oh, no, his given name is Paul but he didn't feel that had enough flair so he changed it to Remy when we were in college. College is where he discovered himself, he says."

"I'm going to take a leap here and guess that Remy is…"

"Gay?" she supplied, and Wade nodded. "Yep. Out and proud. It was a mild upset in the family when he came out but now, I don't even remember what he was like before."

"Are you close?"

Morgan paused and a flicker of a shadow crossed her expression but it cleared quickly as she grabbed another pear slice. "We're as close as we can be without being siblings, I guess. He's a good man. Even if he does poke his nose where it doesn't belong now and then."

"Isn't that what family is for?" he asked drily. He couldn't remember a time when his siblings weren't offering opinions, solicited or not. "My siblings are pretty good at being bossy. I think Simone was the bossiest," he said, recalling how his baby sister had been a pro at getting what she wanted from whoever and whenever. "Or maybe we just indulged her a lot. I don't know. But the other two are pretty bossy, too."

"Strong genes," Morgan said, shifting on the sofa. "Your mother is a very strong woman. It stands to reason she'd pass on that trait to one or more of her children."

"That she did. I like to think of myself as pretty even-keeled but maybe I ought to ask my employees first before I own that opinion."

"What do you do?"

"I'm the superintendent of a national park in California."

Her brows went up, impressed. "Really? Which park?"

"Yosemite."

"Ah, beautiful country. I'd been there once before I started college. My girlfriends and I took a California road trip. We started at San Francisco and ended in San Diego. It was a wild time. We did all manner of fun, exciting, scary and sometimes boneheaded things." She stopped and her expression softened with the memories. "Yes, those were some good times. I think everyone should take a road trip like that before starting college. Sort of like sowing your oats before you buckle down. Have you ever taken a trip like that?"

He shook his head. "No, I'm not what you'd call spontaneous," he admitted, though it seemed an incongruous statement to make when he'd just made love to a woman he barely knew. "I like to plan things out."

"Well, we had to plan a little bit but we wanted things to be free to flow."

"Are you a hippie at heart?" he teased.

Her tone became wistful as she answered, "Maybe at one time." She shook her head and continued, "But that was a long time ago. Now my life is very scheduled and structured."

"Which way do you like better?"

His question seemed to scratch at something personal that she hadn't meant to share and he could see her withdraw. "I'm sorry... did I say something?"

"Of course not," she said, trying to laugh but he sensed something there, beneath the surface. She glanced out the window and her expression changed as she rose quickly, going to the window. "Damn it," she said under her breath, and when he followed her, he knew exactly what the problem was.

"Guess I should've paid more attention to the weather conversation we had earlier," he said, watching as the snow coming down blanketed the area, making the driveway impassable at this point. "Damn."

"I need to call Remy," she said, distressed. "I have a full client load and he'll need to cancel and reschedule for me."

He needed to make a few calls himself. His sister and brother were, no doubt, going to be filled with questions that he didn't want to answer. Changing his mind about calling, he sent a quick group text to his siblings: Snowed in at a friend's house. We're safe. Don't worry. Tell Mom I'll see her tomorrow.

Wade listened to Morgan as she talked with Remy and deduced that Remy had already rescheduled appointments and the multitude of messages he'd left were to let her know. When Morgan clicked off, she smiled ruefully and confirmed what he'd already figured out. "This is why I put up with Remy's flamboyant nature. He'd already called my clients. So…it's just you and me until the storm lets up and the plow comes through to clear the road. You okay with that?"

"I only have one problem with that scenario," he said gravely as he pulled her to him.

Her eyes widened as he nuzzled her neck. "And that would be?"

Wade lifted his head long enough to quip, "We're all out of condoms."

"Well, it's a good thing my sister probably has a few stashed in the spare bedroom," she said, groaning when his tongue flicked out to taste the hollow of her neck. Wade sang *Hallelujah* in his head as he renewed his efforts to taste every inch of her gorgeous body. She tasted of fresh rain and sensual promise and he couldn't get enough.

Thankfully, she seemed to feel the same. Morgan gripped his hand and led him out of the living room toward a bedroom. He was already hard and ready to go.

And, hot damn, more condoms were stashed in the bedside table.

This was the best snowstorm of his life.

MORGAN FELL EXHAUSTED against the bed, unable to believe how many times they'd had sex. It was as if both were trying to make up for lost time and it was a sprint to the finish line. "I think I need a break or else I might never be the same," she admitted breathlessly, rolling her head to cast Wade a silly grin. His chest rose and fell with the same harsh breathing as hers but he managed a brief nod of agreement.

She laughed softly, deliriously sated and content. She wanted this feeling to last forever. And if wishes were snowflakes... A sigh rattled from her chest, and Wade rolled on his side to face her. He looked devastatingly handsome with his dark hair mussed and his lips red and swollen from their epic kissing bouts. And she'd been right—Wade was an excellent kisser.

"Can I say something as cheesy as 'penny for your thoughts?'"

She smiled. "What if my thoughts aren't worth that much?"

"I'm sure they are. Tell me."

"It's nothing. I was just thinking that this is so out of character for me and I should feel guilty but I don't. I suppose I should analyze that, right?"

"Why?"

"I don't know. I think I'm supposed to feel guilty. I mean, you are the last person I should be sleeping with."

"We haven't done any sleeping," he reminded her silkily, and she laughed. Wade grinned, saying, "I'm giving you a hard time. I know what you mean. I never planned to sleep with my mother's therapist. That sounds so sordid. And I never truly believed that line people use when they say, *it just happened,* but I guess that's exactly the situation between us. Neither of us planned this but I'm not sorry, either."

"If I tell you that this has been the greatest sex of my life will your ego go crazy?" she asked, mildly teasing, but she wasn't lying. She'd never known such glory in a lover's arms and now that she'd tasted it, she wanted more. "It's going to be a challenge to find someone else with your skill."

"Stop, my ego can only take so much before it hits maximum density," he said with a chuckle that warmed her to her toes. "You're no slouch in the bedroom. How is it that you're still single?"

Ah, a question that she couldn't actually answer with any hint of honesty. She shrugged. "Just busy with work. No time to date."

Wade reached over and tweaked her nipple gently. "Their loss and my gain," he said in a low, sultry tone.

She groaned and fought the urge to lean toward him. They were officially—*completely*—out of condoms and as sexy as Wade was and the prospect of more sex with him was a good one, she wasn't going to engage in unsafe sex. She made a mental note to replace her sister's stash. "So…why are you still single?" she asked, turning it around on him. "How is it that no one has snatched you up?"

"Same story. Too busy with work."

"So there's no one waiting for you at home? No girlfriend waiting hopelessly in the wings for your proposal?"

He hesitated for the briefest moment then said, "Well, I was seeing someone before I left for Alaska but it wasn't working out so I ended it. Seemed like a mercy, honestly. She was looking for more than I was going to give and I didn't want to end up hurting her."

"How did she take it?"

"Um, well, she wasn't happy about it," he admitted, shifting in discomfort. "She thought… I don't know. It was a hard conversation."

"What didn't work for you? I mean, are you averse to all commitment or just commitment to her?"

He chuckled as if not sure how to answer

because either answer might paint him in an unflattering light, and he finally replied with a helpless shrug. "I really don't know. I never considered myself a commitment-phobe but if I were to examine my dating track record, it might look pretty suspect."

She smiled at that. For a tiny, infinitesimal second she imagined what life would be like with Wade Sinclair, which was patently ridiculous because she didn't actually know him aside from his bedroom talents. She didn't know if he liked ketchup on his scrambled eggs or if he flat-out hated eggs. And yet she was perfectly willing to sink into a fantasy of her own making, featuring herself and the man who could turn her to pudding with a touch.

Wade took a moment then said, "I want to say I just haven't found the right person."

"I have clients who are in love with the idea of love and they're constantly pushing away what is real for the hope of something that only lives in fantasy," she shared, watching him for a reaction. She hoped that wasn't the case with Wade.

"I'm not hoping for the perfect relationship," he assured her. "I know people are flawed."

"Then what are you looking for?" she asked.

"This going to sound stupid, given what's going on with my family, but I want what my parents have—or had. My parents always seemed so in love with each other. It was embarrassing at times to watch them fawn all over each other like two teenagers. But as I got older I realized I wanted that. I wanted that *feeling* they obviously shared. I know it's possible because my siblings have it with their significant others. I've never seen Miranda so happy, and Trace is finally content to live among people, rather than tucked up in a tree somewhere and it's all because of their mates. I should've loved Elizabeth—she was everything I thought I'd ever want in a woman— smart, sexy, accomplished. But..."

"But you lacked chemistry," Morgan finished for him, and he nodded. David had been everything she thought she should want, too. And because of that, she'd been wild about him. "That pesky chemical process in the brain can be such a pain in the ass," she said with a short smirk. Maybe if she'd been less enamored and crazy in love, she might've seen the warning signs.

"It's more than that," he said quietly. "I know all about the science of *love*. I studied biochemistry in college. I'm talking about more than infatuation. Up until Simone died, my parents had never stopped looking at each other like they wanted to disappear in a bedroom together. The heat in their eyes was enough to scorch a room. Whether or not that's unrealistic, I don't care. I want it."

Morgan swallowed the lump that had risen. She admired his courage, his determination not to settle. Someday he would make some lucky woman very happy. "I hope you find it," she murmured, hating that she was so damaged inside that she always drew parallels to her life with David. David wasn't normal, by any stretch of the imagination, and if she was going to move beyond the past, she had to stop making connections to it.

As if zeroing in on her private thoughts, he asked, "What was your husband like?" startling her with the innocent question. Instantly, her throat went dry and her smile froze. Wade noticed her stiffen inadvertently and frowned. "Are you okay? I'm sorry if I overstepped. I was just curious. Forget I asked." He reached out to rub her shoulder and then gestured for her to come to him, murmuring, "Come here, sweetheart," and she scooted closer, turning so that her backside pressed against him. His arms closed around her, and she smiled, but the tension remained in her body. She wanted to tell Wade about David, but why? She didn't want to burden him with the knowledge that she'd been living a lie in her marriage and that her husband had died in this very house. But there was something so honest and open about Wade that called to her battered heart and she had to consciously fight the urge to lay it all at his feet.

"Tell me about Simone," Morgan ventured, needing to change the subject before she embarrassed herself. "My sister isn't a very good source of information. What was she really like?"

He sighed, and she bit her lip, hating that she'd used a very painful subject as a diversion but she couldn't share with Wade what had happened in her marriage to David. How would it look if it was discovered that a therapist had been locked into an abusive marriage? The knowledge could wreck her career. Who would trust her to help them through their crises if she hadn't been able to help herself?

A delicate shudder passed through her, and Wade mistook the reaction as one of cold and pulled the blanket over them. "Simone was a force of nature," he said quietly, but Morgan felt the pain of his loss like a physical thing. "Sometimes I can't quite believe she's gone, even though it's been eight years. She had this cute laugh and every now and again— usually when I haven't had enough sleep—I could swear that I hear her laughter out there. Weird, huh?"

"The power of suggestion is a mighty thing. Maybe you caught sight of someone who reminded you subconsciously of your sister and your brain pulled the memory of her laughter from the cache."

"I knew there was a logical explanation," he said, tightening his hold around her. She felt wonderfully secure and could remain in that position with Wade for the rest of the day. "Glad I'm not losing my mind."

"You're not." She paused, curious about what had happened after Simone died but reluctant to bring up anything that might be more appropriate for a therapy session. But she wanted to know Wade's perspective. "I know we promised not to talk about your mother's case but I'm curious…what happened after Simone died? Did the family just fall apart?"

"Pretty much."

Wade's flat answer cut at her heart. Such

pain. Such heartache. "Did you leave Alaska to escape the memories?" she asked, holding her breath. Would he answer? She wouldn't blame him if he didn't. "You don't have to answer if it's too personal," she tacked on.

Wade released her, and a chill sliced through her at the loss of his body heat snuggled against her. He swiveled to a sitting position with his back to her, leaning on his elbows. "I don't know. Maybe. I was young and I saw an opportunity so I took it. At least that's what I told myself but now that I'm looking backward, I guess you're right… staying here wasn't an option for me."

"What about your siblings? Why'd they stay?"

He straightened with a shrug. "I never knew. Well, that's not entirely true. Miranda stayed to help out our parents and then she got pregnant. As for Trace…I don't know why he stayed other than he had a job here that enabled him to disappear for weeks on end. I made the offer for them to come to California but both declined."

"Do you miss your brother and sister?"

"Yeah. Sometimes. Other times…I don't know, I think I just bury all those kinds of feelings under work. Easier that way."

Yes, she knew how that worked. "Do you think that if your family had been given some kind of closure, things would've worked out differently?"

He glanced at her sharply. "What do you mean?"

"I mean, if perhaps the police had caught the person responsible for hurting Simone."

Wade drew a deep breath and on the exhale shrugged as if he didn't like to think about *what-ifs*. "It is what it is," he said as he rose. "I'm going to shower. Care to join me?"

"Are you sure that's a good idea?" she asked, climbing from the bed. "We don't have any protection left."

"There are other ways to have a good time," he reminded her as he clasped her hand and tugged her close. She smiled and practically purred in his arms, liquid feminine heat already slicking her core at the suggestion. "And as I seem to recall, you really like some of those other ways."

"Oh, I do," she agreed with a hearty nod. She lifted on her toes and kissed him hard and deep then said, "I'll go get fresh towels!" and bounded off to the linen closet, all manner of sad, tense or scary thoughts leaving her head, and for that she was grateful. Reality would intrude soon enough, and she wanted to preserve this unexpected bit of heaven for as long as possible.

## CHAPTER SIXTEEN

THE SNOW HAD stopped around three in the afternoon and by five the plow had come through and cleared the roads, which meant that it was time for Wade to get back to reality, even though he found himself dragging his heels.

"So...this was fun," he said at the door, prompting a laugh from Morgan. He grinned, loving the sound of her laughter. He curbed the urge to reach out and pull her back into his arms. He was trying to leave, not start something they couldn't finish. "I never imagined something like this would happen but I'm not sorry that it did."

"I'm not sorry, either."

"Great. Neither of us has an ounce of regret. I guess the bigger question is, do either of us have an ounce of sense?" he joked.

"Nope. It doesn't seem as if we do because we both know that logically this wasn't wise."

"Right. So...where does that put us?" he asked.

"It puts us in the same exact spots we were

in before I invited you over for coffee. I am your mother's therapist and you are leaving as soon as possible. That's the best part about our hookup—it's temporary."

She was right. So why did he feel a twinge of disappointment? "Of course," he said, forcing a smile. He didn't want to seem like the kind of guy who didn't know when to take a hint but he secretly wished she'd been a little more reluctant to turn him loose. A guy had his pride, after all.

He wanted to kiss her goodbye but he didn't. Instead, he had to be content with the smile he sent her way that he hoped communicated all the feelings he had bound up inside. "I'll see you in a few days," he said. At her raised brow, he added, "At my mother's hearing with Adult Protective Services."

She exhaled as if she'd been holding her breath and she nodded with a bright smile. "Of course. Good evening, Wade. This was a lot of fun."

Fun. Yep. That's what it'd been. And that was it.

Wade made his way to his car and slowly pulled out of her driveway.

He'd had a great time so why was he left with the vague feeling of dissatisfaction?

Possibly because for a small slice in time he'd played with the idea of taking her to dinner and going backpacking together and bringing her out to California to see his neck of the woods. And even though that kind of thinking wasn't welcome or encouraged, he'd still done it.

He rubbed his forehead as if trying to rub out the disturbing slant of his thoughts but he had to admit, Morgan was hard to forget. She made him feel alive and vibrant, something other relationships had never done. It wasn't as if he'd never had a good time with his previous lovers but there was something indefinable about Morgan. He wanted to know more than just surface stuff about her. And he particularly wanted to know what caused the shadow behind her eyes that she tried to hide.

But digging into her personal life wasn't appropriate, given the parameters of their relationship.

As much as his brain kept throwing all sorts of pleasurable scenarios his way, he made a concentrated effort to stop because the bottom line was, Morgan was right. They had no future together and neither were looking for that kind of attachment, anyway.

He'd made it back to his hotel when his cell

phone went off. When he saw it was Elizabeth, he sighed and took the call when his conscience wouldn't allow him to send her to voice mail again.

"Hello?"

"Wade? Where have you been? I've been calling for days and you haven't picked up or returned a single phone call."

Wade tried not to bristle at the possessive tone in her voice and tried not to start the conversation with a brusque reminder that they were no longer seeing each other. "I've been caught up with family stuff and haven't had the time to call. I'm sorry," he added because he felt obligated to offer something. "What's going on? Everything okay?"

"No, everything is not okay," she said, a mild tremble in her voice that immediately put him on alert. "You know, I have a life, too. When you ignore me like this, it makes me realize that you are not the man I thought you were."

"I'm sorry," he said because he didn't know what else to say. He tried to take into account that their breakup was still very fresh and likely raw, but he really didn't want to spend much more time listening to Elizabeth bitch him out for perceived character flaws. "I'm still hoping we can be friends," he said, trying to gently remind her that he'd never made promises about their relationship.

"Well, we've got some things to figure out," Elizabeth said, her voice quivering. "And I need you to come home soon."

He frowned. "What sort of things?" That queasy feeling in his gut had just tripled.

He heard sniffling in the background, and he gripped the phone harder but he waited, the seconds ticking by with agonizing slowness, until she said in a pained whisper, "I'm late."

And the bottom dropped out of his world.

MORGAN WANDERED HER house in a sated, content state, going about cleaning up the house on autopilot, smiling as she remembered in great detail everything she and Wade had done only hours prior, humming beneath her breath. What a lovely difference from the other memories crowding her brain most times. For a blessed second, she could almost forget the double life she was living and just be a woman enjoying the company of a man.

And what a man. She stopped and leaned against the granite countertop, the cool, smooth surface chilling her arms but she was too happy to care. A small sound of happiness escaped, and when she lifted herself again, her silly smile froze when she saw her sister standing there watching her with a frown. "Oh! You startled me," Morgan said, pushing a lock of hair behind her ear and wondering if her sister had seen Wade leaving the house.

"Was that Wade I just passed?"

Damn. That answers that question. "Um..." Should she lie? Too late, Mona's gaze narrowed. Morgan went with the truth. "Um, yes."

"What's going on?" Mona asked, getting straight to the point. "Was it related to his mother's case?"

"No, not exactly," she hedged, not sure how much she wanted to reveal to her sister. "It was nothing, really. He came over for coffee and then the storm covered the roads for the afternoon so he had to stay. He's actually a very nice man. A gentleman."

"Uh-huh. And he just happens to be super-hot. That doesn't hurt, does it?" Mona cast a speculative glance at the spare bedroom—her hookup room—and said, "I wonder if I took a look in the bedside drawer I'd find a few condoms missing?"

Morgan couldn't help the immediate blush heating her cheeks at her sister's accurate speculation, and Mona gasped as she pointed an accusatory finger. "You slept with him, didn't you? Oh, my God, you little hypocrite," Mona said with growing outrage. "I can't believe you slept with Wade. After all that crap you gave me, you just swooped in and threw yourself at him. Not cool, Morgan. Not cool."

Morgan frowned. "Now, wait a minute. I am not a hypocrite," she said, irritated. "There was a very good reason why I didn't want you with him and it had nothing to do with personal gain."

Mona crossed her arms. "Oh? And what would that be?"

Morgan opened her mouth but snapped it shut again. Crap. Maybe she didn't have a good reason. "All right, fine! I didn't want you with Wade because the idea made my skin crawl. Are you happy?"

"A little," Mona admitted grudgingly. "So…are you really into him or something?"

"Something like that, but I'm conflicted by my own feelings so I want you to know that I would ordinarily never do something like this."

"Like what?" Mona, already bored with her own supposed outrage, went to the pantry to find something to eat and began rummaging.

"What's the big deal? He's hot and you're single. Seems all signs point to *go,* to me. No wonder you haven't found anyone you want to date yet. You're turning into a fuss bucket of worry." Mona grabbed Morgan's favorite stash of chocolate chip cookies—the ones that cost $6 for each tiny box—and ripped into them without asking, per usual. "Here's the thing. I will forgive you for giving me hell over Wade if you share details. And spare nothing. I want to know everything. I want to know what I'm missing out on."

Just as Mona was about to bite into the first cookie, Morgan snatched it out of her hand and snagged the box, too. "Forget it," she said, ignoring Mona's *"Hey!"* and stuffed the box back into the pantry with a pointed look Mona's way before saying, "I don't kiss and tell. Besides, I need you to keep this between you and me. I can't have word getting out that I've slept with the son of one of my clients."

"What's the big deal? He's an adult. I'm sure you didn't tie him down and have your wicked way with him against his consent. Or did you? You're such a little vixen."

"I'm not a vixen by any means," Morgan protested behind a smile. She couldn't help herself. Thinking about Wade prompted a smile that was hard to suppress. But her sister could be a loose cannon. She sobered. "I'm serious, Mona. I need you to keep this information to yourself. If word got out that I was sleeping with him, it could affect my career."

Mona sighed dramatically and flounced onto the sofa. "Oh, screw the haters. As if they don't have sex. Okay, fine. Between you and me…was it good?"

Morgan felt like a teenager again and she desperately wanted to share a little something with someone, and perhaps her sister could keep a tiny secret. For once. It was a risk but she felt like a risk-taker today so she settled next to her sister and began to gab. "Okay, I'm trusting you to keep your lip zipped." Mona made a zipping motion on her lips and Morgan continued. "Well, it sort of just happened. We went to yoga last night and then I invited him to coffee the next morning and then I made the offer to have coffee here. Once we were here…well, you know."

"That's it?" Mona screwed her face into a disappointed scowl. "That's the most boring hookup story I've ever heard. Where's the romance? The flair? The details that will make for a good story later in life?"

"Unlike you, I don't seek out drama for the sake of a good tale later."

Mona sniffed as if the insult rolled off her back and said, "Well, at any rate…was he good? Did he manage to ring your bell? Sometimes those buttoned-down business types are pretty wild behind closed doors."

Was he good? How could she answer that question without revealing too many details? He was, without a doubt, the best lover Morgan had ever had but she certainly didn't want to tell that to her sister. "He was very skilled," she answered, almost primly. "Very attentive and dedicated."

"You really suck at this sharing-details thing. You make it sound like he was a suitable job applicant. I want details—*real* details. Or else forget about it because this story is already putting me to sleep."

Morgan stiffened in indignation. "I don't suck at telling the story. I just don't want to reveal too many intimate details and run the risk of oversharing."

"Which is exactly the point of telling a story. I told you all about that hookup that I had with Bran and I didn't leave out any detail."

"Yes, I remember." Talk about overshare.

Although, by the time Mona had finished, Morgan found herself just a wee bit envious of her sister's carefree attitude toward sex. Mona had no problem enjoying a man simply for what hung between his legs and nothing more. "Unlike you, I like to leave a little something to the imagination."

Mona shrugged. "Suit yourself. So he's decent in the sack? I wish I'd been able to sample some of that action."

"Well, I for one, am very grateful that you did not. And I'm going to ask that you keep your hands to yourself, please. The idea of you going after a guy that I've slept with really grosses me out."

Mona laughed. "You're such a little Puritan at heart. Fine, I'll keep my hands to myself and you can have Wade all to yourself."

Ah, having Wade all to herself…she liked the idea of that too much.

Mona caught her dreamy expression and said, "I'm just glad you're finally seeing someone—secret or not. You deserve it."

"Thank you," Morgan said, smiling at her sister. Sometimes when Mona wasn't being a self-absorbed twit, she was actually pretty sweet. "Feels kinda good to just be me. Not the doctor, just me. Wade makes me feel comfortable in my own skin." For the first time in years. God, David really had done a number on her, which she'd known intellectually, but it hadn't actually sunk in until this moment. "Is it weird that I like him so much so quick?" she asked.

"You're asking me?" Mona asked wryly, and Morgan laughed.

"You're right. But okay, just for the sake of argument…do you?"

To Morgan's surprise, Mona sobered and shook her head. "Not at all. I think that when something clicks between two people—and I mean, *really* clicks—time doesn't actually matter and you should just accept wherever fate is going to take you."

Oh, that wasn't something Morgan would ever do. She wasn't the kind of woman who took big risks in a relationship or in life. That's why she'd been so quick to accept David's offer of marriage. He'd seemed a very good match. Very stable. Very dependable. Ha! What a joke. The only thing she'd come to depend upon with David was his capricious cruelty. Fate had a funny sense of humor.

*Stop thinking about David.* She was so tired of battling his ghost, both in her head and in this house. "Is it too early for wine?"

she murmured, needing something to calm her nerves.

"It's never too early for wine," Mona said, and Morgan agreed, rising to open a bottle. "Although not a red—the last one was a little too earthy for my tastes. How about a nice, light white?"

"I think I have some Barefoot somewhere in the wine cabinet," Morgan said before taking a look. "Aha, yes, here it is," she exclaimed, grabbing the bottle and glassware. "So," she began, using the opportunity to switch subjects. "Since I'm so bad at telling intimate stories, why did you come over in the first place?"

Mona's expression lit up, happy to talk about herself again. "Oh! Yes, that's right. I came over for a reason. Seems your date with George wasn't a waste, after all. I ended up getting a buyer for a few of my pieces with the potential of a commissioned piece, as well."

Wow, that was big news. Maybe that meant that Morgan wouldn't have to pay Mona's rent next month. "That's wonderful. Who was the buyer?"

"I don't know him and I don't care as long as his check clears."

"Good attitude. So which prints did he buy?"

"Do you really want to know? I know you're just humoring me. Don't get me wrong, I love you for it but those kinds of details really aren't necessary. All that matters is he likes my work, I get validation as an artist and I don't have to beg you for money. It's a win-win all the way around."

Morgan couldn't argue with that logic. "Should we open a bottle of champagne, instead, to celebrate?"

Mona grinned. "Champagne gives me gas. I'm good with the white. Crack open that Chardonnay and let that bad boy breathe. But please promise me you won't break out that stinky cheese. I loved David, don't get me wrong, but that cheese is flat-out gross. In fact, I think if you put it outside, it would scare away the wildlife." Mona seemed to reconsider and then added, "Unless having the cheese around helps you to be stronger…"

"Stronger? How would cheese make me stronger?" Morgan asked, confused.

"Well, you know, because the cheese reminds you of David and whatnot. I mean, you're the therapist. If you think hanging on to that dumb cheese is the way to heal and move on…then, I guess I'll stop teasing you about it."

*Oh, for God's sake.* In that instance, Morgan saw herself through her sister's eyes and the picture was not flattering. *Cheese as a therapy tool?* More like something that continued to hold her hostage. Like everything associated with David. Morgan had been insulating herself from prying eyes for so long—even before David had died—that she'd completely lost sight of what normal was supposed to look like. "I hate that cheese," she admitted in a soft murmur. "I never liked it. I always thought it smelled like a dirty armpit and tasted just as bad." She met Mona's perplexed stare and made a decision that she was going to stick to. If she had to, she'd avoid the dairy aisle or switch grocery stores so that cheese did not inadvertently end up in her cart, *ever again.* "And I'm not going to buy it anymore." And this time, she meant it. Truly.

"Well, hallelujah," Mona said, breaking into an unsure grin. "Are you okay? You seem a little pale."

"I'm good."

"Are you sure? You seem a little more fragile than usual."

*Fragile?* "Why do you think I'm fragile?"

"Don't get your panties in a twist. I wasn't insulting you," Mona assured her but it must've been the day Mona had marked on her calendar to think of someone aside from herself, because she seemed filled with stuff to say to Morgan about life in general. "Listen, I'm just saying that most people would be ready to move on after three years of mourning. Why do you think I'm not mad as hell that you and Wade hooked up? Frankly, I'm just so happy that *someone* knocked the cobwebs off that dusty shelf that I don't care who it is."

Morgan exhaled in irritation. "Maybe it wasn't because of David that I haven't been dating," she flat-out lied. "Maybe I'm just consumed with work and haven't had time."

"Who knew my beautiful, smart, responsible sister is also prone to lying through her damn teeth?" Mona mocked sweetly, startling Morgan with how close Mona had come to the real truth. Morgan had spun so many lies she didn't know how to keep them straight anymore. "Listen, I know you're keeping everyone who could possibly keep you warm at night at arm's length because you're afraid no one's going to measure up to David. I get it, he was a tough act to follow, but at this rate you're gonna die alone."

Why did her thoughts immediately zero

in on Wade? Wade wasn't looking for commitment and she wasn't emotionally available so why did she yearn to spend more time cuddled up to him? She rubbed her forehead, tired of her own bullshit. "I don't understand why our conversations keep ending up on the same topic. I'm fine and I like my life the way that it is. Yes, I miss David." *How did she manage those words without choking?* "But it's more about being busy than trying to fill my social calendar. I promise. Now can we please go back to celebrating your accomplishment and drop this subject?"

But Mona had a bone and she wasn't letting it go. "And why do you work so much?" she demanded, then answered herself. "It's because you're trying to fill a hole with work instead of trying to fill a hole with something else."

Morgan's cheeks burned. "Mona, you are so crude sometimes," she said as she poured the wine and slid a glass over to her sister. "Sometimes I don't even know how we share the same DNA."

Mona accepted the glass and agreed. "You and me both, sister. Sometimes I just don't understand how your brain works. But that's what makes you *you* and I love you just the

way you are because that's how you love me."
Mona took a swallow and smiled with pure
joy. "Yeah, that's the stuff. You always have
the best wine," she said with a happy exhale
as if she'd just unloaded a heavy burden and
was ready to kick off her shoes and just chill.

Morgan's eyes burned with sudden tears at
the unexpected affection from her little sister,
and for a moment she was paralyzed by the
urge to tell Mona exactly what kind of person
David was. The reasons why she always had
good wine and disgusting European cheese
on hand were because David had beaten the
reasons into her. She wanted to tell her about
the bruises she'd always managed to hide beneath long-sleeved shirts or bulky sweaters
or the wounds that were invisible to the eye.
David's abuse of choice had been a punch to
the gut because it didn't leave the same kind
of marks, and any mark he did leave behind
was easily concealed. She especially wanted
to tell Mona about the baby but as desperately
as she needed to share with someone, she silenced the words with a long swallow of wine.
Mona had adored David. What good would it
do to destroy her illusion or memory of him?
It wouldn't change a thing except it would
ruin her sister's ideal and at the end of the

day, Morgan was still Mona's big sister and she would do anything to protect her. "I'm really proud of you, Mona," she said with love in her voice. "You're very talented and you have the sense of self to know that you can do what you are good at and make a living, too."

"Hear, hear!" Mona said, lifting her glass with a grin. "Now, if you could just let Mom and Dad know and assure them that I'm not going to end up homeless, that would be great. I swear if Dad offers to get me a job as a secretary at one of his old cronies' businesses one more time, I will scream."

"I will talk to Mom and Dad," Morgan promised. "I'm sure they'll be very happy to know that your art is finally selling. You know they just worry about you."

"Yeah, I know. But I'm going to be okay. Just like you're going to be okay. Eventually, you're going to meet someone amazing and even if he can't replace David, you're going to find happiness with him."

If only that were true. If only she could latch on to Mona's prophecy as gospel instead of the rosy-eyed proclamation from a young woman who didn't know all the facts that it was. "Well, from your mouth to God's ear,"

Morgan said with a small smile. "But in the meantime, I think I'll just focus on work."

"Well, it's your decision. But you know what they say…use it or lose it."

Morgan laughed. "You're impossible. Simply impossible. Not everything is about sex in life."

"No, but sex is pretty damn important."

Before Wade, Morgan would've adamantly disagreed. But now…she was beginning to understand Mona's point of view because even though she shouldn't, she was already trying to figure out a way to finesse another opportunity to enjoy Wade in her bed. Maybe Mona was right. She should've enlisted the help of a bed partner to erase David's memory from her brain. And she couldn't think of another person she'd rather ask to help her than Wade Sinclair.

She hid a slow, private smile behind the rim of her glass. Oh, yes…she was definitely open to another round with that sexy man.

No doubt about it.

*Reckless, thy name is Morgan O'Hare.*

# CHAPTER SEVENTEEN

WADE DIDN'T KNOW how the phone stayed at his ear because he could no longer feel his fingers. "What are you talking about?" he asked when his throat worked again. A fine sheen of sweat popped along his hairline and he actually felt sick. "There must be some kind of mistake. We were always cautious."

"Nothing is one hundred percent," she reminded him with a resigned sigh. "I guess you must have really industrious swimmers."

"Are you sure? I mean, have you talked to a doctor yet?"

"No, but I know what my body feels like and something is definitely happening that's out of the norm. I'm never late. Ever."

He shifted, unable to believe he was having this conversation when prior to this phone call he'd been basking in the afterglow of an amazing sexual encounter with another woman. Ah, God, Morgan. What was he supposed to say to her? He didn't want to tell her but then, should he? Too many questions.

Wade closed his eyes and prepared to ask the question he never imagined asking a woman. "So…if it's true that you're pregnant…are you planning to keep the baby?"

"Of course I'm keeping the baby," Elizabeth answered sharply. "You know I'm Catholic and abortion is out of the question. Frankly, that you would even ask tells me that you're not interested in coparenting with me."

"That's not true," he disagreed quickly but his head was spinning. A baby? Kids had always been in the plan *eventually* but he'd figured he was light years away from that reality, seeing as he hadn't found *The One* to build a life with. *Ah, hell.*

He rubbed his forehead, wiping away the sudden nervous sweat, trying to remain calm. "I didn't mean that I don't want to be a part of the child's life but it wouldn't be right of me to assume anything in this situation. Neither of us was planning to parent together so this is a bit of a shock."

"No, what was a shock was you breaking up with me before you left for Alaska," she said, surprising him with her pointed statement. He started to protest but she cut him off, determined to have her say. "We were dating for quite a while…most people at that stage in the relationship start talking about taking it to the next level, so when you came to me I had assumed that you were going to ask me to marry you, not break my heart and throw me away."

Wade stopped himself from saying they never really had a relationship but rather a mutually beneficial sexual partnership that sometimes included dinner, because he knew he'd come out sounding like the jerk even if it was true. "Elizabeth, I'm sorry that you were hurt. I was under the impression our relationship was more *casual,* something without labels that we both enjoyed, but there was no express understanding that it was going somewhere deeper." The heavy silence on the other end made him wince but before he could try again, she cut in with a cool tone.

"So what you're saying is I was a convenient booty call?"

"No, of course not." *Yes, sort of.* But he hated that term. "I care for and respect you as a friend and a professional woman."

"But you have no interest in marrying me, even if I was pregnant?"

"Well, no," he answered with a frown. "Do you really think two people should marry if there's no love, just because there was an unplanned pregnancy? Statistically, that's a recipe for resentment, which is not a healthy environment for a child. I'd rather coparent with someone I respect than force myself to marry and potentially grow to hate because she forced me into something I wasn't interested in."

"Maybe you should've gone into contract law rather than administration," she said, the masked pain in her voice cutting at him. He'd never meant to hurt Elizabeth but it seemed he'd done just that. What would Morgan think? The fact that his immediate thought was worry about Morgan gave him pause. Morgan wasn't a factor. True, but for some reason, he couldn't stop thinking of her reaction to all this because it did matter.

There was a sniffle on the other end and Wade closed his eyes against the sickening lurch in his stomach. "I'd held out hope that you would love me like I loved you," she admitted in an embarrassed whisper. "I'm such an idiot."

"No, you're not," he said. "I'm sorry you're going through this. I feel like a jerk."

"Me, too," she said, her voice catching. "I never saw myself in this position. This is the kind of thing that happens to women in different social situations. Not me."

He didn't blame her for the hint of bitterness in her tone. "I don't know what to say that won't make it worse. Everything that comes to mind seems trite even if it's coming from an honest place. What can I do to help?"

"I'd like you to come home," she said, sniffing again. "I feel alone in this."

"You're not alone," he tried assuring her but he wasn't sure how much more help he could really be at the moment. "But I can't come home just yet. Things with my family are still volatile and it's taking longer than I imagined it would to sort things out."

"Not that I'm not sympathetic to your family's problems, but how are you managing to take so much time off? You're the superintendent of a national park. You don't have the luxury of gallivanting around the countryside for an indeterminate amount of time without losing your job."

Wade frowned at the subtle accusation in her tone. "What are you implying? That I'm not coming home for a reason?"

"I'm just saying there's no need for you to be evasive. I would prefer honesty. Perhaps if you'd been honest from the start of our relationship I wouldn't be in this position."

"Elizabeth, I was honest. I can't control what you chose to hear. I'm not that kind of man," he said, fighting a growl. He tried to keep in mind Elizabeth was likely hormonal and emotional and not in her right mind. "I'm trying to get things figured out here with my family. Hopefully, in two weeks I can leave."

"I guess if that's all you can offer...fine. I'll be in touch."

"Elizabeth..."

"I can't talk about this anymore. I have to go."

"Elizabeth, wait—"

But the line went dead, and he knew she'd hung up. He shook his phone in frustration and then sat heavily on the bed. How could the day go so wrong in such a short time frame?

Wade's heart pounded with an unhealthy beat against his rib cage, and his head was crammed with all sorts of unhelpful nonsense. *Please don't be pregnant.* What would Morgan say to this new development? Would it matter? It wasn't as if they were building something to last. But would she hold it against him that he might be having a baby with another woman? "Damn it," he muttered, letting his phone roll from his hand so he could scrub his palms across his face. This was just fabulous. *Fab-u-lous.*

Wade slowly rose from the bed, lost and a bit angry, with no one to talk to about it. He couldn't call his brother because Trace was still holding a grudge against him, and he couldn't call Miranda because she had enough on her plate as it was without adding his drama to it. All he had was himself. And right now, he was terrible company with absolutely no advice to give.

What were the odds of Elizabeth getting pregnant when they'd used every precaution? Would she lie about something like that? No, she was a professional woman, not some gold digger looking for someone to bankroll their life. Hell, Elizabeth might even make more money than he did. Well, it was probably a tie. He made a pretty good living. His phone rang and he snagged it, hoping it was Morgan but it was Miranda.

"Hey, there you are. Everything okay? I got your text about being snowed in at Morgan O'Hare's house but why were you there in the first place?" she asked, not missing a beat.

"Seems weird to hang out with your mother's therapist."

"It's not weird," he disagreed, wincing when he heard his defensive tone. "We have a lot in common and we went out for coffee."

"And ended up at her house? What happened to coffee in an actual coffeehouse?"

"Was there a point to this call?" he asked, irritated.

"Geesh, you're grumpy. And yes, there was a point to my call. Mom is being released from the hospital and she needs a place to go. She can't stay with Florence anymore because she needs aftercare, which means she has to stay with me or Trace. And since Trace lives in the boonies and I live in town, it makes sense that she should stay with me and Jeremiah."

Criminy, that news ought to go over like a turd in a punch bowl. "Let me guess. You need me to help tag team Mom so she'll go along with this idea."

"I hate to agree but yes. You know she's not going to go willingly and we can't take the risk that she'll drag herself back to the house before we've had a chance to get it cleaned up. Oh, and about that, Trace has the cleaning crew slated for Friday so clear your schedule."

Friday...that was in four days. Good. He was glad things were finally moving. Maybe with some luck they could get this whole situation figured out by Monday and he could be on a plane by Wednesday at the latest.

"When are you breaking this news to Mom?" he asked. "I'd rather get this over with quickly so we can deal with the aftermath."

"We can do it now if you like. I'm just about to get off work. I could meet you at the hospital."

"Might as well. The news is going to overwhelm her, no matter what. What's the news on Dad?"

Miranda sighed. "Nothing new. He's still rotting in jail and refuses to come out. Personally, I feel it's a different form of escapism. So he's not sitting in the shed anymore, but he certainly isn't helping Mom, either."

Wade agreed. But he could only handle one problem at a time. "Fine, he can stay there. Besides, if he's not going to be helpful I don't want him around."

"I just don't understand why he's acting like this. It's like a pod person came and stole our dad and left this loser in his place. I mean, he looks the same but he's not the same. I wonder if that's how Mom feels, too. Maybe she'd be less hostile if Dad wasn't so checked out. That has to be hard on her."

Wade didn't have the answer. Right now, his whole life had taken on twisted proportions. Everything felt out of place. Including him. And the worst part? All he wanted to do was go back to Morgan's. The past few hours spent with her were the best he'd had in years and it wasn't just about the sex. Although that'd been pretty spectacular. He refocused his stubborn brain and said, "All right, I'll meet you at the hospital."

"Great. Don't forget to wear your body armor."

Wade smiled grimly as he clicked off. Miranda may have been joking but it was a fairly accurate warning for the fight that was coming. He could only imagine what the collateral damage was going to be like. But one thing he knew for sure, Trace wasn't getting off the hook. If he had to be in on the dirty work so did his brother.

He quickly dialed Trace's cell phone number and to his surprise his brother picked up. He half expected the call to go to voice mail. "Hey, Trace, you probably already heard but Mom's being released from the hospital tomorrow and that means she's going to have to stay with Miranda."

"Yeah, I know. Miranda and I talked about it. I offered to take her but it doesn't make sense for her to be out in the middle of nowhere in her fragile state."

Wade couldn't help himself and chuckled, even though there was nothing humorous about the situation. "Sorry, it's not funny. I guess my nerves are just a little worn because hearing Mom being described as *fragile* was never something I would've imagined."

"Yeah, I know what you mean. So are you and Miranda going to the hospital right now to tell her?"

"Yes. I was hoping you could meet us there. I think she needs to see that we're a united front."

"Okay. I can meet you there in five minutes. Did Miranda tell you the cleaners are coming on Friday?"

"Yes. How much is that costing? I can pitch in, if you like."

"It isn't cheap. Between the organizer and the cleaners it's going to eat up the paycheck that I got for that reality show pilot. So if you'd like to help that would be great."

Wade was frugal by nature and had plenty

in savings, although he'd been eyeing a new Jeep, but this was far more important. "I'll write you a check when we meet at the hospital."

"Thanks."

"No problem. Hey, Trace, how long are we going to be angry at each other? Seems now is the time that we need to come together."

"Yeah, I know. I don't know why I was so angry. Maybe I'm just mad at the situation. Our whole family has gone to crap and it's nothing the way it was when we were young. How am I supposed to have kids in this kind of environment? How am I supposed to introduce my kids to their grandpa, the felon? And grandma, the crazy hoarder?"

Kids? Wade winced at the reminder of Elizabeth's phone call. This wasn't the way he wanted to have kids. He'd always imagined that when he had children, he'd be married to their mother, happy and content. But if Elizabeth was truly pregnant, the reality would be nothing like the fantasy in his head. And now his brother was thinking about having kids, too? Trace would have a family the normal way—with a woman he loved. "Don't let our parents screw up your plans. If you want kids, have them. You'll be a great dad."

"How do you know? Hell, for a couple years I was a really terrible brother. How do you know I'll be a good father?"

"Because I just know. You love kids and you always have. Besides, someone has to pass on those tracking skills. It's a dying art, you know. I was never as good as you and I've gotten really rusty."

"That's what happens when you sit behind a desk all day." Trace was teasing but there was some truth to it. Tracking was a skill you lost if you didn't use it. The last time he put his tracking skills to use was the night Simone died. He tried not to think of that night very often. Somehow Trace must've known where his mind had gone because he sighed and said, "I'll see you at the hospital." Nobody wanted to remember the night Simone died.

"Miranda said we should wear body armor."

Trace laughed but he knew there was truth to that joke, as well. "Good idea." And then he clicked off.

Wade had meant what he said. Trace would make a very good father. But what kind of father would he be? A weekend father. The Disneyland dad. He hated that idea. He wanted to be there for homework, for baseball games, for dance recitals, whatever his child was involved in—he wanted to be there. But he didn't want Elizabeth. He knew that with certainty.

Maybe she wasn't really pregnant. Maybe she was just late and this was all a big mistake.

*Please...don't be pregnant.* That seemed a terrible thing to pray for but it was the truth, just the same.

# CHAPTER EIGHTEEN

WADE AND HIS siblings arrived at the hospital nearly simultaneously. They didn't waste time on small talk because they knew what was coming and they wanted to get it over with as quickly as possible. When they walked into Jennelle's hospital room her gaze narrowed with suspicion when she saw all three of her children.

"What's this about?" she asked, looking to Wade for answers and ignoring Trace and Miranda. "Something tells me you've come bearing bad news. Let me guess—you're putting me into a home. Is there a place where ungrateful children stow away their parents they no longer have a use for?"

"Stop being so dramatic. Nobody is putting you into a home. Mostly because no one would take you," Miranda muttered. "If you could stop being so mean for about two seconds things would get a lot better, you know."

Wade shot Miranda a look that said, *slow down, slugger,* and Miranda gave him a subtle nod to say she'd try. Of the three, Miranda had taken the brunt of their mother's bad attitude, and he hated that. Wade came to stand by her bedside and tried a disarming smile. "How are you feeling today, Mama?"

Jennelle didn't trust him any more than she trusted his siblings and that much was apparent. "You're up to something. Something no good, I wager. What's this about?" she asked, going straight to the point.

"Mama, there's no need to draw lines. We're all on your side, even if that's hard to see right now," he said. "Just try to remember that."

Jennelle sniffed and looked away. "This is what a mother with a broken heart looks like. Get used to it. Now what do you want?"

Trace tried jumping in. "Mother, we have good news," he said, breaking a charming grin that had always been his saving grace. "The hospital is going to release you tomorrow, which means you don't have to choke down bland hospital food any longer. Lord knows you've done nothing but complain about it the entire time you've been here. Not that I blame you. That stuff looks pretty gross."

"You mean I get to go home?" The hope

in Jennelle's voice made Wade wince. When no one rushed to correct her, she clasped her hands together with a smile. "Thank heavens. I'm so sick of this place I could scream. Lord knows my flowers are probably dead by now."

Miranda shook her head. "Mom, your flowers are dead because it's winter. Not because you haven't been there to tend to them," she said, shooting a quick glance at Wade for reinforcements. "And no, you can't go home. You're going to come home with me, Jeremiah and Talen. This will give you an opportunity to spend more time with your grandson. You're *only* grandson."

"Me, go home with you? I'd rather sleep outside."

*Oh, come on, Mama. Why do you have to make it so hard to be on your side?* No one had ever accused Jennelle Sinclair of being a pushover, that was for sure. Time to be the bad guy. "Mama, stop being so mean," he admonished, trying to be gentle but firm. "Here are the facts—you can't live on your own and Florence can't take care of you any longer. Trace lives out in the middle of nowhere and Miranda lives in town. It makes logical sense that you will stay with her while we figure out an alternative."

"And what I want means nothing? I just get to be tossed around like an old potato with no opinion as to where I land?"

Miranda bracketed her hips with her hands. "Yes, that's right. You old potato. Don't you get it? You brought this upon yourself. If you hadn't ruined the house you could still live there. But no, you had to fill it with so much crap that it was condemned. This is no one's fault but your own. Stop trying to blame every single person you come into contact with for your own problems, which coincidentally, are also now *our* problems because we have to take care of you. So stop being so ungrateful, you mean old bitty."

"Miranda!" Wade shot his sister a look. *"Was that necessary?"* Miranda shrugged but her eyes glittered as if she was holding back tears. Whether they were tears of frustration or hurt, he wasn't sure. They could've been a combination of both.

Jennelle gaped at Miranda's outburst and her eyes watered, and Wade knew he had to smooth things between Miranda and their mother before World War III happened and they were all collateral damage. "Mama, this is a temporary arrangement," he promised her. "And this is a great opportunity to spend some quality time with Talen. You've always said that you don't get enough time with your grandson. Well, this is your golden opportunity."

"Leave my grandson out of this. I won't be bamboozled into accepting a false truth. Just come out and say what's truly happening. Don't try and pretty it up," Jennelle quipped darkly. "I wasn't born yesterday, and I can see right through your machinations."

"Can't you see that we're trying to help you?" Trace begged in a tone that betrayed his frustration. "Throw us a bone, will you? We're doing everything in our power to help you get back into your house. All we're asking is for just a little bit of help on your end."

Jennelle's upper lip seamed to a tight, stubborn line before she said, "I've seen it before. First you're tied to a bed, forced to drink pureed grilled cheese from a straw and the next, all your possessions are given to Goodwill and you're left with nothing but the clothes on your back. I've seen it happen, though I never imagined it would happen to me."

"What are you talking about? Who have you seen this happen to?" Trace asked, irritated. "No one is going to force you to drink a pureed cheese sandwich."

"Gladys Monker," Jennelle answered in a strident tone. "She broke her hip and then her family stuck her in a home. She died of a broken heart a year later."

"She died of pneumonia and she had dementia," Miranda corrected her, shaking her head. "Good try, though. Not to mention, Gladys was, like, a hundred years old and you said yourself, her family waited too long to intervene on her behalf."

Jennelle glared at Miranda for daring to interject facts into her dramatic storytelling hour. She closed her eyes and shrugged. "You say pneumonia. I say broken heart. Her children betrayed her. Plain and simple. Same as me."

"Mama," Wade warned, causing Jennelle's eyes to open warily. "You have to stop attacking people who are trying to help you. You had a heart attack. You have needs that Florence cannot help you with. Plus it's not fair to your friend to have to take care of you when you have three kids who are trying their damnedest to help. Stop pushing away the very people who love you. *Please.*"

"I wish to speak to Wade alone," she declared, her bottom lip trembling. Miranda and Trace made sounds of frustration but left the room. Once they were alone, Jennelle turned to Wade, beseeching his help. "You're the only one who truly loves me, son. Those two people don't care about me or my comfort. They'll just throw me in a home as soon as your back's turned. I guarantee it!"

Wade sighed, praying for patience. "Mama, that's not true. I don't know what happened to you. You used to be a little more levelheaded than this. Something's gone wrong inside your head and your heart if you truly think that your children would do something like that to you. We love you and we're worried."

"Why is everyone so worried? I was doing just fine before everyone poked their noses where they didn't belong."

He wasn't going to have the same argument with her. He didn't have the energy. "The facts remain the same. Your house is condemned and you cannot move back until the cleaners have done their job. Dad is in jail and there's no one else who can help. Pushing away the very people who are turning their lives upside down to help you is very rude."

"I don't need anyone's help."

"Really? Because from where I'm standing, I see a stubborn woman who would rather cut off her nose to spite her face because she's so blinded by her own pride to see what's right in front of her."

His mother blinked back tears. "I never thought I'd see the day when you would turn on me, too, Wade."

"I'm not turning on you," he said, gentling his voice because he knew the truth was a bitter pill to swallow but it had to go down just the same. "But you raised me to be a straight shooter and always speak the truth, even if it wasn't pretty. So I'm not going to lie to you just because it might be easier. Trace is paying for cleaners to come and clean the house in the hopes that we can salvage your home. But there's a chance that we won't be able to save that house." He let that truth sink in because he really needed her to understand that there was no going back to the way it was before. "There's a lot of interior damage caused by rot that might not be able to be fixed. I want you to know that. And on Friday when the cleaners come, you need to be there to see what's happening and you need to be a part of the cleanup because this is your mess."

He drew a deep breath to say what really needed to be said but definitely wouldn't be appreciated. "And the fact of the matter is, Simone died a long time ago. We have to let her go. We can't change the past no matter how much we would like to. No matter how we punish ourselves it won't bring her back."

*Let her go.*

Wasn't that what he needed to do, too? Had he truly been punishing himself all these years with her memory? Was it true that the root of his insomnia had Simone's name written all over it? His knee-jerk reaction was to deny the thought and push it away but if he could plainly see that his parents were suffering the effects of unmitigated grief, why couldn't he see that in himself? "It doesn't matter how many rooms you fill up with stuff or how many boxes of cereal you collect. She's never going to come home *ever again.* Stop trying to replace Simone with inanimate objects. It's not going to work."

Jennelle clapped her hands over her ears as tears welled. "Stop! Stop saying these terrible things. I don't want to hear it," she cried, but Wade couldn't stop. Not now. Things had gotten to a place where going forward was the only way to survive.

"Mama," he said, gently pulling her hands away from her ears. "We all loved her and we all miss her but we have to move on. Because we're still living. Remember that,

Mama? Remember that you have *three* other children? This has to stop. Sometimes I don't even know who you are when such mean and hateful things pour out of your mouth. It's not you. You didn't raise us to be petty and small, which is why I can't reconcile what I see in the woman before me. And I'm sorry if what I have to say is harsh but I expect more from the strong woman who raised me and that's just the way that it is."

Jennelle's lip trembled and a tear escaped to slide down her cheek. He felt bad for being harsh but damn it, it had to be said. For a long moment she remained silent until she said in a choked voice, "I don't mean to hurt anyone. Sometimes things come out of my mouth before I can stop them and then I can't take it back."

"I know," he said, wiping away the tear and fighting his own. "We need to work on that. Because you've been saying some really awful things to your own children. To Miranda, particularly. She's trying so hard to help you and all you do is push her away. Lord help you, there will come a day when you will succeed in finally pushing her away for good. And then you won't have any contact with your grandson or any other grandchildren that may come. Is that what you want?"

"She doesn't let me see Talen anyway," she retorted mournfully. "She prefers that Indian woman over me."

"I don't believe that but even if a tiny bit of that statement were true, maybe you should ask yourself why? Maybe Talen's other grandmother doesn't judge Miranda for every little thing that she does or doesn't do. A person can only take so much before they break."

Jennelle's bottom lip trembled. "And what about all of you? You never visit, you don't call…Wade, you haven't been home in eight years. That's a mighty fine glass house you're sitting in. Why haven't you come home? Not even once?"

He fell silent. He wouldn't lie to his mother but he wasn't quite ready to admit the truth aloud. "Mama, I've got some things to work out in my head, too. Simone's death screwed with us all. Things just fell apart and I couldn't face it. I'm sorry." He could've come home. He chose not to. Simone's ghost had kept him away and he was ashamed to admit it. He drew a deep breath and let it out, his insides shaking like the legs of a newborn fawn. "The thing is, we've got a long road to walk and it would go a lot more smoothly if we didn't have to fight you every step."

"You're asking a lot of me," Jennelle said, looking away. "My whole life has been destroyed and I'm not supposed to be upset about it?"

"No, I understand that things are not ideal but we're trying to fix it. Can you trust us, just a little bit, to get you where you need to be?" Jennelle lifted one shoulder in a helpless gesture, as if she didn't even know where to start, and Wade took that as a tiny step in the right direction. "How about this, Mama…consider this an opportunity to get to know Talen better and then it's something positive rather than a negative," he suggested. "Things are going to change in this family. They have to. Otherwise, we're just delaying the inevitable. This family is going to implode and there'll be nothing and no one around to pick up the pieces."

Jennelle said nothing. Wade wasn't fool enough to harbor hope that his mother had had an epiphany but he wasn't above hoping for a little luck that the tide was finally turning their way. He'd meant what he'd said. He felt bad that Miranda had been bearing the brunt of their mother's rage when they all should've been there to help her. But they'd all bailed. His father included.

Shame followed the private admission, and he knew the biggest piece of the puzzle was still missing. "I'm going to find a way to get Dad out of jail," he announced, making up his mind. Jennelle looked very vulnerable and sad and he wondered how fragile his parents' marriage was right now. "It isn't right for Dad to hide out and expect everyone else to do the work when he should've been there for you."

"It's not your dad's fault," Jennelle said, surprising Wade with her defense of her husband. "He's had a lot to deal with."

"No, Mama," he disagreed. "We've all got stuff on our plates. Nobody gets a pass. Not even Dad." If it was time for everyone to start dealing with the past, Zed Sinclair didn't get to sit it out. This shit had gone on long enough.

And if he had to drag the man out of his cell with his bare hands, he would do it. Wade stepped forward and pressed a kiss on his mother's forehead. "I have some errands to run. Do me a favor, bite down on that sharp tongue of yours before you say something you can't take back. I will be here tomorrow to help you get settled into Miranda's house. Promise me you'll be nice," he said.

She nodded reluctantly, and he took that as an important step. Now he just needed to find a way to get his father out of that jail cell.

He met his siblings in the hallway, away from Jennelle's doorway. Miranda was biting her fingernail, a habit she hadn't quite lost from childhood, and Trace paced in small steps. Both stopped when he said, "Okay, she's calmed down a bit. She'll be nice. I think."

"How'd you manage that?" Miranda asked, spitting out a tiny sliver of nail. "Did you perform an exorcism?"

Trace barked a short laugh, but when Wade didn't share their laugh, he sighed and said, "Okay, so moving day tomorrow. She say anything else?"

"She said plenty. Nothing new. Listen, let's all try to remember that this is a pretty big transition, okay? Don't take the bait even if she throws it at you. Sometimes she can't help what comes out of her mouth."

"You're asking us to be the bigger person?" Miranda asked wryly. "I've spent my adult life being the bigger person with Mom. It's getting old."

"Well, seeing as she's going to be your roommate, you might want to keep the status quo."

"Good Lord, heaven help me. Maybe we should put her in a home." Wade shot her a dark look and she shrugged. "I'm kidding. Sort of."

"In the meantime, I'm going to see if I can get Dad out of jail by Friday."

"Why?" Trace asked. "It's not like he's going to be much help."

"Because I think it'll help Mom deal with the cleanup. She feels alone. Her husband abandoned her to that house. If we can see that, she can, too."

Miranda nodded, flushing with shame. "You're right. It's hard to remember when they were different. Always laughing, hugging and kissing...they're like different people now. They probably haven't had sex in years."

"Blech," Trace said, his face wrinkling in disgust. "Thank you for that lovely visual. I could've gone my whole life not thinking about my parents' sex life."

"Hey, a healthy sex life is integral to a healthy marriage," Miranda quipped, and Trace made a gagging sound.

Wade bit back a grin, recognizing that

Miranda was deliberately trying to gross out her brothers. Miranda had always been a bit of a troublemaker, and he'd loved that about her. Somewhere along the way, they'd all lost a bit of themselves and it was high time they reclaimed it. "Wish me luck," he said, turning to leave. "And remember…be nice."

"I'll kill her with kindness," Miranda promised with false sweetness. "And if that doesn't work, a good, old-fashioned pillow over the face will."

Wade laughed and kept walking. He knew she was kidding. At least he hoped she was.

# CHAPTER NINETEEN

"WHY THE SUDDEN need to spring clean? It's not even spring yet," Remy said, idly picking through the clothes hanging in the large walk-in closet of Morgan's bedroom. "And am I on the clock? If not I've got better things to do with my time unless you're going to share what's going on in that cuckoo brain of yours."

Morgan exhaled a short breath and shot Remy a look that said *keep working* but said, "Yes, you're on the clock."

"Mmm-hmm. So what are we doing here, looking through David's dusty drawers? You should've unloaded these ancient threads three years ago."

Yes, she should've. But when it had come time to throw it all out, she'd hesitated. If she were truly grieving, would she be in such a hurry to get rid of his things? She hadn't wanted to seem anything but the grieving widow and thus, the clothes had remained as David had left them—perfectly organized by color and type—as if he were going to walk through the door at any minute. "Do you see anything you like?" she asked her cousin as he eyed a particularly fine Calvin Klein suit. "You're about the same size, right? You can have whatever you want."

"Are you kidding? Don't tease me when Calvin Klein is on the line." He pulled the dark navy suit and made a sound no man should make when talking about clothes. "This is exquisite and so classic. Your David had impeccable taste. Are you sure he wasn't gay?"

"He was pretty straight," Morgan said. "And homophobic."

"Ohh, honey, that's a dead giveaway that he was hungering for something he would not allow himself to have."

Morgan suppressed a shudder. It was hard enough to remember David period, much less try to imagine him with another man. "Well, guess it doesn't matter now. Help yourself to whatever you like. Everything else is going to Goodwill."

Remy chortled like Tim Gunn at a runway show and began picking through the suits, exclaiming here and there at his good fortune.

"Not that I'm not tickled pink but I have to ask…what's happening with you, sugar pie?"

"Nothing. Just time to let go."

"It was time to let go of that man the minute his body cooled. He was a dirty, rotten SOB—with impossibly gorgeous tastes in clothing—and you're better off without him. But why now?"

She didn't know. Something felt different inside her. Maybe it was breaking the seal on her self-imposed celibacy post-David that had made the change. Maybe it was spending time with a man who was an overall good person and not just surface deep. Everyone thought David was a good man but that was because no one actually knew him. Except Morgan.

"David had wanted to start trying for a baby," she said, pausing at the dresser. "Can you imagine?"

"It was a blessing in disguise that you lost that baby," Remy said, pursing his lips at the sad memory. "And an even bigger blessing that you didn't get knocked up again afterward. Can you imagine, indeed. That man… you should've pressed charges when you had the chance."

"And who would've believed me? David was a pillar of the community. Beloved, even.

I doubt anyone would've taken a police report even if I'd tried to report the abuse. I would've gotten a stern talking to, to try and work things out, and then David would've punished me even more for embarrassing him." She shook her head at the idea. "No, there was no out for me except the way it'd happened."

Remy shot her a warning look. "That's a terrible burden to carry around, sister. Someday those shoulders are gonna bow from the weight. Are you at least coming out of your fake mourning?"

"It's not fake. Not exactly. I am a grieving widow." Grieving the loss of her ideals, hopes and dreams, at the very least. "I wonder how things would've been different if I hadn't met David but someone else, instead."

"You're in a philosophical mood today. Fate is a funny thing."

"Sometimes I wonder how I ever fell for David's charm in the first place. Perhaps I'm just jaded now because I feel I'm not even the same person in my memories."

"You were a young, idealistic girl and you were taken in by the idea of marrying a rich, successful man who appeared to dote on you.

How were you supposed to know he was going to turn out to be a sadistic bastard?"

She shrugged. "I'm a therapist. I should've seen some kind of sign."

"Would you have paid attention? We see what we want to see. I never told you this but in college, while I was out discovering my true self, I thought I'd fallen head over heels in love with the first man I'd slept with. I put up with a lot of bullshit from him and it included abuse."

"Remy...you were in an abusive relationship?" She gaped, shocked that her flamboyant, outspoken cousin had found himself in an abusive situation such as herself. "What happened?"

"The first time? I told myself we were both emotional and things just got out of hand, and the reason he hit me was because he was scared of the idea of losing me. I thought his freakout was a testament to my worth. I mean, why not? No one had ever cared that much about me to raise a fuss if I wasn't around. It felt good to be so madly desired for once. But it got harder and harder to stick to that thinking after he kept beating the shit out of me."

Morgan stared, stunned by Remy's revelation. "How did you get out?"

Remy smiled. "I may be a flaming queen but I was raised by a hard-living fisherman. One night he came at me—pissed off because I'd dared to make a joke about his hair—and I realized that SOB didn't love me, and he sure as hell didn't deserve me. And then I laid him out. After that, I collected my things and walked away. Best damn thing I ever did. Just as it was the best damn thing *you* ever did by getting away from David."

Tears burned behind Morgan's eyes, so incredibly thankful for her wild, outlandish cousin who kept her secrets and felt safe enough to share a doozy of his own. If only she'd had Remy's courage and had walked out on David before that night. "Why couldn't I have inherited some of that bravery?" she whispered, mostly to herself, but Remy caught it and scowled as he tossed the suit in his hand to the pile growing on the bed.

"Don't do that," he warned, shaking his head. "You are braver than you know. Braver than you give yourself credit for, and you need to stop beating yourself over something that was an accident."

"Is it an accident if you wanted it to happen?" she dared to ask, lifting her gaze to

Remy. "So many times I wished David dead…
what if I made it happen somehow?"

"Listen to me…he slipped and fell down the
stairs. That's all anybody ever needs to know.
Now wipe that look off your face and hold
your head up. You're acting like the judge,
jury and executioner are coming to dinner.
He was a rotten man and he deserved what
he got. Who cares if you wished it a thousand
times? I wish to win the lottery every damn
day but it hasn't happened yet. Our thoughts
don't manifest into reality and I don't care
what the self-help gurus say. David's death
was a *happy* accident. Leave it at that."

A happy accident. She wished she could
embrace that perspective. Maybe if she could
lose the crushing guilt that she carried every
day, she could actually move on.

But move on to what? She looked to Remy.
"Have you ever considered moving away
from Homer?"

He shrugged in answer and made a silent
exclamation of joy at a wool coat he found.
"Honey, home is where you make it. I can live
anywhere I choose." He cast her a pointed
look. "And that goes for you, too. I've long
thought that maybe it's time for you to move
away and start fresh someplace else."

She waved away that idea. Move away? Where would she go? Her home was here. "This is where I belong. I have no interest in moving away. Besides, I've built my practice here. I wouldn't want to start over someplace else."

"Why not? Sounds fun to me. You're in a rut, girl. You need something—or someone—to shake you loose."

Morgan couldn't help the private smile at Remy's comment because it conjured all manner of delightful memories spent shaking things up with Wade. What would it be like to say goodbye to everything she'd ever known and start fresh? Somewhere where David's ghost didn't dog her every step? Where no one knew she'd ever been married to the horrid man? That would be fantastic.

And impossible.

She was firmly entrenched in her life here. She had to take the good with the bad. That was being a grown-up.

"Sometimes being a grown-up isn't all it's cracked up to be," she murmured. Without missing a beat Remy snapped his fingers and nodded.

"Amen to that."

Morgan smiled and pushed away thoughts that bordered on dangerous. Her life was here. And that's where it would stay.

# CHAPTER TWENTY

WADE WALKED INTO the jail with one purpose—to convince his father to let them bail him out and come help them with Jennelle. He had no idea how he was going to do that, seeing as his father had already been given many opportunities to get out of jail. But Wade hadn't come all the way to Alaska, disrupting his own life and career, for his dad to hide out in jail.

As before when Wade visited, Zed was led into the receiving room and for as long as Wade lived he would never fail to wince at the memory of his father in shackles. There are just some things you can never imagine are going to happen and this was high up on that list. Wade waited for his father to sit before he started talking. "I've come to get you to see reason," he started, determined to make his dad see what a mistake he was making. "This business of you hiding in a jail cell while everyone else cleans up our family's mess is unacceptable. Talk to me, Dad. What's going on with you?"

ZED LOOKED AS if he'd aged ten years in the time that he'd been incarcerated, and it hurt Wade in a deeply private place to see his dad so diminished but he needed to focus. "I need to try to understand what's going on because right now I'm at a loss. Help me to understand," Wade pleaded with his father, feeling much like a young kid again, trying desperately to understand why the man who had once been his hero had regressed to a sad, pathetic mortal.

Zed glanced away, shame in his gaze. "You think I don't want to be there for your mom? Of course I want to be there. But I'm not what she needs right now. She has you kids, and you guys can help her through this. I'll just get in the way."

"She doesn't need us, she needs *you*. She's falling apart. You guys have been together since you were teenagers, and you can reach her in a way that we never could. We need you, Dad. Don't abandon us now."

"Come on, Wade. You're not babies anymore. You're grown adults. I don't need to hold your hands any longer."

"We're not asking you to hold our hands. We're asking you to help us pull Mama out of a really bad situation that you helped put her in." Wade couldn't help the rise in his voice as his temper got the best of him. "What you're doing is *hiding,* not helping. Don't try to tell yourself anything different. You can sit in this jail cell and pretend that you're doing everyone a favor but the truth of it is, you're being a coward. I'm sorry but there's just no pretty way to say it. Take responsibility and help us to help this family. Do you think that it doesn't hurt to see Mama pushing away every single person who loves her because she's swimming in grief? Grief that you won't help heal?"

"What am I supposed to do about it, boy?" Zed's cheeks colored as he leaned forward, his eyes flashing with a hint of his former spirit. "I'm no therapist! Don't you think I have my own issues? Am I in any shape to be helping anyone else with their pain? If you can't see that I would make it worse, then you're blind."

Wade clenched his fist. "No, you're wrong. You locked yourself in that shed and you buried yourself in drugs to escape your shame for letting down this family. I get it but you can come back from that. You don't have to wallow in self-pity forever. If you don't watch out, your wife will be dead before you come to your senses. She almost died in that house as it is. *Do you hear me?* She almost died! And where were you? Sitting here in this jail cell. How is that helping your wife? How can you continue to let down your family? The man I knew, the man who raised me, he wouldn't have stood for this bullshit. Do you hear me? *Bullshit!*"

Wade had never spoken to his father in that way but he couldn't help it. What was going on wasn't right and Zed had taught him to stand up for what was right, and sometimes that meant going against the stream.

Whether Zed was rattled by Wade's impassioned speech, it didn't show. The man was a rock and a stubborn mule to boot. "Have you said your piece?"

"Would it matter? Does anything I have to say matter to you anymore?" he retorted bitterly.

"I've done a lot of wrong and I sure as hell have no authority to throw stones, but you have a helluva lot of nerve coming in here and pointing fingers when you walked away from the family eight years ago. You skipped off when we all needed the family to rally, so don't sit there and point your fingers and raise your voice as if you are innocent in any wrongdoing. You hide behind your excuse that you had a job to go to—but what you did was run away. Don't try to sell it to me any other way."

Wade opened his mouth to protest but what could he say? His father was right. He'd run as quick and as fast as he could. How could he stay after what had happened with Simone? After he had failed to find her? How could he look his father in the eye and not see failure staring back at him every single time?

"I shouldn't have left the way I did," Wade admitted quietly. "I didn't know what else to do. If I'd stayed in this town I would've lost my mind. So I left. Is that what you want me to say? Well, there you have it. My confession. Yes, I bailed. I bailed on my family because I couldn't handle the thought of confronting Simone's ghost around every corner. I failed to find her. I was her big brother. I was supposed to protect her. But I failed. I couldn't live with myself if I'd stayed." Wade leaned back in his chair and covered his face with his hands. Pain, sharp and unrelenting, sliced across to his heart as he suffered the echo of his guilt and suffering but it was a wound that needed lancing. It'd taken eight years for him to admit that he shouldn't have bailed and a weight fell from his shoulders that he hadn't realized he'd been carrying.

"You didn't fail," his father said roughly. "Bad things happen and there's no rhyme or reason to it. Simone got caught up in something terrible and we might never know why. Don't bear that burden, son."

Wade scrubbed his face and ground the moisture from his eyes. "You don't blame me?"

"Why would I? No more than I would blame Trace or Miranda. It was just Simone's time and that's the part that we have to get right with."

"I can't get right with it, Dad. I just can't."

"I know, I know. Getting right with it… that's the struggle. Every day. Why did such a sweet girl get cut down so young, so brutally? The questions kept me awake at night. While your mother fought nightmares, I fought insomnia."

God, Wade knew insomnia well. Seems he'd inherited that particular trait from his father. Whereas Wade used work to occupy his brain, his father had resorted to marijuana.

What a slippery slope it is managing emotional pain.

"At first, the dope helped me sleep. And then it turned into something more, something I needed to function but then I wasn't really functioning. I was just existing. And I didn't have the strength to hold your mom up because I didn't have the strength to hold myself up. I turned down Rhett's and Trace's offers to pay my bail because I knew I needed to be here. I needed this time to get my head on straight—to let the smoke clear from my brain. And for the first time in a long time I have clarity. But with that clarity comes the realization that I don't deserve to ride in on a white pony to save the day." Wade stared in shocked silence at Zed. He couldn't fathom his father's position but he could plainly see Zed's pain. "I'm a burden to your mother— just one more thing for her to worry about at the end of the day. And I never imagined I would be that. But I am. I'm trying to give your mother time without adding to her burden, don't you see that?"

"But you're not doing that, Dad. She's drowning without you. You're standing on the shore and watching her go under water saying 'I can't save her. I can't save her' but you can. She needs you, more than any time in her life. She's turning into a bitter, angry woman." Wade took a deep breath. "And she's killing Miranda—your other daughter. Mom's squelching Miranda's spirit and stomping on all the love that a mother is supposed to have for her children. It's as if she can't help herself and all sorts of mean things come popping out of her mouth at Miranda's expense. I wouldn't have believed it if I hadn't seen it myself."

"She's always been harder on Miranda," Zed agreed in a soft, aggrieved tone. "I don't know why."

"It's gotten worse. Please, Dad…please come home."

A torturously long moment stretched between them, and for a second Wade was hopeful that his father might finally agree, but Zed gave a slow, definitive shake of his head and Wade's hope plummeted. "I can't. I'm not ready. I wish that I were, son. I really do."

"Tomorrow they're doing the cleaning on the house. She's going to need you more than ever. We need you. We're all going to be there. You know it's going to be difficult for her to have people going in and out of the house looking at all of her embarrassing mess. But if this cleaning doesn't work, they're going to condemn the house permanently and Mom will have nowhere to go. Do you understand? This is bigger than your pride. This is your wife's home. The place where she raised her children. The place you built! It has to mean more than your pride. It has to mean more than your shame for failing her. I need you to rise above all of that and be the man you once were. The man I remember. The man I miss."

In all of his life Wade could remember his father crying on three occasions. The first time was when they'd lost his favorite hunting dog, Butch, to a bear mauling. The second time was when Trace broke his leg skiing and had to be airlifted to Anchorage in order to save his life. And the third was the morning that they found Simone. But as Wade watched, a tear snaked down Zed's cheek, and Wade knew his father wasn't going to budge. Wade was looking at a broken man—a man whose soul had been crushed by circumstance with no hope of survival—and it was all he could do not to cry himself.

There was nothing more he could say. The situation was out of his hands. His father had made up his mind that they were better off without him, and Wade didn't know what to say or do to change it. His dad had already admitted he had demons to slay, and he thought the best place to battle them was behind bars.

Wade let out a heavy sigh and pushed away from the table. "I came here to change your mind. When I set out and walked into this place, I swore I wasn't leaving without you. But I can't really force you to do what's right. You think that your family doesn't need you and you think that your wife is better off with you in here. All I can say is you are wrong. There was a time when I thought of you as the wisest of all men. And I know it's unrealistic for fathers to remain their sons' heroes for the rest of their lives but I never thought that you would stop being my hero. But today, you did."

Wade stood on stiff legs and walked away. There was a wealth of pain crashing over his heart, crying out for his father but he had to accept that his father had made his choice. He would have to do his best to be the stand-in head of the household for his family. If his father were thinking clearly that's what he would've wanted.

# CHAPTER TWENTY-ONE

"PERFECT," MIRANDA MUTTERED, glancing up at the dark skies overhead as the cleaning crew and organizers gathered in their parents' yard. Wade followed Miranda's gaze and nodded in agreement. That's all they needed to make things worse: rain. Already their mother was glaring at everyone as if they were the enemy and she was the lone defender of her property. Miranda sighed and looked to Wade. "Might as well get this show on the road, right? It's not as if it's going to get better."

Wade gave a minute shake of his head but he agreed. There was no sense in putting off the inevitable. Jennelle was going to pitch a fit no matter what.

Morgan pulled up and he used that excuse to break away from Miranda. He wanted to be anywhere but here at the moment. Maybe Morgan could give him some words of wisdom to bolster his resolve.

Morgan's cheeks instantly pinked in the biting cold, which only gave her porcelain skin a fresh hue that immediately made him think of the other times he'd made her blush—and moan—and he had to shelve those thoughts before he made a fool out of himself in front of God and country. "Hi," he said, smiling. "Ready for this?"

"Are you?" she countered with a small smile of her own but she was the consummate professional both in her manner and her expression. "This kind of cleanup is hard on everyone, not only the hoarder. There are bound to be some memories that pop up as we go through the process."

"I'm not sure how. That house is not the same house I grew up in. I don't even recognize it anymore."

"You will. Once we dig down to the bones, you'd be surprised what comes up. It can be very cathartic but it can also be very painful," she warned him in a gentle tone that warmed him in places it shouldn't. He didn't know if she was this way with every patient's family or if he was special but he'd like to think it was the latter. "How is your mother today?"

"Ornery as ever. Bound to insult or offend someone before the day is out," he answered. "But the doctor said she's healthy enough to participate as long as she doesn't do any lifting."

"Well, we have people for that so no worries there. And how are you doing?"

"Terrible," he admitted, tapping his chest. "I think I might have a heart attack, myself. There's a tightness right here that makes it hard to breathe. I don't know why this is stressing me out so much."

She graced him with another soft smile. "Because your subconscious knows that house has both painful and beautiful memories. You haven't been dealing with any of them since you left. Today is the day you will. It's natural to be apprehensive. Just don't run from it."

"Funny, 'cause that's exactly what I feel like doing and then I feel like a jerk for even thinking it."

"It's natural," she assured him. "If at any point you need a breather, let me know. This is about the family's process, not just your mother's."

He nodded and knew he should keep the conversation professional but he suffered the overwhelming impulse to reach out and touch her. He knew that wasn't appropriate, and she likely wouldn't appreciate him drawing attention to their private dalliance so he kept his hands to himself. But his gaze must've burned with hunger for Morgan's breath caught and she gave a slight shake of her head. "You must've read my mind," he murmured so only she could hear him.

"I guess I did," she admitted, glancing away, searching to catch any stares their way. "We need to keep it professional. I don't need anyone finding out about us."

*Us.* He wished there was an *us* to discover. "I know." *You look beautiful today.* The words danced on his tongue and nearly tripped from his mouth. "Assuage my ego and tell me that I'm not the only one feeling something here."

She laughed softly as her gaze darted with guilt. "You are not alone. But I can't do this here. You and I need to be professional right now." She took a tiny step forward, acting as if she was flicking something from his shoulder so that she could whisper, "But tonight I'm free if you want to come by...I'll even cook."

He grinned. "Can you cook?"

"You'll just have to wait and see."

"That's a date, Ms. O'Hare," he promised, his mood lightening. "Anything I should bring?"

She met his gaze boldly. "Condoms. Lots of them." And then she left him to struggle with his sudden erection as she went to talk to his mother. Crafty woman…oh, he would delight in the payback—and so would she.

HAD SHE REALLY just told Wade to bring condoms? She pressed a gloved hand to her cheek, unable to believe she'd been so saucy. *Ohhh Lordy*…what was she doing thinking about sex with Wade when she was supposed to be focused on the task at hand? *Get your head on straight.*

She approached Jennelle Sinclair, whose expression hovered somewhere between horrified and mortified as total strangers converged on her property, and her daughter, Miranda, who looked ready to go into battle. "Good morning, ladies," she started with a smile but only Miranda returned the gesture. Jennelle merely sniffed and looked away. A work in progress, that woman. "How are you feeling, Jennelle?" she asked, drawing the older woman into the conversation. "This is a big transition, and I want you to feel comfortable that nothing is being done without your consent."

"That's grizzly poop and you know it," Jennelle spat, embarrassing Miranda.

"Mom, stop it. Don't start off the day with

your sharp tongue," Miranda warned, shooting an apologetic look Morgan's way. "I'm sorry. She's impossible to wrangle on a good day much less a stressful one."

"Don't apologize for me. I've done nothing wrong. I'm the one being forced to suffer strangers going through my things, riffling through my underwear drawer and passing judgment on my life just to satisfy some government agency's opinion that I am safe to live on my own."

Miranda's face showed her frustration, and Morgan stepped in to intervene. "May I have a word with your mother privately?" she asked Miranda.

"Be my guest. Maybe you could dose her with something to change her personality?"

"You'd like that, wouldn't you?" Jennelle said with a scowl. "Go on, make sure those people don't trample my yard."

Miranda grumbled and walked away, leaving Morgan with Jennelle. "I know this is very hard," she started but Jennelle cut her off.

"You don't know anything, girlie. You don't know what it's like to be forced from your home or to lose something so precious you don't know how you'll ever recover. Don't patronize me with your doctor speak. We both know I have no choice in the matter. I just want to get it over with so I can return to my life."

"Jennelle, you won't heal if you don't commit to the process. You have the opportunity to start fresh and heal the wounds with your children. Isn't that worth the sacrifice?" Morgan withheld a sigh when Jennelle didn't respond. The older woman was too stubborn for her own good. Empathy for Wade's family's situation bordered on the unprofessional as she fought the urge to sharpen her voice with the older woman. "Well, the cleaners and organizers are here so let's meet with them and see how the day is going to go. The weather is not on our side, it would appear, so we need to use each moment afforded to us."

"Then I'll hope for snow," Jennelle muttered, which Morgan ignored. Jennelle was not an easy woman on a good day. It made her wonder what she'd been like before life dragged her down to this bitter place.

They walked over to the assembled group and to Morgan's surprise, Jennelle kept her mouth shut when Morgan thought for sure she'd have a few gems to share as they detailed how they were going to go into the house, room by room, pulling everything out and placing it in piles to sort and toss.

Morgan's gaze found Wade's, and a tingle erupted in her stomach at the banked promise in his eyes. Lord, that man was sexy. He did crazy things to her sense of self that she didn't quite trust but she craved just the same. For those reasons alone she should've rescinded her offer for tonight but she knew with a certainty wild horses couldn't force her to say those words. For the first time in her life, she felt out of control of her own emotions and it was addicting.

An hour into the cleaning process, as multiple cleaners dressed head to toe in hazmat suits and breathing apparatuses worked like bees to clear out the residence, the first meltdown occurred.

"What are you doing? You've ruined an heirloom!" Jennelle screeched, her hands shaking as she held a broken porcelain figurine. Wade, Miranda and Trace were around her, trying to calm her down but she was quickly gathering speed and Morgan rushed over to help. "You said they would be careful! You promised!" Jennelle cried to Miranda, and Miranda looked chagrined at the oversight.

"Jennelle, come talk with me for a minute," Morgan encouraged her, drawing her away from her children so that the woman could gather her wits. Sometimes patients needed to remove themselves from the situation and those associated with it in order to calm down. "Talk to me about the heirloom."

"What does it matter? It's broken," she cried, big tears rolling down her cheeks. "It's never going to be the same. Ever."

"No, it won't," Morgan agreed solemnly. "But accidents happen and we have to learn how to move on."

"This wasn't an accident," she said vehemently, wiping at her tears with her free hand.

"And how wasn't it an accident? Do you feel someone broke your heirloom purposefully?"

"I don't know but it's broken and that's all that matters."

"Why don't you show me where you had this heirloom," Morgan suggested, knowing it was likely the heirloom had been broken long before she'd noticed, and the movers had simply tossed it in the trash pile because that was the rule: anything broken or ruined had to go.

Jennelle paused, not sure if she wanted to

comply as if she knew where Morgan was going with this but she nodded reluctantly, and Morgan followed the older woman into the house where a bustle of activity continued unchecked. Jennelle's face soured into an unhappy pucker as boxes upon boxes of garbage and who knows what were taken from the house, and for a moment it was hard for Jennelle to focus on the task at hand so Morgan gently helped her along. "Jennelle? Show me where the heirloom was."

By this point, her children had slowly come to stand near their mother, waiting anxiously for her answer. Clearly, Miranda was bothered by the fact that something truly precious to her mother might've been inadvertently damaged while the men appeared openly perplexed by their mother's reaction.

Morgan wanted to explain that this was a normal reaction for a hoarder and it usually had nothing to do with the actual item in question, but right now she needed to focus on Jennelle as this was part of the healing process. Every lost treasure was metaphorical for something else in the hoarder's mind, although they rarely realized this at the start. "Well, it was over by the mantel," Jennelle answered, though her lip quivered when she realized the mantel was still covered by an assortment of things. "Or maybe it was in the kitchen...I don't remember but I know it was in a safe place."

"Mom...nothing in this house is safe," Wade murmured regretfully. "There's a chance it was broken without you realizing it."

Jennelle whipped her head around to scowl at her son. "That's ridiculous. I may have a collecting problem but I know where to put things to keep them safe."

"Mom, if that were true, we wouldn't be sorting through a pile of trash right now," Trace said, pointing toward the huge tarp laid out on the front yard covered with items that needed to be sorted, though most of which was going to end up in the trash bin.

"Tell your children about the heirloom... what was it? What did it mean to you?"

"What does it matter?" Jennelle asked bitterly, fighting tears.

"Please, Mom...we want to know," Miranda said in a gentle tone that caught Jennelle off guard. The mother-daughter dynamic at work was so complicated and needed further help but one crisis at a time. For a long moment Jennelle simply stared at the pieces, lost in herself until she started sharing in a halting voice.

"It was a gift from your father when we were dating," Jennelle answered, staring at the broken pieces in her hand. "It was the first gift he'd ever given to me. I kept it all these years because each time I looked at it, I remembered how much he loved me then."

Morgan nodded in understanding, knowing a little bit about the complex nature of Jennelle's relationship with her husband. Everything in this poor woman's life was shattered. She was going to need so much help putting it all back together again.

"Mom, we can try and fix it," Wade said, gently taking the pieces from his mother. "It might not be the same but we'll do our best to make it right."

Morgan had a feeling Wade wasn't only speaking about the broken figurine, and it warmed her heart in a breathtaking way that he was so gentle with his mother in spite of all the trouble she'd caused. "Trace, can you find some glue?" he asked his brother.

Miranda piped in, snapping her fingers. "I have Super Glue in my purse."

"That should work," Wade said, and Miranda went to her Range Rover to retrieve it. Trace rubbed his mother's shoulder and shared a look with Wade that no doubt was about their father, and Morgan knew whatever differences the brothers had, they shared a common disappointment in how their father had abandoned their mother. "Mama, you're so brave to go through with this," he said. "I'm proud of you."

She looked up, tears filling her eyes. "I don't feel brave," she admitted. "I feel like everyone is staring at me in my skivvies."

Wade chuckled and gathered his mother in his arms for a quick hug. "Well, that's probably natural, right, Dr. O'Hare?"

"Absolutely. And Trace is right. What you're doing is incredibly brave and even though it's difficult, when we're all done, you're going to be so much happier."

Morgan could tell that Jennelle wasn't sure on that score but she jerked a stiff nod and within moments, Trace, Wade and Miranda were able to glue the shattered pieces back together again. Somewhat satisfied, Jennelle allowed work to continue and for a few hours, progress was swift until the time came to go into Simone's room.

Then meltdown number two happened.

And this time no amount of cajoling was going to make a difference—Jennelle would not allow anyone near that room.

# CHAPTER TWENTY-TWO

JENNELLE LOCKED THE door behind her and ignored her children's pleas to open the door, going to sit on Simone's bed. Her entire body ached and she just wanted to close the door on everything that was happening that felt out of her control. As she always did, she allowed the energy of what she believed was Simone's spirit soothe her ragged nerves. No one understood a mother's agony at losing a child. No one understood that it never went away. It was a dull, permanent ache that pounded away at her nerves and her sanity until she couldn't remember a time when she didn't suffer this horrible pain. So when the pain became unbearable she always came here.

In this room she could forget that her life was falling apart more rapidly than she could piece it back together again. In here was her sanctuary.

"Mom, please open the door." Miranda's plaintive tone reached Jennelle through the thick oak. "Don't do this. We were doing so well."

She could hear the disappointment in her daughter's voice but Jennelle couldn't deal with that right now. It was too much. Everything was too much to bear at the moment. Jennelle closed her eyes and breathed deep the quiet of the room, picturing in her mind her youngest daughter's smile and sparkling eyes. Lord, she'd been such a beauty. Maybe that had been her downfall. Boys had always flocked to the girl.

Too many nights Jennelle had lain awake fretting that she'd somehow missed the warning signs somewhere. Maybe if she'd been less lenient with Simone, she'd still be here. Maybe if she'd refused to let her and Miranda get a place together, she'd have been home that night. Or maybe if she and Zed hadn't been so adamant that all the children work for their own car, Simone wouldn't have had to rely on her sister for a ride home that night. The multitude of maybes wore on Jennelle's soul like a collar cinched too tight.

She picked up a framed photo of Simone and her girlfriend, Zoe. They'd been inseparable, those two. Until Simone had died and then Zoe had slowly stopped coming by. It was as if Zoe hadn't been able to handle seeing the hole that Simone had left behind. Jennelle hugged the photo to her chest, catching her breath as tears robbed her of coherent thought. They wanted to tear down this room and take Simone from her. This was all she had of her baby girl. Everything—everyone—was gone.

This room was all Jennelle had left and right now, she wanted to die in it.

The insistent knocking on the door had stopped and sudden silence followed. Jennelle waited, cocking her head subtly to listen for the sounds of people but she heard nothing. It was as if everyone had evacuated the house. Was it too much to hope for? Jennelle swallowed and hugged the picture frame closer. And then she heard the most unlikely of voices.

"Jen...open the door."

Zed? A lump formed instantly in her throat and she couldn't speak. Was that her husband? No, that wasn't possible. She was losing her mind. Her husband was not here. He was choosing to rot in jail, far away from her and her troubles. "Come now, Jen...open this door."

The quiet authority in her husband's voice

was impossible to ignore. It'd been so long since Zed had shown an ounce of interest in anything that she'd forgotten that at one time he'd been the solid head of the household. "Zed? Is that you?"

Only Zed called her Jen. It was his nickname for her and always had been. She rose on unsteady feet and opened the door cautiously. A tiny cry followed when she saw her husband, a man she'd loved with all her heart since she was fifteen, standing there looking older than he ever had but with something in his gaze that had been missing for a very long time—quiet strength. "What are you doing here?" she dared to ask, lifting her chin.

"What I should've done a long time ago," he admitted, reaching for her hand. "It's time, girlie."

A soft, vulnerable spot deep inside her trembled at the way he'd always been able to get through to her with so few words. This was Zed…the man she'd always known was the one for her and had been so lost without, but she wasn't ready to leave that room. She shook her head as tears sprang to her eyes again. "I can't."

"You can." He held out his hand, focusing his gaze on her. "We'll do this together."

"This is all I have of our little girl," she said, her eyes streaming. Why didn't anyone understand? "I can't let her go."

He shook his head gravely and pointed at his heart. "She lives here. Not in that room."

And with that she crumpled, but Zed was there to catch her, pulling her tightly to him. She clung to him, sobbing big, ugly tears that poured out of her soul, lancing the wound inside her, until she couldn't manage another drop of moisture, and even then her shoulders shook with the magnitude of her loss. "I miss her so much," she whispered to her husband, forgetting that they were not alone, though everyone had respectfully gone outside to wait out the storm. "I want her back."

Zed didn't say anything, mostly because Jennelle knew he felt the same. She'd always known, just as he'd known her feelings, too, but neither acknowledged that simple truth to one another. "She was a strong girl. This is no way to honor her."

Lord, she knew that. Deep in her broken heart, she knew. Simone would've been horrified at the way Jennelle and Zed had completely fallen apart. Jennelle buried her face against her husband's chest. At one time he'd been robust and hale but time had taken its toll. Even though she felt the ridge of his chest bones under her cheek, she clung to him, desperate to feel him against her again. In his arms, she found the sanctuary she'd been trying to recreate with Simone's room and shuddered with relief that he had returned to her. "What do we do now?" she asked, looking to him for guidance.

"We start over." He motioned to their kids who were waiting outside anxiously. "And we stop fighting each other. Time to make amends. All of us."

She nodded, the fight going right out of her. She was wrung out emotionally and didn't have the strength to argue, not that she would've. For the first time in a long time, she had nothing to say.

WADE SHARED SHOCKED looks with his siblings, and he knew they were all thinking the same thing and it was along the lines of "Holy shit" that their dad had suddenly shown up when all attempts to get him to budge had been met with futility. But something must've trickled down to that stubborn heart because here he was. When he emerged with his wife, Wade could only stare.

He looked to Trace, and Trace shrugged.

"I'm guessing he finally took Rhett up on his offer to spring him."

"I guess so," Wade said, still amazed but so thankful. His father was probably the only one who could wrench Jennelle out of her funk. Morgan, sensing the window of opportunity had been flung open, motioned for the cleaners to continue with the cleanup and once again, people were scurrying to and fro, trying to beat the storm that seemed to be gathering power above them. They worked side by side, moving impossible amounts of junk, broken-down boxes and things best left unnamed as slowly but surely, the house became an empty but dirty shell.

"That's about all we can do today," Morgan said to everyone's relief as they stretched sore muscles and wiped away sweat in spite of the bitter temperatures. "But this was an amazing job you all did today. Jennelle—" she turned to Wade's mother and smiled "—you did a wonderful job pitching in and making this part of your process. How do you feel?"

"Tired but good," Jennelle admitted, casting a shy look at her husband. "Real good."

"Excellent. Tomorrow we do massive cleanup. From what the engineers tell me, there is no structural damage to the home—

which is lucky because I've seen houses with so much damage there was no saving them. New paint, some new fixtures and new furniture and you're going to be able to sleep in your own bed. Would you like that?"

Jennelle nodded, tears filling her eyes. "I'd like that very much. But where am I staying tonight?"

"I'll spring for a hotel room for you both," Wade offered. "Something tells me you two could use some private time to talk things out."

Zed's subtle nod of thanks caused a lump to rise in Wade's throat, squeezing out any other words he might've said, but his dad understood.

Morgan smiled and said, "I'm very pleased with the progress today. I will see you all bright and early tomorrow, assuming the storm doesn't dump a ton of snow tonight."

Wade made a point to avoid watching Morgan go, even though his gaze stubbornly wanted to refuse. It wouldn't do any good to let anyone else in on their little secret. He sure as hell didn't want to explain to anyone something he didn't understand himself.

"Dad, what happened?" Miranda asked, once it was just their family again. "Don't get

me wrong, I'm so happy to see you here but…
we all tried to get you out of that jail cell but
you were stuck like glue."

"Does it matter? He's here now," Jennelle
said, speaking up in defense of her husband.
"I don't want any fighting."

"Yes, it does matter," Trace said. "And
we're not fighting. We're asking a simple
question. I think we're entitled to that."

A part of Wade wanted to side with their
mother and just let it go but another part of
him wanted answers, too.

"It's cold and I'm frozen to the bone. Questions and answers can wait," Jennelle said,
putting her foot down. She looked to Wade.
"We will happily take you up on that hotel
room offer. The Orca has always had nice
rooms and a very tasty continental breakfast,
if I recall properly."

"You got it, Mama," Wade said, withhold-
ing a sigh. He could wait another day or two
to get the answers and so could his siblings.
He looked to his dad. "You driving?"

"You can drive," Zed said, linking fingers
with his wife in a protective manner that
Wade recognized from his childhood. His
parents had always been very affectionate,
very touchy-feely. He couldn't remember a

time when they weren't hugging or kissing and embarrassing their children with their antics. After Simone, that part of them had died, too. So many changes, so many hurts. He rubbed at his eyes, ready for this day to be done. "Let's load up, then. I'm tired and ready to hit the shower."

Miranda and Trace climbed into their respective vehicles and after one last look at the property, still shocked at the amount of trash that filled the bin, Wade did the same. It was definitely time to put a pin in this day.

It wasn't until he had settled his parents into their hotel room and he'd showered himself and was heading to Morgan's house that he realized something else was eating at him that was a foreign irritant, one that he'd never felt before. A sense of longing tugged at his thoughts, reminding him of everything he didn't have in his life and hadn't realized he wanted up until this moment. Family was everything. And he'd abandoned each and every one because he couldn't deal with the pain.

But the rub? He loved his life in California. He enjoyed his work and frankly, he enjoyed the milder winters. He wasn't much for the bone-chilling cold of Alaska anymore. Even though it snowed in Yosemite, there was a huge difference in the chill factor of thirty degrees versus five degrees. Hell, his first winter in Yosemite he thought it was downright balmy in comparison to what he'd been accustomed. He'd even been teased about his short-sleeve shirts while everyone else was bundled in wool scarves and turtlenecks.

He didn't want to move back to Alaska but he also didn't want to go back to the personal life he'd been living. Something had been missing for a long time and he'd been reluctant to admit it. Maybe that was why he'd been lukewarm about a commitment to Elizabeth because he didn't trust letting someone get that close. He wanted what his parents had—that deep, enduring love that survived the ugliest moments, tarnished but still strong—but he had to be willing to let someone in first.

That was the key, right?

Yeah, just like closing your eyes was the key to sleep.

# CHAPTER TWENTY-THREE

MORGAN'S NERVES FLUTTERED, and she sipped her wine as her gaze found the clock to check the time again. Would he come? Had he changed his mind? The day had been terribly emotional. She wouldn't begrudge him the need for some peace and quiet after everything that had transpired. But what an incredible breakthrough. As Jennelle's psychologist she was pleased with the progress and she actually had hope that everything was going to fall into place for the Sinclair family now that some major hurdles had been achieved. She allowed the wine to sit in her mouth for a split second, savoring the faint woodsy flavor of the dry red before swallowing, closing her eyes briefly. *Just relax. Stop being so nervous. If he comes, fine. If not, oh, well. Not the end of the world.*

But when the polite knock sounded at the door, her heart leaped and she couldn't stop the grin that followed. When she opened the door, every rehearsed smile or sexy grin went out the window, and all she could do was bite her lip and undress him with her eyes.

"I wasn't sure you'd come," she admitted in a husky tone that sounded far more Rita Hayworth than she'd ever thought she was capable. But judging by the way he stepped over the threshold and immediately captured her mouth with his, he liked it.

Their tongues tangled as he leaned into her, bending her over his arm as he plundered her mouth like a man determined to taste her soul, and she shuddered with pure desire at his masculine touch. He vibrated with raw emotion that was heady and addictive, and she lapped at it like a kitten with a bowl of milk. Somehow her wineglass safely left her hand and she was lifted into his arms and carried without a sound to her bedroom.

For a moment she was unaware and didn't care where they ended up but when he placed her gently on the bed, she realized she was in her own bedroom rather than the spare. A chill doused her ardor and she forced a light smile as she said, "I'm partial to the spare bedroom for our fun," she said, hoping her request didn't make her appear strange. Well, of course it was strange! If only she had the guts to admit that the reason she didn't want to have sex with Wade in her actual bedroom was because David's ghost still dominated the space. And the space in her head. Wade's subtle frown confirmed her biggest fear, and she babbled a hasty explanation. "It feels so decadent and taboo to make love in a bed that isn't your own."

"Ahh, like hotel sex?" he surmised, and she bobbed a quick nod. With that understanding his grin returned, and he did an about-face and headed for the spare bedroom. She nearly shuddered with pure relief, but a sliver of guilt dogged her excitement. He deserved to know the truth about her and why she was so damn weird but she didn't want to ruin what they had going on, especially since they were on borrowed time. The sharp realization that Wade was going to go back to California filled her with a sadness that was hard to hide.

"Are you okay?" Wade asked, gently placing her on the bed. "You seem a little off. We don't have to do this if you're not into it."

The concern in his voice destroyed her. He was such a kind, giving man. He deserved far better than she could ever give him. Besides, he had enough on his plate; he didn't need her drama, too.

Forcing a bright, seductive smile, she pulled

him to her and sealed her mouth to his. She was going to enjoy every stolen moment to its fullest, and she wasn't going to think about anything else. "Does it look like I'm not into you?" she asked, pulling away to stare into his beautiful, expressive eyes. She smiled as a pleased grin lifted the corners of his mouth as they fell back onto the bed. He towered over her and she framed his face with her hands, desperate to capture the moment and freeze it in her memory for later. "Has anyone ever told you that you have the eyes of a poet?" He chuckled and shook his head as she caressed him. "Well, you do. Someday you're going to make one woman incredibly lucky."

A shadow passed over his expression and she wondered what secrets Wade Sinclair carried in his heart. She wanted to know the story behind every scar, every whispered promise. But that wasn't her place.

Tears stung her eyes, and she squeezed them shut. "Kiss me, Wade," she urged him, desperately needing his touch to blot out the sadness that crept along the edges of her joy like a noxious fog on an otherwise beautiful landscape. Wade didn't hesitate, slipping his tongue into her mouth to seek out hers, and they danced and tangled, building a passion that was so hot that it threatened to burn them both to cinders, and yet neither would ever dream of stopping. Morgan shuddered with feminine power as Wade plunged himself deep inside, a perfectly snug fit that wrenched groans of ecstasy from their lips as they lost themselves in the heady pleasure of giving over to a lover's touch completely. Sweat beaded their bare skin and the musk from their lovemaking scented the room with passion and desire. They were cocooned in their own world of naked skin and ravenous need—and nothing else mattered. This was happiness, this was joy. Morgan wept with the overwhelming sensation of being so utterly pleasured by a man whose sole intent was to bring his woman to a clenching, shuddering conclusion before he tumbled into his own.

Minutes ticked by before Morgan could speak or breathe normally, and she was not alone. Wade collapsed beside her, his chest rising and falling rapidly as he tried to catch his breath. "You're going to be the death of me," he said in a husky but happy groan. "I've never met a woman who matches me in the bedroom. It's my dumb luck that you would be here in Alaska."

She laughed softly, too sated to care about

anything at the moment. Morgan rolled to her side to regard Wade with a silly smile. "You are ruining me for other men."

"Really? Good."

His answer sent a thrill chasing down her spine. For a second she could pretend that they had a future together. "Now is the time when you say that I'm ruining you for other women," she teased, surprised when his smile faded. "I'm sorry...I was kidding. I don't want to kill the moment between us," she said, distressed.

Wade immediately kissed her fears away, murmuring, "You have ruined me for other women. That's a fact. But you can see how that poses a problem for us both."

She nodded. "Yes."

"Can I share something personal with you?" he asked, and she quickly nodded, instantly aware and on alert. She desperately wanted to know who Wade Sinclair was beyond the surface but was that her right? Probably not, but she wanted to, anyway. Wade, seeing that he had her undivided attention, said, "I don't know how you feel about this and I don't know if I'm qualified to say I know what love at first sight feels like because I don't know if I've ever truly been in love, but there's definitely something between us that I don't understand and it's a pretty strong emotion. When I look at you, I feel... *home*. I know that doesn't make sense," he admitted as if embarrassed, and her heart leaped with wild abandon at his admission.

"It makes perfect sense," she admitted in a soft voice, her pulse fluttering like a mad butterfly. "Because I feel the same."

Crazy hope flared in his eyes before it dimmed as he asked, "So what does that mean for us?"

"I don't know. I don't think it can mean anything because we live in opposite worlds and the commute would be a bitch," she admitted in a pained, wry tone.

"True enough." He sighed and laced his hands behind his head, staring at the ceiling. "You know, I'm not this guy who does spontaneous things like this with a near stranger. I'm the kind of guy who plans things out and does things that make sense. What we're doing doesn't make any sense whatsoever and yet, I crave it like a drug. Logic tells me I should put some distance between us but I can't bring myself to do it. What does that mean, Doc?" he asked, half joking but clearly not entirely.

"Sorry, I'm off the clock," she answered,

not wanting to delve too hard into his motivations for fear of uncovering something she didn't want to know. Morgan rested her head on his chest and lightly trailed her fingers down his belly to the coarse hair of his groin. His penis lay against the wiry patch of hair and she threaded her fingers through the hair idly. "Would you think it's weird if I told you that I love the smell of a man's groin area? It's filled with pheromones that really do something for me."

"I think that's pretty damn sexy," Wade admitted, and Morgan giggled when his formerly quiet and spent member began to slowly awaken again. "But then everything about you is damn sexy in my opinion."

She glanced up at him. "Really? You're not just saying that to get lucky again?" she teased.

"Well, there is that. But no, you're unlike any woman I've ever met. And that's incredibly good in my book."

"*You're* incredibly good in my book," Morgan said, thrilling when his gaze darkened with fresh desire. He rolled her to her back and tortured her with slow, teasing kisses that ignited a need so hot that she didn't think she could contain it within her body. She bucked and cried out as he held her down, anchored between her thighs so that she couldn't escape the pleasure barreling down through her nerve endings, soaking her in sweet oblivion.

"Wade!" she gasped, sweat dampening her brow, gulping lungfuls of air as she came down from her cloud. Her heart hammered almost painfully against her breastbone, but her body was numb to anything but the wonderful pleasure still radiating from her clitoris as her womb continued to tighten in soft, receding waves.

"Ohh, Wade..." *I think I love you.* She bit back the words before they escaped her mouth but it'd been so close. Fear of saying something so personal and revealing effectively quelled the feel-good vibrations thrumming through her body, and she quickly rose from the bed with a hasty "be right back" thrown over her shoulder as she disappeared into the bathroom and shut the door behind her.

Morgan flipped the light and stared at herself in the mirror, almost unrecognizable in the fluorescent light. Her hair, normally coiffed into submission, hung in wild strands that practically screamed *I've been rolled hard and it was good,* and a tiny laugh escaped when she realized in her entire marriage to

David, not once did she feel this free, so filled with delicious abandon.

David… What a number he'd done on her. How had she gotten so twisted up and turned around with that man? She'd been sold a bill of goods with that one. She'd mistakenly thought she was marrying a good man with traditional values but instead, she'd hitched her wagon, as her dad would say, to an abusive asshole. And even though he was dead, he still ruled her life with an iron fist.

*Because you let him.*

That tiny voice spoke quietly but with authority and it was true. She allowed her memories of the past to mess with her present and it was time to let it go. Remy would be so proud. This was a breakthrough. She could feel it. Whatever had been wrapped so tightly around her soul had snapped, and she could breathe again. Sure, that restrictive band had been metaphorical but it'd felt tangible, too. There'd been times when she couldn't draw a deep enough breath and actually suffered anxiety when she thought of David. But he was gone. And he was never coming back. Never again would she tremble in fear at the sound of the front door opening, mentally checking everything that he insisted had to be done before he came home from work, or fretting over if his meal was prepared to his specifications. Done. No more. *Finit.*

*Hallelujah.*

A smile found her mouth. She could take the next step. Maybe even with Wade. What did that mean? She wasn't sure but she was willing to take that first, tentative step.

She leaned toward the mirror, fixing her stare on herself, holding her gaze to say in a fierce whisper, "David doesn't live here anymore. He's not welcome in your house or your heart. For God's sake, let him go."

Pulling away, satisfied, she flipped the light and exited the bathroom.

# CHAPTER TWENTY-FOUR

FOR A LONG MOMENT, Wade simply enjoyed the good feelings that were typical post-sex but as he waited for Morgan to return from the bathroom, he realized he couldn't keep spending time with Morgan without telling her what was happening in his life. Somehow it just seemed wrong, even though neither one of them had made promises to the other about some kind of commitment. That was the thing, though; he realized he wanted a commitment with her. But how could he make a commitment to Morgan when back home Elizabeth might be pregnant with his child?

He wanted to see Morgan more—so much so that he would be willing to entertain a long-distance relationship if Morgan was willing—but he couldn't take that step with her without first telling her what was going on. And the idea scared him silly because what if she hated him? What if she turned him away? He'd never been so invested in a relationship that he couldn't walk away if things didn't work out, but he had a hard time imagining not being with Morgan. Somehow, in a short time frame, she had become an important part of his life, and he was already thinking of how he could fit her more securely into his life in California.

It was jumping the gun—something he'd never done in his life—but it still felt right. Everything about Morgan felt so right. He admired her calm strength, her quiet counsel and her professional acumen, not to mention he could lose himself in her body for weeks and happily forget the rest of the world existed. Never in his life had he felt this way about another woman. That in itself made him realize that Morgan was different. And so how could he walk away? What if she was *The One?* He was fairly certain that when he looked at Morgan it was the same way that Trace looked at Delainey or Miranda looked at Jeremiah.

The bathroom door opened and Morgan emerged with a tremulous smile wreathing her beautiful face. She joined him on the bed and climbed beneath the covers with a shiver. "One thing about my bedroom is that it has a fireplace, unlike this one," she said, grinning. "What's with the serious face? I leave for a few minutes and everything changes. Are you okay?"

"You're beautiful," he said, staring into her eyes. "You're the most beautiful woman I've ever seen. And each time I'm with you I fall a little harder."

"Fall? What do you mean?" she asked, a little breathless. "I mean, one might think you were saying that you were falling *in love* with me. But it's too soon for that, isn't it?"

"Yes. Yes to both. You and I both know that this is infatuation but it's the best damn infatuation I've ever experienced in my life. Which leads me to believe that I'm falling in love with you, as well. And I'm not ashamed to admit that, but I feel I need to disclose some things before either one of us decides to take things further. I only want there to be honesty between us, and I can't in good conscience go any further without telling you a few things."

"Is this the part where you tell me you're a cross-dresser? Because I don't think you'll fit into my panties."

He shook his head with a small, pained chuckle, wishing he could joke away the seriousness of his situation. "No, not a cross-dresser. Not a sexual deviant in any way and not a criminal. I'm pretty ordinary. I work too hard, I don't take enough vacation and sometimes I spend way too much time behind the desk. Those aren't my issues. My issue is far more complicated and if we're to go any further it could seriously impact our relationship."

"Oh." Morgan sobered, realizing the gravity of the situation. Seeming to mentally prepare herself she said, "All right, what is it?"

"This isn't easy for me to say and I'm still in shock about it myself. I told you earlier that before I left for Alaska I had a semicasual dating relationship with a woman named Elizabeth, which I broke off because I knew we weren't going to go where she wanted the relationship to go. A few days ago she called to tell me that she might be pregnant. And that if she is…the baby is mine."

Morgan paled and her fingers fluttered to her chest as she sucked in a tight breath. For a long moment she said nothing and the silence was worse than if she'd started yelling. Not that she had anything to yell about, per se, but one never knew how people were going to react to bad news. And Wade didn't know much about Morgan except for how he felt about her.

"A baby? Wow. This changes things a bit." Morgan slid from the bed and grabbed her robe, tucking it around her and tying tightly. She couldn't have looked more unapproachable than if she'd grabbed armor and pointed a spear at him. "I can see why you wouldn't be in a rush to share that kind of information. It does change things. A lot."

"I don't even have confirmation yet if she's truly pregnant but she seemed pretty sure. She said she's never late and…well, she's late this month," he said, watching as Morgan seemed to withdraw further as he spoke. Wade grimaced. This was what he'd been afraid of.

He climbed from the bed and tried to gather her in his arms, but she stepped back. He frowned, trying to explain. "If she's pregnant, and I have no reason to assume the baby isn't mine, obviously I want to have a relationship with the child but that doesn't mean I can't have a relationship with you, too."

"Actually, it does mean that because I am no way interested in being a mother," she said brusquely. "Particularly a mother to a child who isn't mine."

"I see. I was hoping that maybe… I don't know… I know it's asking a lot but I was hoping that you wouldn't bolt. I just found out myself so I'm still in a bit of shock, but I could never abandon a child of mine. It's just not in my DNA."

"Of course. I would expect you to do nothing less. You're a good man and I'm sure you'll make a fabulous father. But I'm not cut out to be a mother or stepmother. I have a thriving practice here and a life I enjoy. I'm not ready to give all that up to raise somebody else's child. No matter how infatuated I might be with its father."

Wade winced. Everything she said made sense but it cut just the same. He wasn't sure what he'd been hoping for but the scenario had played out as he'd feared. He sighed, suffering an acute sense of despair for having lost something he hadn't even really had in the first place. "I understand. I'm sorry. I should have told you about the baby the minute I found out."

"There's no need to apologize. Your personal business is your own. We never made any promises to one another nor did we make a commitment. We were enjoying each other's company for a brief time. But in light of this new information, I'm sure you can understand how I don't think it's a good idea that we continue sleeping together."

He nodded, suffering a wretched, sinking feeling that he'd just lost something precious. He struggled against the urge to fall to his knees and beg her to stay with him. "Of course. God, I'm so sorry. I feel I ruined everything. I think you and I could've been great." She jerked her head in a short nod but otherwise remained silent. What else could he say? The silence between them yawned and he knew it was time for him to leave. "I'll just get dressed and get my things."

"That would be best. Thank you."

Talk about going from heaven to hell in a space of ten minutes. Wade collected his clothes, dressed and left. But he was pretty sure he left a piece of his heart in Morgan's hands because he felt as if he were missing something vitally important to life. He would never wish ill on someone else but at that moment he was mad at the situation, and mad at how helpless he was to change it.

As he pulled out of the driveway he grabbed his cell phone and quickly dialed Elizabeth's number. When she answered sleepily, he said in a terse voice, "We need to talk."

He wanted to know whether or not she was pregnant.

*Now.*

"What's the matter? Is everything okay with your family?"

Wade didn't waste time on pleasantries. "I need you to take a pregnancy test. Now."

The sleep cleared from Elizabeth's voice as she answered quietly. "I already did, right after we talked last. I couldn't wait for my doctor's appointment next week."

He held his breath. "And?" His future rested on this one answer.

"And it was positive." His world crashed down around him and the air disappeared from his lungs. Elizabeth was pregnant. He was going to be a father. He'd lost the woman that might've been *The One* but he'd gained a child. Why did it have to be either/or? He swallowed and forced the words out. "Are you sure? Sometimes those tests are unreliable," he said, his voice cracking like a schoolboy.

"I took two. Both were positive. And I've been throwing up since yesterday. There's no doubt."

"Okay." He needed to think. "Ah...I don't know what to say except I will do my best to be there for you."

"Thank you." Elizabeth's quiet gratitude made him want to cry. This wasn't how it was supposed to be. Conversely, he knew with a certainty that made little sense, if Morgan had come to him and said she was pregnant with his child, he would've leaped with joy. It was simple—he loved Morgan. And he'd lost her.

Elizabeth made a sound like a yawn, drawing attention to the time difference. "I was going to call as soon as I found out but I'd needed time to process and so I'd decided to tell you in the morning. I feel as if I should apologize but I didn't do this on purpose and I never imagined that I would get pregnant before I was married, so I really have nothing to apologize for."

"I know. I don't blame you. You don't need to apologize. We'll get through this and we'll be good coparents."

"It's not that easy for me, Wade," she said, her voice choking. "I was in love with you, even if you weren't in love with me."

"I'm sorry," he said, feeling wretched. "I'm so sorry. Whatever you need, I'll make sure you have."

He imagined her biting her lip as she held back tears, and he cursed himself for being a clumsy clod with someone else's heart. What could he say? Nothing. All he could do was try and be a good coparent. That's all he could offer.

Elizabeth seemed to understand this and let out a shaky breath. "I'll let you know what the doctor says, the due date and whatnot."

"Thank you."

Wade thought the conversation had reached its natural, if not painful, end, until she asked, apprehensively, "Are you seeing someone else? It's probably none of my business but I need to know."

He sighed. Should he lie? No, that wasn't fair to Elizabeth. She deserved the truth, even if it made him uncomfortable to share. "I was," he admitted, adding for her benefit, "It happened while I was here and was completely unexpected."

Her breath hitched but she said, "Does she know about the baby?"

"Yes. I told her this evening."

"And how did she take it?"

"Not as well as I'd hoped but I wasn't surprised. That kind of news under these circumstances never goes well."

"Who is she? Your high school sweetheart?" The jealousy that Elizabeth couldn't quite quell stung with betrayal, and he wondered if a lie would've been a kindness. "I had a feeling this was going to happen," she said. "It was my biggest fear that you'd run across someone you'd once loved and thought had got away. You see it on Facebook all the time. Those social media sites encourage people to get in touch with their past and then it ruins lives."

"She is not someone from my past. I barely knew her when I was younger," he said, hoping his answer softened the blow. "I want you to know that I didn't plan this."

"No one ever does."

He sighed. This conversation was deteriorating. Thankfully, Elizabeth seemed to agree and said, "I'll call you when I have more details."

"Thank you."

Elizabeth was a strong woman but he could hear the hurt in her voice, even if she tried to hide it. He'd never meant to hurt her, but he didn't know how an unplanned pregnancy caused by an extended one-night stand could ever turn out well.

Wade tossed the phone to the other seat with a heavy sigh. He supposed that conversation wouldn't have gone well, no matter what. He felt bad for Elizabeth but he felt worse for himself. Perhaps it was selfish of him but right about now, he figured he'd received the worst end of both of those conversations. Naturally, both ladies would likely disagree but he was going to wallow in a bit of self-pity...at least for the night.

# CHAPTER TWENTY-FIVE

LATER THE NEXT day Morgan met Mona for lunch but only because Mona wouldn't shut up and leave her alone. If she'd had her druthers, Morgan would've ordered in and had something delivered to the office but Mona wouldn't take no for an answer.

Her chatty sister was the last person Morgan wanted to spend time with right now. Her mood had nothing to do with her sister, but the fact was, Morgan wasn't good company for anyone. After Wade had left she'd wished she'd had the courage to pick up the phone and ask him to come back so she could explain herself, but her fingers were made of ice and she neither reached for her phone nor made any other attempt to contact him because she was shamed by the lies that had spewed from her mouth without her control. To think she had actually said that she didn't want to be a mother? Nothing could be further from the truth. But losing her own child had been such a terrible blow that she thought she would never recover. It was a private pain she nursed and protected in an unhealthy manner but until that moment, her painful secret hadn't raised its ugly head.

"What's with the sour face? I have great news to share. So you know that art buyer I told you about? He has turned into a cash cow. He adores my art—not surprising because I am an amazing artist—but even more so than that, he has *connections* to more people who love my art. In fact, he's even paid in full for his commissioned piece." Mona reached into her purse and pulled out a stack of cash and pushed it toward Morgan. "Here is the money I owe you. Bam! I told you I was good for it. Granted, it took me a bit longer than I thought it would, but here it is. Paid in full."

Morgan startled at the pile of cash and quickly scooped it up and stuffed it in her purse. "Mona, a check would have been fine. You shouldn't walk around with this much cash on your person. I'm very happy for you but before you paid me off you should pay Mom and Dad. That would go a long way to getting them off your back."

"Already did, smarty-pants." Mona beamed. "I told you I'm making bank. Admit it, you never thought your little sister would be doing so well with her art."

True, Morgan had had her moments, particularly whenever she'd been writing her sister another check to cover her rent. "It doesn't matter what I thought because you're obviously doing well on your own. Good for you. I'm glad it's working out for you."

Mona made a face. "Wow. That's all I get? I finally become self-sufficient and all I get is a tiny little pat on the back that feels more perfunctory than anything else? Sad. Very sad."

"What do you want, Mona? A cartwheel? I haven't done a cartwheel since I was in high school so you're out of luck."

"Now I get sarcasm? Fabulous. Let's start over. Why don't you tell me why you're being such a stick in the mud and maybe I can help your problem, and then you can get a second chance at being a little more enthusiastic over a major milestone in my life. Okay?"

"Mona, life does not revolve around you. I know that's hard to accept but sometimes people have things going on in their lives that don't affect you in the least."

"Fair point. However, I don't care about those people. I care for my sister. So tell me why you're being such a butthead and maybe we can figure out a solution."

Morgan pinched the bridge of her nose, praying for patience. "Mona, I'm really not up to lunch today. Maybe we can take a rain check."

"Nope. No rain checks issued. Tell me what's going on. I'm all ears. Besides, maybe the drama is interesting for once in your life. Did one of your patients go cuckoo? Well, crazier than usual."

"My patients aren't crazy," Morgan corrected her. "And no, it's not about my patients. Not exactly."

"It's about Wade, isn't it?" Mona snapped her fingers, excited. "Sister, now you have to tell me what's going on. That hunky boy toy is the most interesting thing you've done in years."

"He's not a boy toy. He's a grown man and I don't want to talk about Wade."

"Why not?"

"Because I don't want to. Why do you always question every single thing that comes out of my mouth?" Morgan snapped.

"Morgan, my dear, you are wound tighter than a drum. Sometimes I think if you shoved a piece of coal up your ass, a diamond would pop out eventually. Given how many people would love to have a sister to listen to their troubles and dispense wisdom, I don't see why you're so reluctant to share."

"Wisdom? That's what you call this? I call it badgering."

"Well, it's all a matter of perspective. So did you guys break up or something?"

"You have to be dating in order to break up. So no, we did not break up. But we are no longer going to be seeing each other."

Mona groaned. "Great. What did you do to chase him off?"

"What do you mean, 'what did you do?' What makes you think I did anything?"

"Because it's your personality. But don't worry, we can fix it. Just tell me what you said and I will think of a plausible excuse for why you said it."

Morgan glared at her sister and decided to just lay it all out there—not because she believed Mona had anything of value to add but because she knew if she didn't, Mona wouldn't shut up and give her some peace. "Before Wade left California, he got another woman pregnant."

Mona's mouth dropped open and for a second there was blessed silence but she recovered quickly. "Wow. Didn't see that coming. Okay, is it his girlfriend or his wife?"

"What does it matter?"

"It matters a lot," Mona answered, giving Morgan a look as if she'd just asked the dumbest question on the planet when Morgan didn't see the difference. Mona exhaled and quickly explained. "A wife has a ring on her finger. A girlfriend doesn't. And that would make Wade fair game."

"Not fair game," Morgan disagreed heartily and not for the first time worried about her sister's moral compass. "When a baby is involved, it changes everything. And to answer your original question he said they were only casually dating when she got pregnant, but he only just found out while he was here in Alaska so it was totally unexpected and unplanned."

"Oh, that's not so bad. It's not like he was cheating, right?"

"No, he wasn't cheating but he still got a woman pregnant, and I don't have any interest in dating a man who is about to be a father to a child who doesn't belong to me."

"Yeah, that's a pickle but it doesn't have to be. You used to love kids. What's the problem? You'll probably have to share custody one week on, one week off, which once you get into a schedule it's not so bad. I dated a guy who had a kid and it turned out fine. I didn't break up with him because of the kid issue—it was because he snored and I couldn't handle it anymore. I wasn't getting any sleep."

Morgan glared, irritated that Mona was being so flippant about the situation. "I'm not concerned about the custody issue. I…" Why was she talking about this with Mona? It wasn't as if she could share her true feelings because then she'd have to reveal David's nature, and she swore she wouldn't do that, not for David's sake but for Mona's. Morgan buttoned her lip and grabbed the menu. "Let's just order and drop it."

"No. You're going to tell me who shoved that stick up your ass because you weren't always like this. You changed, Morgan. You used to be fun. What happened?"

"Drop it, Mona."

"I will not."

"You are the biggest pain in my butt."

"Ditto."

The two sisters stared each other down, much like they had when they were kids, neither willing to back down. But in that moment

Morgan realized that her sister wasn't a little kid anymore. Maybe she didn't need to protect Mona. Which meant maybe she didn't need to keep David's secret anymore, either. Morgan lowered her menu and set it down.

After a deep breath, Morgan said, "You're right. I used to love kids. And I wanted lots of them. But that all changed when I had a miscarriage."

Mona's eyes widened. "You had a miscarriage? When? You never told me that."

"Mona, there are a lot of things I've never told you. And I don't know if you're ready to hear this but I might never have the courage to tell you again so here it goes."

"You can tell me anything," she protested. "That's what I'm trying to get across to you. I'm here for you."

"David killed my baby."

Mona gasped and drew back as if she'd been struck. "What? I'm sorry, what did you say?"

"David killed my baby," Morgan repeated, her eyes filling at the memory. As expected, Mona was floored by the revelation.

When she could speak again, Mona said, "You're going to need to fill in the blanks because I'm so confused right now. And horrified. And a bit sick to my stomach."

"Maybe I shouldn't have said anything," Morgan said, wondering if she'd made a mistake in sharing. But there was a part of her that desperately needed to unload this heavy burden, and the prospect of doing just that pushed her forward when Mona jerked a short nod for her to continue.

"No, please. Tell me," Mona said, her voice softening. "I don't know what to say but I think I need to know this."

Morgan nodded and continued, her voice flat and emotionless—not because it didn't hurt like blades going through her chest but because it was the only way she could get through the telling. "David was very particular about appearances. Everything had to be perfect. Including me. Every day I was required to log my weight and I was allowed a two-pound variance. Anything above a two-pound difference and I was punished."

"Punished?" Mona's tone trembled as if afraid. "What do you mean?"

"His preferred punishment of choice was a punch to the stomach because it didn't leave marks. Not that he didn't leave marks, mind you. Sometimes he couldn't control himself and his punishments became frenzied. That's when he left marks that I had to find a way to hide."

Mona covered her mouth on a horrified gasp as her eyes filled with tears. "Morgan... I didn't know..."

"No one knew."

"Why? Why didn't you tell someone?"

"Tell them what? I couldn't do that. What would people say? I'm the one who helps people rebuild their lives. Who was going to trust the counsel of a woman who couldn't fix her own life?" Morgan shook her head. "But that's not the only reason," she admitted, privately ashamed at her weakness. "A part of me hoped he would change. He hadn't always been a monster. I was hoping he would go back to being the man I thought he was. But he never did." She drew a deep breath and prepared herself for the worst memory of her marriage. "The night I lost the baby, David kicked me in the stomach for forgetting to wipe away the soap ooze from the guest bathroom. Neither of us had known I was pregnant at the time. I tried to tell myself that six weeks was barely pregnant but somehow no matter how often I tried to console myself with that, the pain didn't lessen."

"I don't know what to say except that I'm so sorry," Mona said, reaching across to grasp Morgan's chilled fingers. "My mind is blown right now. How could I have missed this? Am I truly that self-absorbed?"

Morgan squeezed her sister's hand. "You didn't see it because I hid it very well from everyone. There was no way I could hold my head up high and admit that behind closed doors David was a mean, abusive bastard who hid behind a veneer of civility and was rotten to the core. I never told you because I didn't want to ruin the ideal you had of him. In some small way I think I was trying to see him through your eyes, too, so I could survive. Not to mention, I was afraid that no one would believe me. You know how people felt about David. I didn't want to take the risk of ruining everything I'd built so I suffered in silence." Morgan lifted her gaze to Mona's and said with complete honesty, "When he died, it was the happiest day of my life."

Mona did nothing but stare, and Morgan knew how she felt. It was a disorienting shock to the system to discover something so heinous about someone you thought was beyond reproach. "I'm so sorry."

A shaky smile found its way to Morgan's

mouth. "Don't apologize. No one knows. Only Remy, and he only knows by accident. If I told people some of the terrible things David did, people would start questioning whether or not he died by accident. My practice would never survive. And so I've protected David's lie, if only to protect myself."

"Wow. I think for the first time in my life, I don't know what to say. I wish I'd been there for you. I feel useless and helpless, even though he's gone and can never hurt you again." Mona's gaze narrowed with rage. "If I'd known...I would've killed him."

Morgan wiped away a tear that'd somehow escaped. "Which is why I never told you. You're such a hothead, you would've done something that you would've regretted for the rest of your life. And besides, it was my problem, not yours. I didn't want to bring that dysfunction into our family's lives. I knew everyone would need to take sides, and I didn't want that to happen, either. The night he died, it was an answer to a prayer."

"Morgan, I'm so sorry." A sigh of pain and sorrow rattled out of Mona, and Morgan caught a glimpse of the woman she could be. "You've always been so good to me. It breaks my heart that I was unable to be there for you in the way that you needed me. I know I've been a screwup for most of my life but I think real changes are coming, and I'm finally on the precipice of actually fulfilling what I feel is my destiny and I want you to grab on to happiness, too. You don't need to worry about me anymore. I want you to worry about *you*. And if Wade makes you happy don't let him get away. So what if he has a baby mama? Who doesn't these days? If you love him, you can work around it."

"I lied to him and said that I didn't want kids. I sounded like a cold bitch."

"So you tell him you overreacted. Besides, it's woman's prerogative to change your mind. If he cares for you, he'll take you back."

"What am I doing? I don't even really know him. We're not two silly teenagers running off to Vegas. We're grown adults with careers and lives. Neither one would be possible to uproot. I'm not even sure why we should encourage this kind of relationship. It's clearly doomed to fail."

"Who says?" Mona asked, shrugging. "You can make it work if it's worth it. And I have a feeling Wade Sinclair is worth it. Besides, you're a psychologist. You can set up a practice anywhere. Maybe California is where you need to be."

"California? You mean move?"

"Yes, you knucklehead. There's more to life than Alaska. Besides, wouldn't it be fun to wear flip-flops all year round? Wouldn't it be fabulous to not have to dig your car out of ten feet of snow? And wouldn't it be awesome if you and your sister got a place together because a fresh start is good for everyone?"

Morgan laughed and wiped her eyes. "I sense an ulterior motive here. What's going on? I thought you hated California."

"Well, now that you mention it, the buyer I was talking about is actually from California. San Francisco, to be exact. He seems to think that my art will be a real hit with the hippies and granolas up in the San Francisco hills. I've had some time to think about it and I've decided that maybe California is where it's at. And besides, I've done everything that can be done here and dated all the men that can be dated, and I'm ready for new frontiers. I'm not afraid to start fresh. And if I go with you, you don't have to be afraid of starting fresh, either. At least until you and Wade decide on a wedding date."

Morgan gasped and tossed her napkin at

her sister. "Don't start walking us down the aisle just yet. We might not even be compatible in the big scheme of things."

"Yeah, yeah. Keep telling yourself that. I've seen the way you look at him and the way he looks at you. It's some true-love stuff and it makes me gag—and a little jealous, if you must know. In all seriousness, don't let this opportunity pass you by. You deserve happiness. I wish I'd known about David a long time ago because then I could've helped you get out of that hell. I can't do anything about the past but I can help you today. You can do this. For once I'll be holding your hand instead of the other way around."

Morgan stared at her little sister, slowly realizing that somewhere along the line her flighty, artistic nutjob of a sister had grown up into a really smart lady. "You would do that for me?"

"In a heartbeat."

And then the waterworks really started. Except this time, Morgan wasn't crying alone.

Maybe Mona was right; a fresh start was definitely on the menu.

# CHAPTER TWENTY-SIX

THE CLEANUP CREWS had worked magic on the house, slapping a fresh coat of paint on the walls, and actually installing a new hardwood floor when it was discovered the old wood had been too badly damaged. And after Miranda and Jeremiah picked up a few new furniture pieces and the personal items that could be salvaged were returned, it looked like a place he could've called home back in the day. He opened the door and walked in, smiling with relief at the fact that the house could be saved, and found his mother in the kitchen, baking, just like she used to when he was a kid.

"Mama...you're baking?" he said, joining her to peek over her shoulder. He inhaled and smiled. "If I'm not mistaken, that's zucchini bread!"

"Your daddy's favorite," Jennelle said, opening the oven to check her bread. "And it's nearly done."

"Where is Dad?" he asked, a frisson of fear

curdling his good mood at the thought of his father going back to his old ways.

"He's in the shed—gutting it out."

Wade released the breath he'd been holding and pressed a kiss to his mother's forehead. "Amen to that."

Jennelle grabbed a plate and sliced up a loaf already made. She handed it to Wade, and he in turn slathered it in fresh butter. "You and butter...you always did like to coat your fresh bread in the stuff."

"That's right. Only way to eat anything breadlike." He took a good whiff of the bread and sighed with happiness. He'd missed his mother's fresh zucchini bread. Among other things. He took his plate to the table and sat down while Jennelle followed. "The house looks great," he said around a hot bite. "It's pretty damn amazing what they were able to do. Are you happy with the results?"

"Very." Jennelle had lost that pinched expression and the dark circles under her eyes, which made him very happy to see. "It was hard watching it all go because there were some good memories in those piles but it was good to watch it go, too. I was holding on too tight to all the wrong things."

"Mama, you don't know what it means to

me to hear you say that. I am so glad. How's Dad doing?"

"He's taking it day by day. But an honest man does an honest man's work and so he's been out there gutting out that shed so he can start carving again. I think that's what he needs to find himself."

Wade agreed with a nod, taking a moment to enjoy his bread. "Have you had a chance to talk to Miranda or Trace?"

She sighed. "A bit. It's hard. Miranda has a lot of reasons to be mad at me. I don't know why I took everything out on her but I did. And Trace is still not sure about Zed and his change. Of all you kids, Trace had the biggest issue with your dad's addiction."

"He'll come around."

"I hope so."

"Are you going to keep seeing the counselor for your hoarding?"

Jennelle grimaced. "I hate that word, but yes. I don't want to go back to that way of living ever again. Seems like another world apart from the world I live in today, even though it was just a few days ago."

"What changed?"

"Everything. But Zed helped me see that I didn't need to hang on to Simone so tight that I ruined everything else in my hand. I couldn't see that before. I was so afraid of losing her completely that I didn't stop to see what I was sacrificing. I did a lot of damage to Miranda. I don't know how to make amends for that."

"You start with one day at a time. One act of kindness after another. Forgiveness is a powerful thing. You need to forgive yourself, and Miranda will fall in line. She wants to forgive you. She wants you in her life."

Jennelle nodded slowly but Wade could see uncertainty in her gaze. "It's going to be okay, Mama. Just keep up with your therapy and you're going to be fine. And as long as Dad doesn't slip up and start cultivating again… I think this family can finally start to heal."

"Maybe. I hope so. I really do." Jennelle waited a moment then asked, "So…are you packing up to go back to California?"

He heard the hope in her voice that maybe he was going to stay home but he knew that wasn't the right choice for him. "Yes," he said regretfully. When her expression dimmed, he added, "But I've decided that eight years between visits is too long. From now on, every six months I'll plan to come and stay for a week or two if I can. Besides, I'll be here for Miranda's wedding, for sure. How's that sound?"

Tears brimmed in his mother's eyes. "I'd like that. I miss you so much, son."

"I miss you, too, Mama."

While Wade finished up, they made small talk, plans for the property and whatnot and then Zed walked in, going straight to the sink to wash his hands. When he returned, he had a plate in his hand, piled with fresh zucchini bread.

Zed eyed Wade's plate. "Don't be eating all my zucchini bread," he warned, and Wade chuckled as his mother shushed him.

"There's plenty to go around," she said, smiling with genuine happiness. It'd been so long since he'd seen that joy in his mother's face, it almost caused tears of gratitude to spring to his eyes.

Jennelle disappeared back into the kitchen, leaving father and son alone. He had two choices: one, gloss over everything that had happened by not talking about it or two, just put his questions out there and hope for an answer. He opted for the second choice because he didn't think he could go forward in his life without knowing. "What made you change your mind?" Wade asked quietly.

Zed took a bite of his bread and savored it for a long moment. When he finally spoke, his answer was simple and to the point. "A boy who'd grown up to be a good man helped me to see how I was being a coward."

*Oh, hell.* The tears he'd held back for his mama leaked from his eyes. He ground them out but his shoulders shook, betraying him with the involuntary motion. Zed clapped a hand on his shoulder with knowing, and Wade didn't have to say a word. This was the man who'd taught him everything he knew about being a man, about keeping his word when given and following through with promises. He knew with one look at his father that no matter what, Zed would stick to his promise to remain sober and the one reservation he'd been holding on to evaporated into the wind. "If you need help, I'll pitch in on your fines," he offered, wiping at his eyes. "I don't mind helping out to get you back on your feet."

"I made the mess, I'll clean it up," Zed said, returning to his bread, stopping briefly to smile at his son with a solemn, "but I appreciate the offer. You're a good boy."

"Thanks, Dad."

"Tell me what your plan is…when you go back. Are you happy in California?"

"Yeah, I really like my job and what I do in the big scheme of things. Looking out for a national park is a big responsibility, and I take it seriously."

"What about a wife? You seeing someone?"

"Not exactly." His situation was complicated, but he knew his parents would want to know some details. "I should tell you that there's another grandchild on the way." One brow went up, but his father waited for him to explain. "I didn't want to say anything until I knew for certain but the woman I was seeing casually...she told me she's pregnant."

"You going to marry her?"

Wade's cheeks flushed. "No. I don't love her like that."

"Baby changes things."

"I'll be a good coparent but I can't marry Elizabeth."

"Why not? Love can grow out from friendship."

"Yes, and if I didn't feel something for someone else I might consider it but the fact is...I think I've fallen in love with another woman."

"That's a tangled mess you've got there, son."

"Yeah. Pretty much. Any advice?"

"I'm probably not the one who should be handing out advice. You've got a good head on your shoulders. But I can say this...I always knew it was your mother for me. I knew it from the moment I laid eyes on her. And I wouldn't let no one or nothing stand in my way of having her. If that's the way you feel about a woman...don't hesitate. Listen to your gut."

"I wish it were that simple," he said with an unhappy sigh. "She has a career here and it wouldn't be right to ask her to give it all up for me."

"You're right," Zed agreed, pushing his empty plate away and leaning forward on his elbows. "But maybe she wouldn't be giving it up if she made the choice on her own. You have to make your case. If it's supposed to happen, it will."

"Dad, I never knew you were such a romantic."

"Well, I guess parents can hold on to their mysteries after all." Zed winked and pushed away from the table. "I've got to get back to work. Don't be a stranger, son. We miss seeing your face around here." And then his dad left out through the back door. Jennelle returned and saw that Zed had left his plate, and she scooped it up with a frown.

"That man wouldn't know how to put away a dish if his life depended on it," she groused, and he smiled at the familiar complaint as she added, "Well, I suppose I can't throw too big a stone on that score anymore, huh?"

"Probably not," he said, chuckling. After Jennelle had cleared the table, she returned with a sigh as she sat in the chair formerly occupied by her husband. Wade allowed his gaze to wander his mother's beloved face, and he knew things were going to continue to improve. "Mama…I have something to tell you," he said, knowing there was no easy way to break the news. At her expectant expression, he continued with a resigned sigh. "I'm going to be a father."

Jennelle sucked a wild breath and her hand went to her chest, momentarily alarming Wade. "I don't understand. I didn't know you were serious with someone. Why didn't you bring her with you?"

He shook his head. "It's not like that, Mama. We were having a casual relationship and the pregnancy is very unexpected. She plans to keep the baby and we're going to coparent together."

"Coparent? I've never heard of such a thing," Jennelle said, a touch of her old orneriness showing through. "Wade Neal Sinclair, if you've gotten a woman pregnant you need to marry her."

"I can't do that. I don't love her. I think I love someone else."

"Oh." Her mouth formed a soft O as she digested the information. She rubbed her forehead, overwhelmed and trying to find firmer footing. "I don't know what to say. I know you'll do what's right. If you say you're going to be a good father, even if you're not with the mother, then I trust you will be."

"Thank you, Mama. It's all very new and frankly, scary."

Recovered, Jennelle sighed and said, "Well, you know, hearing those words uttered by your teenaged son is every mother's nightmare but you're a man now and frankly, you're not getting any younger. And neither am I, for that matter. I'm ready for more grandchildren. I have a lot to make up for with Talen but I can start fresh with the new ones. Bring 'em on." He stared in mild shock at his mother's quick about-face, and she shrugged. "What? My house is nice and clean and I'm ready to start the next chapter in my life, which includes the pitter-patter of little feet that I can send home after I sugar them up. Grandchildren are the reward for all those years of hard parenting. And I'm ready to enjoy the rewards."

A slow laugh bubbled up from his chest as relief followed. His family was going to be all right. "Okay, well, that's good to hear. I'll let you know when I know more."

"Sounds good. Now tell me about this other woman you fancy yourself in love with," Jennelle instructed him, and he hesitated. Should he tell her about his feelings for Morgan? The words hovered on his tongue but in the end, his mother shocked him yet again. "My son, you were always so easy to read. You have feelings for my doctor, don't you?"

"Um…what makes you say that?"

"The way your eyes lit up whenever she was around. And the way her eyes light up the same around you." When Wade didn't protest—what was the point?—she smiled and said, "I approve of Dr. O'Hare. She's a smart cookie and she doesn't waver easily. You need a strong woman, and I think she would do nicely."

Was his mother playing matchmaker? "It's not that simple, Mama…"

"Oh, pooh, it is. It's as simple or as complicated as you make it. Talk to her."

"I tried."

"No...really talk to her. Make her see what you see and trust me, she'll fall all over herself to be with you."

He loved his mother's confidence in him but Morgan had already expressed her feelings about being a stepmother. Still, there was a piece of him that knew he had to talk to Morgan at least one more time before he boarded a plane to go back to California.

"Maybe you're right, Mama," he murmured, rising to press a kiss to her forehead. "I have some errands to run. I'll see you tomorrow before I head out."

"You bet your sweet tail you will. Don't even think about boarding that plane before giving me a chance to make you a home-cooked meal. I'm thinking of inviting everyone over for halibut and rice."

"Sounds delicious, Mama. Can't wait." And then he practically sprinted for the door.

# CHAPTER TWENTY-SEVEN

MORGAN WAS JUST packing up her office to leave for the day when Wade walked in. She wasn't going to lie—her heartbeat sped up when she saw his face, and she couldn't help the tremulous smile that followed.

"I see you two have a lot to talk about," Remy said, closing the door behind him, leaving her and Wade alone.

She was deliriously happy to see him but her mouth hadn't got the memo because she immediately blurted, "What are you doing here?" before she could stop it. She winced and tried to make amends, saying. "I mean, not that I'm not happy to see you. I'm just surprised after our last conversation. I didn't think you'd want to see me after how things had ended."

He walked toward her, and she backed up until her rear bumped the desk and she could go no farther. He invaded her space in a deliciously masculine way, and it was all she could do not to melt in a puddle of want and feminine goo. Was it because he was so damn handsome? Was this some kind of evolutionary process at work? She didn't know. All she knew was that when she was within close proximity of Wade Sinclair, she became a riot of hormones.

"It occurred to me that you and I have a lot more to say and before I board my plane I'm going to say it."

She licked her lips, curious and hopeful. "Oh? I mean, yes. I'm glad you came by because I have a few things I would like to say to you, too." Morgan nodded, clearing her head so that she could actually make sense instead of babble. "I'm really sorry I came off as such a coldhearted bitch when you came to me and shared your situation. It was unbecoming of me and I'm so sorry. I think I panicked a little and ended up saying a few things that were actually untrue."

"You don't need to apologize. The news came as a shock to me, as well."

"No, I do need to apologize. And I need to explain. Can we sit down for a minute?" Morgan gestured toward the small sofa in her office, and Wade reluctantly backed away. Her hands fluttered as she took a seat. "I could use a glass of wine to steady my nerves but as you can imagine, I don't keep alcohol here."

A wry smile twisted his mouth as he sat beside her. "Understandable," he said. Wade saw the tremble in her hands and gently folded them into his own. "You really have nothing to apologize for, but I'm happy to listen to whatever you feel you need to say."

She graced him with a grateful smile and then drew a deep breath before beginning, thankful for his willingness to listen, and then braced herself to share her biggest, darkest secret. "I don't want to go into a very long story so I'm just going to say it. For many years I was in an abusive marriage and the consequence of that relationship was a miscarriage caused by my husband. He messed with my head for a really long time. And I didn't realize how truly messed up I was until you came into my life. When you said that you would be having a baby in your life my knee-jerk reaction was to put as much distance as possible between me and that child. But when I stopped to think about it, I realized that wasn't how I felt at all. A child is a blessing no matter how it is conceived and if you are ready to embrace fatherhood then you deserve someone who will embrace it with you. I didn't think I deserved to be that person, and that's why I said what I did."

"Why would you blame yourself for something that someone else did? You didn't ask to be abused. I would never blame you for something like that."

"Remember when I told you that I was looking to put my house on the market? Well, I'm selling because my husband died in that house and I'm tired of running into his ghost every time I turn around. I'm ready to make a fresh start and I can't wait to unload that giant monstrosity. I never liked it from the start. Everything about that house reflected David's style, not mine."

"Is that why we couldn't make love in your bedroom?"

Heat flooded her cheeks, but she nodded. "Yes. David messed with my head in a million different ways and as much as I hate it, he's still in there sometimes. But I think I'm ready to make a change. And with that change I can finally let David go."

"How did David die? If I may ask."

Morgan closed her eyes briefly as the scene flashed in her memory. How many times had she relived that night? Too many to count. The funny part was, as horrific as the night was, when she envisioned it she never wished for a different outcome. That was perhaps where the guilt came in. "David was very particular in the way he wanted his house to look. The bathrooms had to be scrubbed twice daily with fresh linens always available. He lived with some sort of phobia that people would judge him if his house wasn't perfect. Which meant that it was *my* job to make sure that everything remained as pristine as possible. I had to ensure the right wines were always available at a moment's notice and of course, the right food to accompany and complement the wine so that everyone always saw David and me as the consummate hosts. On the night that I miscarried, David had lost his temper over a tiny drop of soap that I'd somehow missed when I did my second cleaning for the day. He threw me down and kicked me in the stomach so hard that I miscarried."

"What a rotten son of a bitch," Wade growled, his fist actually tightening. "If he were alive I'd punch him in the face."

Morgan smiled at Wade's show of chivalry but she had to get through this before she lost her nerve. "The night he died I was trying to get away from him. He was going to beat me because I'd forgotten to pick up his dry cleaning. It'd been a terrible day at the office with a suicide attempt, and I'd been emotionally exhausted by the time I got home. But none of that mattered. He was enraged because it was his favorite suit and he'd planned to wear it the next day for a business meeting. He told me that I had purposefully set out to humiliate him and that he had to teach me a lesson. I ran but just as I reached the top of the stairs he grabbed me by the hair and yanked me back. But something inside of me snapped. I started kicking and screaming and fighting back. He tried to drag me back into the bedroom but I wasn't going to let him. Somehow he got turned around and the next thing I knew he lost his balance and he went tumbling down the stairs. I heard his neck snap and he died instantly."

"Was there an investigation?" he asked.

She shook her head. "There was no reason to doubt my word. There were no marks on David that weren't supported by a fall down the stairs. It was chalked up to a tragic accident. But ever since his death, I've had to wear this mask so that no one questioned what had seemed like a perfect life. My practice depended on everyone believing the lies that David and I had created. But I think it did more damage to me than I ever could've realized by keeping up the charade. I'd been keeping people at arm's length for so long that I'd forgotten what it was like to want more. And I definitely want more, Wade." She lifted her gaze to his. "I want more with you."

For a long moment Wade just held her gaze, and fear began to creep into her thoughts—did he think she was some kind of murderer? Was he second-guessing his feelings for her?—but she need not have worried. He clasped her hands more tightly and said, "I'm humbled that you would share such a painful chapter in your life with me. You don't have to wear the mask anymore with me. I promise to keep your secrets for as long as you want me to. I can't begin to understand why I feel the way I do with you. All I know is that when I'm with you, I feel complete and I never realized until I was with you that I was actually missing something. I've fallen deeply, irrevocably and utterly in love with you, Morgan O'Hare, and I want to know what we should do about it."

Tears sparked in her eyes and for a moment she couldn't speak. Her throat closed with the sweetest emotion that she'd ever known and all she could do was nod because she felt the same. Irrevocably and utterly. "Ditto," she managed to whisper, and he gathered her in his arms to hold her tightly. "I'm ready to make a fresh start. I swear it. I'll follow wherever you go."

"Are you sure? Your practice is here. Your family is here."

"I'm ready to make a new life elsewhere. There are too many people whom I have to pretend with here. I'm actually looking forward to going someplace where nobody ever knew me as David's wife."

Wade nodded in understanding and pressed a soft kiss to her lips as he said, "Then would you do me the honor of moving with me to California while we figure this stuff out? I live in a small cottage in a national forest. It has one bathroom and not nearly enough closet space but it has the most glorious view of every sunrise and sunset."

Her voice broke as she nodded. "Sounds perfect. Yes…yes to everything. As long as I'm with you, everything else is just window dressing."

And then he really kissed her, pouring all the love and emotion from his heart into a song without words. But no words were needed. They'd said what needed to be said, and they knew that they would always be stronger together rather than apart. She knew it wouldn't be easy—she still had issues to work through, and he had baby-mama drama to figure out—but for the first time in a very long time she was excited for the future.

A future with Wade Sinclair—and whatever that may bring.

# EPILOGUE

FOR THE FIRST time in eight years, the entire Sinclair clan was crowded into their parents' home for a final dinner before Wade boarded a plane for California in the morning. On the menu, Wade's favorite—his mama's halibut and wild rice.

"This is exquisite, Mrs. Sinclair," Morgan said, openly delighting in his mother's cooking. "I've never been a huge fan of fish until now. This is amazing, truly."

A welcoming smile wreathed Jennelle's face as she said, "Situations have changed and it's time that you call me Jennelle. No more Mrs. Sinclair. You're no longer my doctor and if my son has his way, you're going to be the next Mrs. Sinclair in this family. Am I right?" She sent a meaningful glance Wade's way, and he nodded, causing Morgan to flush prettily. He hadn't asked her yet but it was on his mind, and the only reason he hadn't done so was because he didn't want her to feel pressured. But there was no doubt in his mind that he wanted her for his wife.

"Uncle Wade, are you coming to my mom's wedding?" Talen asked around a hot bite. "I'm going to be the best man."

"Wouldn't miss it, buddy," he assured his nephew then looked to Jeremiah. "Are you ready to jump feetfirst into this crazy family?" he teased. "It's kind of like being in a gang. Once you're in, you're in for life."

"Sounds good to me. I can't wait to marry Miranda," he said with a warm smile, which his sister returned.

Wade turned to Trace and Delainey. "No regrets for not having a big wedding?"

"None at all," Delainey assured Wade, actually shuddering at the idea of a lavish affair. "I don't think I could handle everyone staring at me. Besides, I wasted too much time caring about all the wrong things, and I'm done with that." She shared a sweet look with Trace and added, "Plus we're too busy focusing on other things…right, babe?"

Trace answered with a mischievous smile that spoke volumes, and Wade was willing to put money on the possibility that Jennelle would have her pitter-patter of little Sinclair feet before too long.

Talk flowed easily around the table as the evening wore on, and Wade knew it was going to be hard to board that plane tomorrow morning, especially since Morgan was staying behind to close up her practice in Homer and prepare to make the move to California, but he knew this wasn't the end. Things had changed. There was a palpable difference between his parents and his siblings and the air was no longer heavy with tension.

Zed was determined to carve again and thus resume a legitimate trade for his income, and Jennelle was committed to sticking with her therapy, even though, in her words, her new therapist had a funny smile and his eyes were too close together, and she was fairly certain he was squinting at her in an odd fashion. However, as part of Jennelle's therapy, she was also committing to sessions to help heal her relationship with Miranda, and Wade thought that was an excellent idea.

They'd all managed to finally let Simone go and rest in peace. They didn't have the answers—they might never know why Simone had died or who had taken her life that fateful night—but the questions no longer held them hostage. They were ready to move forward—all of them.

*Rest in peace, Simone. Life in the Sinclair household had been on hold for long enough. Time to live.*

And that's exactly what he was going to do.

\* \* \* \* \*

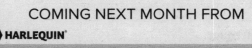
**938 THE SWEETEST SEPTEMBER**
*Home in Magnolia Bend* • by Liz Talley

Of all the wrong men Shelby Mackey has fallen for, this one's a doozy. John Beauchamp is still grieving his late wife, and now Shelby's pregnant with his child. They weren't looking for this, but could that one night be the start of something much sweeter?

**939 THE REASONS TO STAY**
*by Laura Drake*

Priscilla Hart's mother leaves her an unexpected inheritance—a half brother! What does Priscilla know about raising kids? How can she set down roots and give him a home? Then she meets sexy but buttoned-down Adam Preston. Here's one man who might convince her to stay in Widow's Grove.

**940 THIS JUST IN...**
*by Jennifer McKenzie*

Sabrina Ryan never wanted to go home. But, suspended from her big-city newspaper job, that's exactly where she is. Things improve when sparks fly between her and Noah Barnes, the superhot mayor. Doing a story on him, she discovers home isn't such a bad place, after all....

**941 RODEO DREAMS**
*by Sarah M. Anderson*

Bull riding is a man's world, but June Spotted Elk won't let anyone tell her not to ride—not even sexy rodeo pro Travis Younkin. He only wants her safe, with him—but what happens when her success hurts his comeback?

**942 TO BE A DAD**
*by Kate Kelly*

Dusty Carson has a good life—no responsibilities and no expectations. But after one night with Teressa Wilder, life changes in a hurry. Teressa's pregnant and suddenly, she and her two kids have moved into his house. Now Dusty's learning what it really means to be a dad.

**943 THE FIREFIGHTER'S APPEAL**
*by Elizabeth Otto*

To most people, firefighters are heroes—but not to Lena Ashden. She blames them for a family tragedy and is in no hurry to forgive. But Garrett Mateo challenges all of her beliefs. This sexy firefighter wants to win her over and won't take no for an answer!

# The Sweetest September
## By Liz Talley

Shelby Mackey would have been happy
to *never* revisit the night she met
John Beauchamp. Well, that's not entirely true.
It was a good night...until the end. But now
avoiding him is no longer an option!

Read on for an exciting excerpt of the upcoming
book **THE SWEETEST SEPTEMBER**
by Liz Talley...

Shelby took a moment to take stock of the man she had
seen since he'd slipped out that fateful night. John's boo
were streaked with mud and his dusty jeans had a hole in t
thigh. A kerchief hung from his back pocket. He looked li
a farmer.

She'd never thought a farmer could look, well, sexy. B
John Beauchamp had that going for him...not that she w
interested.

Been there. Done him. Got pregnant.

He looked down at her with cautious green eyes...like s
was a ticking bomb he had to disarm. "What are you doi
here?"

Shelby tried to calm the bats flapping in her stomach, but there was nothing to quiet them with. "Uh, it's complicated. We should talk privately."

He slid into the cart beside her, his thigh brushing hers. She scooted away. He noticed, but didn't say anything.

She glanced at him and then back at the workers still casting inquisitive looks their way.

John got the message and stepped on the accelerator.

Shelby yelped and grabbed the edge of the seat, nearly sliding across the cracked pleather seat and pitching onto the ground. John reached over and clasped her arm, saving her from that fate.

"You good?" he asked.

"Yeah," she said, finding her balance, her stomach pitching more at the thought of revealing why she sat beside him than the actual bumpy ride.

So how did one do this?

Probably should just say it. Rip the bandage off. Pull the knife out. He probably already suspected why she'd come.

As they turned onto the adjacent path, Shelby took a deep breath and said, "I'm pregnant."

**How will John react to the news?
Find out what's in store for these two—and the
baby—in THE SWEETEST SEPTEMBER
by Liz Talley, available August 2014 from
Harlequin® Superromance®.**

# LARGER-PRINT BOOKS!
## GET 2 FREE LARGER-PRINT NOVELS PLUS
## 2 FREE GIFTS!

**⊕ HARLEQUIN®**

*super romance*®

## More Story...More Romance